New York *Times* Bestselling A

SIMO
GREEN

GHOST OF
A SMILE
A GHOST FINDERS NOVEL

ISBN 978-0-441-02075-1

5 0 7 9 9

Praise for the Novels of the Nightside

A HARD DAY'S KNIGHT

"Plenty of action packed in from London to Glastonbury . . . should definitely please fantasy action fans."   —*Booklist*

THE GOOD, THE BAD, AND THE UNCANNY

"A fast, intelligently written tale that is fun to read."
                                                    —*The Green Man Review*

JUST ANOTHER JUDGEMENT DAY

"Another unrestrained ride through the Nightside."
                                                    —*Monsters and Critics*

THE UNNATURAL INQUIRER

"Sam Spade meets Sirius Black . . . in the Case of the Cosmic MacGuffin . . . crabby wit and inventively gruesome set pieces."   —*Entertainment Weekly*

HELL TO PAY

"If you're looking for fast-paced, no-holds-barred dark urban fantasy, you need look no further: the Nightside is the place for you."   —*SFRevu*

continued . . .

SHARPER THAN A SERPENT'S TOOTH

"A captivating tale."   —*Midwest Book Review*

PATHS NOT TAKEN

"An entertaining adventure."   —*Chronicle*

HEX AND THE CITY

"[Green's] style is unique, stylized, and addictive."
                                               —*The Green Man Review*

NIGHTINGALE'S LAMENT

"Strong horror fantasy."   —*The Best Reviews*

AGENTS OF LIGHT AND DARKNESS

"If you like your noir pitch-black, then return to the Night-side."
                                               —*University City Review*

SOMETHING FROM THE NIGHTSIDE

"A fast, fun little roller coaster of a story."   —*Jim Butcher*

GHOST OF A SMILE

SIMON R. GREEN

ACE BOOKS, NEW YORK

THE BERKLEY PUBLISHING GROUP
Published by the Penguin Group
Penguin Group (USA) Inc.
375 Hudson Street, New York, New York 10014, USA

Penguin Group (Canada), 90 Eglinton Avenue East, Suite 700, Toronto, Ontario M4P 2Y3, Canada
(a division of Pearson Penguin Canada Inc.)
Penguin Books Ltd., 80 Strand, London WC2R 0RL, England
Penguin Group Ireland, 25 St. Stephen's Green, Dublin 2, Ireland (a division of Penguin Books Ltd.)
Penguin Group (Australia), 250 Camberwell Road, Camberwell, Victoria 3124, Australia
(a division of Pearson Australia Group Pty. Ltd.)
Penguin Books India Pvt. Ltd., 11 Community Centre, Panchsheel Park, New Delhi—110 017, India
Penguin Group (NZ), 67 Apollo Drive, Rosedale, Auckland 0632, New Zealand
(a division of Pearson New Zealand Ltd.)
Penguin Books (South Africa) (Pty.) Ltd., 24 Sturdee Avenue, Rosebank, Johannesburg 2196,
South Africa

Penguin Books Ltd., Registered Offices: 80 Strand, London WC2R 0RL, England

This is a work of fiction. Names, characters, places, and incidents either are the product of the author's imagination or are used fictitiously, and any resemblance to actual persons, living or dead, business establishments, events, or locales is entirely coincidental. The publisher does not have any control over and does not assume any responsibility for author or third-party websites or their content.

GHOST OF A SMILE

An Ace Book / published by arrangement with the author

PRINTING HISTORY
Ace mass-market edition / September 2011

Copyright © 2011 by Simon R. Green.
Cover art by Don Sipley.
Cover design by Judith Lagerman.
Interior text design by Laura K. Corless.

ISBN: 978-0-441-02075-1

ACE
Ace Books are published by The Berkley Publishing Group,
a division of Penguin Group (USA) Inc.,
375 Hudson Street, New York, New York 10014.
ACE and the "A" design are trademarks of Penguin Group (USA) Inc.

PRINTED IN THE UNITED STATES OF AMERICA

10 9 8 7 6 5 4 3 2 1

Ghosts are messages. From the Past, the Present, and sometimes the Future.

ONE

DOGGED BY THE PAST

It's a sad fact that these days, there are more places that used to be factories than there are working factories. And many of these old deserted buildings, left to rot and ruin, have become bad places. Haunted by a past they can't forget and men who can't forgive.

There are lots of ways a building can turn bad. Something terrible happens, staining the environs with enough horror and suffering to poison the psychic wells forever, or just the long years' accumulations of all the petty evils and moral crimes that man is heir to. People make places bad, and bad places make horror shows, to haunt the living with the sins of the dead. People do more than work in factories, and they always leave something of themselves behind.

Which is why a battered old mini-van, with rusting pan-
els and balding tyres, came crashing to a halt in an over-
grown and weed-infested car park, outside the factory
building once owned and operated by Winter Industries. The van's engine fell silent with a series of relieved
coughs, and the slow, sullen quiet of evening returned.
The huge old building stood open and exposed to the
elements, a stark minimalist structure of steel and concrete, looking somehow lost and ill at ease now that it no
longer had a function or a purpose. Broken glass in the
windows, overlapping graffiti on the walls . . . most of it
faded into incoherence, like disappearing voices from the
past. The huge open doors at the front had been sealed off
with yards of yellow police-incident tapes, their ragged
ends whipping mournfully back and forth in the gusting
wind.

From out of the clapped-out old mini-van stepped JC
Chance, Melody Chambers, and Happy Jack Palmer.

The Ghost Finders of the Carnacki Institute.

It was late evening, heading into night. There were
bloody stains on the heavy clouds in the lowering sky,
while the sun hung low above the horizon, giving up on
the day. There were shadows everywhere, long and deep
and dark. The evening light looked stained and damaged,
bruised. The gusting wind made a few half-hearted attempts to kick some leaves around the abandoned car
park but couldn't really be bothered. The factory stood
still and solid, holding darkness within.

JC strode out across the car park, heading for the deserted factory like a general with a battle hymn in his
heart. He was never happier than when he was throwing

himself headlong into life-and-death action, with the world at stake and all to play for, best foot forward and damn the consequences. Which was why he'd had such a hard time finding partners who would put up with him. Most people had more sense. He stopped before the building and looked it over, his fists on his hips and a broad cocky grin on his face. JC loved a mystery, and a challenge, and a chance to kick the unearthly where it hurt.

JC was tall and lean, loud and confident, full of energy and far too handsome for his own good. In his late twenties, he had a rock star's mane of long dark hair, and a rich ice-cream three-piece suit of quite startling style and elegance. He also wore the heaviest, darkest sunglasses he could find, with good reason. Simply standing there in the wide-open car park, he looked like a sheriff come to clean up Tombstone.

Melody Chambers trudged across the cracked concrete, pulling a trolley heaped high with her own very special equipment. Melody was the science geek of the team, and proud of it. She used technology as a weapon to beat the supernatural into making sense. She knew everything there was to know about fringe science and paranormal activity, and what she didn't know she made up as she went along. She firmly believed in the iron hand in the iron glove approach, and only settled for poking ghosts with a stick when she didn't have a better weapon to hand.

Melody was pushing the edge of her late twenties, and pretty enough in a conventional sort of way. Short and gamine thin, she wore her auburn hair in a severe bun at the back of her head, so it wouldn't get in the way. Melody was a very practical sort, first and always. She never bothered with make-up, and wore serious, no-nonsense glasses. Her jeans, sweater, and jacket were dark, practical, and anonymous. She kept several sets in her wardrobe, all exactly the same, so she didn't have to waste time wondering what to wear. But even standing still beside her trolley, scowling impartially at JC and the factory, she blazed with repressed nervous energy waiting to be unleashed upon some poor unfortunate spirit.

And, finally, there was Happy Jack Palmer, taking his time locking up the van and even more time slouching across the car park, to make it very clear to one and all that he didn't want to be there. Happy had just turned thirty and was still bitter about it. He was the team telepath, borderline head-case, and dark cheerless pain in the arse. Because, as he was fond of saying, if you could see the world as clearly as he did, and all the weird and strange things we shared it with, you'd be clinically depressed, too. Happy could Gloom for England, and still take a Bronze in Dire Mutterings.

He might have been good-looking if he ever stopped scowling, and he might have been tall if he ever stopped slouching, but the odds were against it. Prematurely balding and defiantly pot-bellied, he wore a faded T-shirt with the legend *Go On. Ask Me About My Day. I Dare You*, over a pair of distressed jeans that clearly hadn't been threatened with a washing machine in recent memory. He wore slip-on shoes because he couldn't be bothered with laces, and a battered leather jacket that looked like the animal who bequeathed its skin had known a really rough time even while it was still alive. Happy was a Class Eleven Telepath, and would cheerfully have lobotomised himself with a blunt ice-pick if he'd thought for one moment it would keep the voices out of his head.

JC turned to Melody and beamed at her. "Have you got all your toys, Melody? I'm sure you could pack that trolley a little higher if you really tried."

"Eat shit and die, Chance," said Melody. "You couldn't do this job without me and my equipment, and you know it."

"And Happy, Happy, Happy!" said JC, ignoring Melody with the ease of long practice. "Have you locked up the Mystery Machine properly?"

"I wish you'd stop calling it that," said Melody. "It wasn't that funny when we picked the bloody thing up from the rental place, and it's grown exponentially less funny all the way here."

"I can think of worse things to call it," said Happy. "It isn't so much a mini-van as a nearly van. Only the extensive corrosion is holding the bodywork together, and the engine makes more noise than a banshee with bleeding haemorrhoids. The van's about as much use as . . . a thing that's no damned use at all. Oh God, I'm so tired I can't even manage a decent metaphor. I hate long train journeys and I hate car rentals. I swear the Institute goes out of its way to choose something desperate they know will put my back out. Just once, couldn't we have a nice stretch limo? With a chauffeur, and a built-in bar?"

"Dream on," JC said kindly. "Such vehicles tend to attract attention."

"It's budget-review time, that's what it is," said Melody. "We're not even allowed to travel first class on the train any more. I'm going to complain to the union."

"We're not in a union," said JC, staring thoughtfully at the factory.

"I can't believe I volunteered for this job," said Melody.

JC produced a local tourist guide from a jacket pocket with a grand flourish and flipped it open to a relevant page. "Hush, children, and pay attention. Here is useful knowledge, for those who have the wisdom to consult it. The strikingly ugly structure before us was once the pride and joy of Winter Industries. Very successful, from the fifties on into the eighties, at which point all the wheels came off the economy, and a great many once-solid industries hit the dirt. The factory shut its doors for the very last time in 1983, and the whole work-force was made redundant. Thousands of men and women, all laid off in an afternoon. The local economy never really recovered."

"What did they do here?" said Melody, practical as always. "What did the factory make?"

"Apparently, machine parts for other factories," said JC. "And when the orders dried up, the jobs disappeared. Lot of that about, in the eighties."

"Maggie bloody Thatcher," growled Happy. "When that woman is dead, I will piss on her grave. I don't care how long I have to queue."

"Get to the local legends," Melody said to JC. "You know you're dying to get to the local legends."

"Yeah," said Happy. "All the weird shit that no-one believes but everyone talks about."

"Know thine enemy," murmured JC. He flipped through the pages. "Ah yes, here we are. Ghosts, strange animal sightings, UFOs, and Men In Black, all the usual . . . Ah! This is more like it. There are local legends of Big Black Dogges, going back centuries, chasing people down deserted lanes, hunting people at night. And that's *Dogges* spelled the demon way, in case you wondered."

"Big?" sad Happy. "How big?"

"Says here, twice the size of a man," JC said cheerfully. "Always black, appearing and disappearing, and some of them have no head. Definitely not your average Rottweiler."

Happy sniggered suddenly. "No head? How do they smell?"

"Don't even go there," said Melody. "Exactly how dangerous are these Dogges, JC?"

"Reading between the lines, very," said JC. "A lot of local disappearances have been put down to the Dogges, down the years. Apparently it's bad luck even to see one. There's also mention of big cats, attacking sheep at night."

"Cats and dogs? Wonderful," said Happy. "Maybe we can set them on each other."

"Enough talk; time for action!" said JC. He tossed the guide-book carelessly over his shoulder and strode determinedly towards the open doors to the factory. "Time to stare Evil in the face and pull its nose! Give me danger and excitement, Lord, that I might smite the ungodly and send them crying home to their mothers!"

"There's something seriously wrong with you, JC," said Happy, trudging sullenly after him.

"And don't anybody feel they have to help me shift all this equipment!" said Melody, bringing up the rear with her weighed-down trolley.

"It's good healthy exercise," Happy said callously. "And you know you don't like us touching your stuff."

"That's because you always break it!" snapped Melody. "You could break an anvil just by looking at it."

Happy smirked. "It's a gift."

"I'm glad you didn't pay for it," said Melody.

"Children, children," murmured JC. "If we could please all concentrate on the very dangerous and possibly horribly haunted deserted factory before us . . ."

Melody snorted loudly and made a point of striding ahead of JC and Happy, hauling her trolley behind her. JC let her get a fair distance ahead, so he could talk quietly with Happy.

"So," he said brightly. "You and Melody are an item now. How's that working out?"

"I don't know whether we're an item, or friends with benefits, or ships that have crashed into each other in the night," said Happy. "We're having lots and lots of sex, if that means anything. I used to take all kinds of useful little pills, to help make sure the only voice inside my head was mine, and to give me a more positive outlook on things, but these days I seem to be living mostly on bathtub speed and multi-vitamins, just to keep up with her. God, that woman's got an appetite."

"Are you still scared of her?" said JC.

"Hell yes," said Happy.

Melody had almost reached the yellow police tapes when JC called out sharply for her to stop. She did so immediately, looking quickly about her, while JC and Happy hurried to catch up. The three of them stood together, the huge open doors of the factory holding secrets within. Looking into the gloom inside was like looking into a bottomless pit, where the dark fell away forever and ever. JC abruptly turned his back on the dark and looked back over the empty car park.

"Notice anything, oh my children?" he said. "Listen. Listen to the quiet . . . No birds singing, or even flying anywhere near. No insects buzzing, even in this dying dog day of summer. The air is heavy, like a storm that's right on the edge of breaking but never does. This . . . is an unnatural quiet because Nature has withdrawn from this place. This bad place. And what do we know about bad places, my esteemed colleagues?"

"Bad places make ghosts," said Melody. "Hauntings are as much an expression of places as people."

"*Genius loci,*" said Happy. "The spirit of the place because some places are more alive than some people. Did I pass? Please tell me I didn't, and I can go home."

"Gold stars for everyone!" said JC. "And honey for tea. It's quiet here because all the natural things are afraid of the factory."

"If they've got the good sense to stay out of there, maybe we should, too," said Happy. "No? I'm sure I used to have survival instincts, before I joined this team. Can't we start a nice accidental fire and burn the whole building down?"

JC ignored Happy, launched himself at the police tapes, and broke through them with a series of ostentatious karate chops. He strode into the factory, and the others followed him. The temperature plummeted the moment they stepped out of the sunlight and into the gloom. JC shuddered briefly. Walking into the factory felt like diving into a cool dark sea. The only light fell in through the high windows, illuminating the long, dark interior with a series of bright shafts of sunlight, stabbing down from on high. JC and Happy and Melody moved slowly forward, trying to look everywhere at once, their footsteps echoing strangely hollow on the concrete floor. The trolley's wheels creaked loudly. The huge interior of the factory seemed to swallow up the sounds immediately, making them seem small and insignificant.

The long interior stretched away before them, a massive open space, like a museum wing with no exhibits. Everything of value, everything that mattered, had been removed long ago, and the factory was an empty shell. JC looked interestedly about him. Despite the heavy gloom, he still hadn't taken off his sunglasses. Melody stopped abruptly, slamming to a halt, and Happy jumped despite himself. He glared about him while JC looked at Melody and raised a single elegant eyebrow.

"This is where the body was found," said Melody.

They all looked down. There was a dark stain on the rough grey floor that might have been human-shaped if seriously horrid things had been done to a human body. Melody set about assembling her own specially designed workstation, supporting various usual items of scientific equipment. Some of it so up-to-date that so far no-one had even realised she'd stolen it from the Institute's research laboratories. JC and Happy didn't have a clue what half of it was, or what it was for, but they trusted

Melody's high tech to come up with answers to questions they wouldn't even have considered. Melody ran through the details of the murder as she worked, confident that, as usual, she'd been the only one to pay proper attention during the original briefing.

JC always said details got in the way of seeing the Big Picture, and Happy's attention tended to wander a lot.

"The victim," said Melody, "was one Albert Winter, main shareholder of the very successful and influential Winter Group of companies. Interestingly, no-one seems to know what he was doing here; though given that this factory was once a part of Winter Industries, we could probably take that as a clue. If you like that sort of thing. Anyway, the rest of the Winter Group's board were not at all happy with the results of the original police investigation. Mainly because there weren't any. They couldn't explain why Albert Winter had come here, or how he died, or what killed him. Except that it must have been a really nasty death. The state of the body was so bad, even hardened policemen had to run outside to puke up things they hadn't even eaten yet. Anyway, the Winter Group made its displeasure known and put the pressure on, which eventually filtered down to us. The Carnacki Institute does so love a mystery. Particularly when there's a chance to get in the good books of a rich and powerful company. I did mention this is a Budget Review Year, didn't I?"

"Your cynicism wounds me," murmured JC, kneeling down beside the large dark stain. "All that matters is that this is our first case since we were officially declared an A team, after our proud and glorious success against

Fenris Tenebrae, down in Oxford Circus Tube Station. Nothing like saving the world to up your pay grade. But it is incumbent on us to do well on this very important case, or we will be busted back down to a B team so fast it will make our heads spin."

"Or, we could all be horribly killed," said Happy, blinking miserably about him. "By evil forces as yet undetected. Just thought I'd remind you since that part is always mysteriously overlooked in the briefings. I don't like it here. If it were up to me, I'd say we nuke the whole place from orbit. It's the only way to be sure."

"Danger comes with the job," JC said happily. "And the territory. It's what gives our calling its spice! I love the smell of ectoplasm in the evening!"

"You're weird," said Happy.

"Why don't you boys go take a look around this dump," said Melody. "On the grounds that you're getting on my nerves big-time. I have to calibrate my equipment and do a whole bunch of other technical things that you wouldn't understand even if I did explain them to you."

JC and Happy set off in different directions, wandering across the great open expanse of concrete. A thick layer of dust covered the floor, marked here and there with overlapping footprints. Some attempt had been made to keep them away from where the body fell, but it was clear a great many people had taken a keen interest in the murder. There were cobwebs, thick and dusty, but no sign of mice or rats, not even a dropping. The air was deathly cool, without even a breath of movement, despite the many broken windows. Dust motes swirled lazily in the long shafts of sunlight, dropping down from the high windows like so many dimming spotlights. The only sounds in the great open factory were their footsteps, and the occasional electronic chirps from Melody's station. Small sounds, quickly swallowed up and smothered by the heavy quiet. The atmosphere was tense and still, as though something was waiting to happen. As though something had been waiting to happen for some time . . .

JC stopped abruptly and looked thoughtfully about him. He pursed his lips, as though considering an idea he didn't like. "Melody, who is authorised to come in here these days?"

"A couple of night-watchmen, and a local security firm that takes a quick look round, twice a week," said Melody, her hands flying across her keyboard as her various instruments woke up and came on line. "But none of them ever actually enter the building. Apparently, it disturbs them. Disturbs them so much they have it written into their contracts that they don't have to come inside. And how do I know this? Because I'm the only member of this team that ever bothers to do their homework."

"You logged on to the files, on the train coming down," said Happy. "God bless laptops for those of us who are slaves to The Man."

"Is he saying I'm a swot?" said Melody.

"Teacher's pet," said JC, not unkindly. "From your extensive research, do you know if anyone has actually seen anything? Any named or identified thing?"

"Not seen, as such," said Melody. "More heard, or sensed. Everyone says this place has a bad feeling, even if they can't agree why. One night-watchmen said he was followed by something as he made his round outside the factory. But he couldn't, or wouldn't, say by what. But he quit his job the next day and moved to another county. They get through a lot of night-watchmen. No-one stays long."

JC frowned. "If things have got that bad, why hasn't the Institute been called in before this?"

"Because no-one's actually *seen* anything," Melody said patiently.

"Isn't that always how it is?" said Kim Sterling, stepping daintily out of the shadows to join JC. "It's always hard to pin down a ghost."

She smiled brightly on all of them, and they all smiled back, in their own ways. Kim walked a few inches above the dusty floor. She tried her best, but she still rose and fell a few inches in the air as she approached JC. Gravity has no attraction for the dead. Kim was a ghost and had a hard enough time concentrating on the important things, like looking solid and substantial when she wasn't, without worrying about the little things. Like gravity, and consistency. She was a beautiful young woman in her late twenties, now and forever. A great mane of glorious red hair tumbled down about her shoulders, framing a high-boned, classically shaped face. Her eyes were a vivid green, her mouth a dark red dream, and she had the kind of figure that makes men's fingers tingle. Because she was dead, her appearance was an illusion based on memory, which meant that not only did it tend to vary in the details as her attention wandered, but that she could dress in whatever fashion she chose. Today, she was a 1920s flapper, complete with cute little hat and a long string of beads round her neck. She twirled them artlessly round one finger as she stood before JC. She smiled at him, and he smiled back.

JC and Kim were an item, the living and the dead. Everyone knew it wasn't going to have a happy ending, including JC and Kim. But while love is blind, it is also always eternally hopeful.

Kim was a part of the team but couldn't join them in direct sunlight. It dispersed her ectoplasm. So she only worked with them in the dark places of the world, stepping out of the shadows to fight the forces of darkness, all for the love of a good man. Even if sometimes she was scarier than some of the things the team faced. She beamed at JC and tried to slip her arm through his. But her ghostly arm passed right through.

"I'm sorry, JC," said Kim. "I keep trying to intensify my presence, but no matter how hard I concentrate, I can't become solid."

"I keep telling you," said JC. "It doesn't matter. You're here with me. That's all that really matters."

"Young love," growled Happy, staying a cautious distance away. "The horror, the horror . . ."

"What I want to know," Melody said to Kim, "is how you can turn up wherever we are, whenever we need you."

"Because I'm not really here," said Kim. "I impose my presence on the world through an effort of will. So basically, any place is every place because wherever I am is a matter of opinion. So I can be wherever I want to be.

It's very liberating, being dead. You should try it. The physical rules of the world aren't nearly as binding or restrictive."

"Spooky . . ." said Happy.

"Shut up, Happy," said JC.

"You're as spooky as she is these days, JC," said Melody, slapping a particularly recalcitrant piece of tech to show she was serious. "After what happened to you on that hell train . . . It isn't your eyes that changed. I really do need to sit you down and run some serious tests on you."

"No you don't," said JC very firmly. "You just want an excuse to wire me up and poke me with the science stick."

"For your own good, JC," said Melody. "I promise; there wouldn't be that many needles involved . . ."

"You stay away from me, Melody, and from Kim. We are not your lab rats—we are your colleagues. You don't tie colleagues down and threaten them with internal probes . . ."

"Actually," said Happy, "sometimes in bed, she . . ."

"Shut up, Happy," said JC. "Far too much information."

"Ectophile!" said Happy.

JC and Kim made a point of drifting away a little, so they could have some quality time together. JC left footprints in the dust. Kim didn't. Happy glowered after them and went back to join Melody, who was giving all her attention to her equipment as it hissed and purred and blinked coloured lights in an important sort of way.

"I can't believe they're still together," said Happy.

"The dead and the living aren't supposed to be together, for all kinds of really good reasons."

"It'll all end in tears," Melody said vaguely, peering from one glowing display screen to another. "I mean, they can't even touch each other. Ever."

"There is more to love than the physical side," said Happy.

"Couldn't prove it by me," said Melody.

"You worry me sometimes," said Happy. "Actually, you worry me a lot, but . . . JC and Kim worry me more. It's like watching a train crash in slow motion, and not being able to help anyone."

"Sometimes, people have to sort things out for themselves," said Melody. "Even if one of them isn't people any more."

JC and Kim walked happily along together, sticking to the factory wall. Close to each other but not touching. It was easier that way. His footsteps echoed quietly, hers didn't, but they both pretended not to notice. Every now and again they'd walk through a falling shaft of light, and Kim would disappear for a moment.

"I am working on refining my condition," said Kim. "It's not easy. Being a ghost doesn't exactly come with an instruction manual. But I'm sure it must be possible to become solid if I can concentrate in the right way. I can become real, for you."

"It really doesn't matter," JC said patiently. "The living and the dead can love each other, but not as people do. That's the way it is. I found you, and you found me, and I can live with that."

"I can't even get into bed to sleep beside you!" said Kim. "I don't sleep, but I do like to lie beside you. Whether you're awake or not. I can lie down, but if my concentration wavers, I start drifting upwards, and end up bobbing by the ceiling!"

"I don't mind . . ." said JC.

"Well you should!"

They stopped and looked at each other, then they both managed a small smile.

"I've had sex without love," said JC. "Love without sex is better. Sometimes frustrating, yes, but . . . course of true love never did run smooth." He looked at her for a long moment. "Can you feel . . . anything?"

"Mostly, I feel cold," said Kim. "Sometimes, when you're asleep, I run my fingertips down your face, then I think I feel something . . . but it's hard to be sure. I don't have a body, only a memory of one. Mostly, I feel . . . distant. Like I'm hanging on to the world by my fingertips . . . Don't say you're sorry again, JC, or I'll slap you!"

"Like to see you try," said JC. "Look, dead or alive, we're both still human. Man and woman. We care for each other, in a human way. We have that in common, and that's enough. Now, let's get back to the others. They're talking about us, you know."

"You can hear them?" said Kim. "I can't hear them . . ."

"No," said JC. "But if you were them, wouldn't you be talking about us?"

They laughed, and returned to Happy and Melody, and the fully charged electronic equipment. They both fell silent as JC and Kim approached, and Happy did his best to look innocent but couldn't pull it off. Melody didn't even look up from calibrating her short- and long-range sensors. JC indicated to Happy that he wanted to walk and talk with him alone. Happy immediately looked worried and guilty in equal measures, his standard default position. JC laughed and led him away, so they could talk privately. Kim hovered next to Melody, pretending an interest in the high tech, some of which immediately stopped working, in protest to her very existence.

"I'm getting a really bad feeling about this place, Happy," said JC. "And I'm not even psychic. So what are you feeling? What are you seeing and hearing with that marvellous mutant mind of yours?"

Happy scowled, looking around the deserted factory in a decidedly shifty manner. "To be honest, JC, I think opening up in here could be really dangerous. Even with all my mental shields battened down and welded shut, I can't help picking up things. Really unpleasant things. We're not alone in here. Something's watching . . . and waiting. There's no telling what might come jumping out of the shadows the moment I lower my shields."

"Man up, Happy," said JC. "Show some balls and shake them at the shadows. You're the team telepath, the mental marvel, so get on with it. Justify your presence here, or I won't sign off on your expenses claims."

"Bully," muttered Happy. "Can I at least take a few of my little helpers? My chemical companions in need?"

JC sighed. "I thought we were weaning you off those?"

Happy wouldn't meet his gaze, fumbling in his pockets. "Most people take pills to see strange and unusual things, I take pills to keep the weird away. You're the reason I need these things, JC, you, and the job. If you could See the things I See . . . or maybe you do, these days, with those amazing new eyes of yours . . ."

"Stick to the subject," said JC.

"I am! The world isn't what most people think it is," Happy said sadly. "It's a bigger world, and far more crowded. And if you could see what's peering over our shoulders and tugging at our sleeves, you'd fry your neurons with powerful chemicals, too. If you want me to track down what's in here with us, and look it in the eye, I need a little something to back me up!"

"Take your pills," said JC. "You're all grown-up now. You know what you need."

Happy produced half a dozen plastic containers and rolled them back and forth in his hand, squinting at the handwritten labels. He'd moved far beyond mass-produced pharmaceuticals and worked his own mix-and-match magic to produce skull-poppers and mind-expanders of such ferocity they would have made Hunter S. Thompson weep with joy. He finally settled on some fat yellow capsules and dry-swallowed three with the ease of long practice. He straightened up abruptly, as though throwing off a heavy weight, a wide grin stretching across his face.

"Oh yes, that's the stuff to give the boys! Nothing like self-medication to hit the spot!" He giggled suddenly. "Who's the man? Watch me now! Side effects are for wimps! My heart's pounding and my liver's whimpering and my brain is running on nitrous oxide! I'm moving so quickly, I'll pass myself in a minute. Slow slow, quick quick slow suicide perhaps, but it beats the hell out of self-harming. Now, let me See . . . I was right. We're not alone in here. I'm picking up all kinds of savagery, and not only from the murder. Rage, hunger, violence . . . and it's not human. Not even alive, as such. Old, very old . . . Something really bad happened here, JC, and I think it's still happening."

"That's it?" said JC, after Happy had been quiet for a while. "I don't know why I keep you around. Could you be any more vague? There are psychic pets on television who are more specific than you!"

"I'm quite willing to go back and wait in the van till it's all over," said Happy. "Oooh . . . I think my fingertips are floating away . . ."

"Walk on," said JC.

They made a full tour of the perimeter, sticking close to the factory walls. The shadows were growing longer, deeper and darker, as the light falling through the windows slowly faded away. The silence made the wide-open space seem even more oppressive than the encroaching night. It was growing colder, too, far more than the late evening could account for. Their breath smoked and steamed on the air before them; but only Happy could produce actual smoke rings. JC kept looking about him, convinced he could see something about to emerge from the deepening shadows, but everything remained stubbornly still and silent. They finished their tour without result, and rejoined Melody and Kim at the equipment centre.

"Did the police find any physical evidence?" JC said immediately. "Anything useful, or indicative?"

"Not a damned thing," said Melody. "I read the official reports. They didn't turn up a thing. Which is surprising, in this *CSI* day and age."

"Tell me again about the state of the body," said JC. "How did Albert Winter die?"

"Messily," said Melody. "Ripped apart. Bones broken, organs torn out, skin shredded. You'd have to put a man through a wood chipper to do that kind of damage."

"So we are assuming a supernatural death?" said Happy. "A supernatural killer? Oh dear. I can feel one of my heads coming on."

"Could it be a werewolf?" Kim said brightly. "I used to love films about werewolves! I was up for a part in *Dog Soldiers 2*, before I was murdered."

"More likely the Big Black Dogges," said Melody. "They're not just a local legend; you get the same kind of phenomenon reported all over the British Isles. Dogges hunting . . . chasing, headless Dogges . . ."

"How do they smell?" said Happy. "Terrible!"

He broke into giggles again. Melody glared at JC.

"You let him dose himself again, didn't you!"

"He works better that way," said JC.

He slapped Happy casually across the back of the head, and Happy stopped giggling immediately.

"Ow! That hurt!"

"Serves you right," murmured JC. He knelt beside the murder stain again and considered it for a long moment. He gestured for Happy to kneel beside him. The telepath did so, careful to keep out of arm's reach, and glared at the murder site in a sideways fashion.

"Stop that," said JC, not unkindly. "Look at the blood stain, Happy. Tell me what you See."

"Blood," Happy said immediately. "Lots and lots of it, and a hell of a lot of spattering. If a man had done this, I'd have said there was serious passion involved. I'm picking up anger, rage, hatred, revenge . . . But this still looks and feels more like an animal attack to me."

JC nodded slowly. "Any ideas as to what kind of animal?"

"Old," Happy said immediately. "And wild. Not feral, though; there was intent and purpose behind this. And . . . the rush is wearing off, and I'd really like to go home now."

"Your metabolism eats pills alive," said JC. He looked thoughtfully about him. "Bad places make ghosts . . . And this is a bad place. Made bad, long before Albert Winter was killed here. So what makes this factory building a bad place? There's no record of any work disaster, or any great loss of life, and yes, Melody, I do occasionally do my homework . . . The real question is why did Albert Winter die now, when this place has been worrying but basically harmless for so many years?"

"Hush!" Kim said suddenly. "Someone else is here with us. Someone living."

"Retreat into the darkness, my children," said JC. "Let us watch and learn."

They quickly abandoned Melody's workstation to hide in the deepest of shadows at the nearest wall. An old man and a young woman came hesitantly through the open doors and advanced slowly into the great open space of the factory floor. The old man held up an old-fashioned storm lantern before him, the flame's soft yellow glow pushing back the gloom. They moved steadily forward, sticking close together, looking about them with keen interest. Neither of them seemed particularly scared or intimidated.

The old man was a stooped, fragile-looking black man, well into his seventies. He wore a battered jacket over a heavy sweater, faded jeans, and sensible shoes. His eyes were bright, and his mouth was firm, but his wrinkled face had sunk right back to the bone. His head was mostly bald, with little white tufts of hair above the ears. His stride was slow but steady, and he looked quietly determined, as though he had come to the deserted factory with some definite purpose in mind. And for all his evident age and fragility, there was something about the man that suggested he'd survived hard times and could survive more, too, if he had to.

The teenage girl at his side towered over him, big, black, and busty, with a strong face that held rather more character than was good for her. Or anybody else. She held herself with defiant pride and dignity, and wore a long, patterned robe over practical sandals. Her hair had been scraped back in tight cornrows. She walked beside the old man like a body-guard, but there was something in it of family, too. She held a mobile phone to her ear, then waved it about, trying for a signal, before swearing dispassionately and putting the phone away.

The old man stopped abruptly. The girl stopped with him and looked quickly about her. The old man held up both hands before speaking in a firm, rich, and carrying voice.

"Is there anybody here? Be not afraid, be not alarmed. We have come to talk with any who might remain here and to offer any help or aid that might be required. Please, come forward and talk with us. We are not afraid. We are friends."

"Bloody cold in here, Gramps," said the girl. "Cold and dark and a complete lack of comforts. Like most of the places you drag me to. Just once, couldn't we go ghost-hunting in a first-class hotel, or a nice pub, or a decent restaurant?"

"Quiet, child! Show respect for the spirits!"

"I am not your child, I am your grand-daughter, and I'm sure this is bad for me. I'll bet there's mould here, and all kinds of spores, waiting to be breathed in so they can break-dance in my lungs. You're not going to find any ghosts here, Gramps. For one thing, this place isn't old enough."

"Hold your peace, child," said the old man. "You only show your ignorance. Spirits accumulate in the dark places of the world, and this has been a bad place for many years. Have I not told you the old stories . . ."

"Yes, Gramps. Many times. But they're only stories. Something for old men to tell, when they're losing at dominoes and want to distract their opponents."

"Stories have power, child. In many ways. Trust me when I tell you, the past does not lie easily here . . ."

"Well," said JC. "Never let it be said that I don't know a cue when I hear one."

He stepped briskly forward, and waved cheerfully to the startled old man and the girl at his side. "Hello, hello! Welcome to the dark and spooky and almost certainly

haunted abandoned factory! Guided tours a speciality!
Psychic phenomena guaranteed or your money back.
I am JC Chance, of the Carnacki Institute for Finding
Ghosts and Doing Something About Them. May I ask
whom have I the honour of addressing?"

The teenage girl had actually jumped a little when he
appeared, but the old man was made of sterner stuff. He
stood his ground and held his lantern a little higher to
spread more light. He looked suspiciously at JC, and
Happy and Melody behind him. Kim remained in the
shadows, being diplomatic.

"What the hell are you doing here?" said the teenage
girl, moving quickly forward to put herself between her
grandfather and JC.

"I'm JC," JC said patiently. "And these are my colleagues in spiritual affairs, Happy Palmer and Melody
Chambers. Don't let them worry you, they're supposed
to look like that. It helps scare the spooks. We are here
to investigate the unnatural phenomena surrounding the
recent death of Albert Winter. Might I inquire what
you're doing here?"

"Don't tell them anything, Gramps!" snapped the girl,
matching Happy scowl for scowl. "We're not obliged to
tell them anything. We don't have to justify ourselves.
We've got as much right to be here as anyone!"

"Mind your manners, child," said the old man, stepping past her to nod politely to JC and his team. "You
were brought up to behave better than that. I am Graham
Tiley, Mr. Chance. This is my grand-daughter, Susan. We
are here to make contact with the spirits."

"You've seen something?" said Melody. "What have you seen?"

"We haven't seen anything!" said Susan, still glowering at one and all. "But we're . . . interested. There have always been stories about this place, and Gramps lives for all that supernatural stuff, so when the murder happened, there was no keeping him out of here. We haven't done anything wrong!"

"Never said you had," murmured JC. "Let us all put our claws away and play nicely. I think we're all on the same side here. Mister Tiley, would I be right in thinking that you have some personal connection to this place? Something that makes it important to you? You do seem to know your way around . . ."

"I used to work here, long ago," said Tiley. "Haven't been back through those doors in twenty-five years and more. Not since the whole place was closed down, and I was laid off. Along with everyone else. Terrible day. All of us made redundant, just like that, after all the years we gave to the company. Can't say I was ever happy here; it was hard, repetitive work, and nothing much to show for it. But, the more I look back, the more I miss it. Not the work so much as the security. All the familiar faces, and the regular routines, knowing where you were going to be and what you were going to be doing, at every given moment of the day . . . There's security in that, and reassurance. I suppose you never know what you really value until someone takes it away from you." He stopped, and looked at JC. "I don't usually open up like that to someone I've only met. There's something about you . . ."

"People always find it easy to talk to me," said JC. "I'm a good listener. That had better not be sniggering I hear behind me . . ."

"You had other jobs, Gramps," said Susan. "Some of them a lot better paying."

"But they were just jobs," said the old man. "Something to do, in the time that was left to me. Something to keep me busy till the pension kicked in. And they did mean I didn't have to spend so much time with your grandmother. A wonderful woman, my Lily, but best appreciated in small doses . . . She did so love to talk. She was very good at being reasonable, in a very wearing way . . . Where was I? Oh yes. This was the first job I had as a teenager, and I gave this factory the best years of my life. I saw more of this place than I did of my own children."

"They understood," said Susan.

"Did they?" said Graham. "I'm not sure I ever did. Now my Lily's gone, and both your parents work all the hours God sends . . ."

"You've got me, Gramps."

"Yes," Graham said fondly. "I've got you, child."

Susan looked at JC challengingly. "Is that your high tech piled up there? I know state-of-the-art shit when I see it. You really think you can measure ghosts, weigh ghosts, pin them down, and open them up?"

"Sometimes," said Melody.

Susan glared at her. "Who did you say you work for?"

"We're official," said JC. "I'd leave it at that if I were you."

"This is our haunting!" Susan said stubbornly. "We were here first!"

"You can't stake a claim on a spirit, child," said Graham. "We heard things, Mr. Chance. People tell stories . . . and I heard more than enough to convince me there was something out here worth investigating. We might only be amateur ghost hunters, but I do have experience in this field. I am here to offer help and guidance to any lost spirits who might be . . . held here, for any reason. Help them realise that they're dead, but there is a better place waiting for them. Show them the peace and the protection of the Clear White Light."

"Amateur night," growled Melody. "All we need."

"Quiet at the back," said JC. "But the rude lady does have a point, I'm afraid, Mr. Tiley. It really isn't safe here. You should leave."

"Young man," Graham said sternly, "I have cleared seventeen unhappy places and left them calm and peaceful, untroubled by any unquiet spirit. I know what I'm doing. I intend to make contact with whatever troubled soul resides here. You are welcome to stay and help if you wish."

"Help, not interfere," said Susan. "No-one messes with my gramps, not while I'm around."

"And what is it you intend to do?" said JC. "I'd really like to know."

Tiley glared at him suspiciously, not entirely sure he was being taken seriously. "I have my own tried and trusted methods. I shall be about them. You and your colleagues can do as you please!"

And he stomped off into the dark interior of the factory, holding his storm lantern out before him, a pool of golden light advancing into the darkness. Susan looked after him, not sure whether he wanted her company. She scowled at JC.

"Official . . . What kind of official? You're not the police."

"Heaven forfend," said JC. "Let's just say we're professionals. We have a lot of experience in this field, enough to know that what's happening here isn't an ordinary haunting. Albert Winter didn't just happen to die in this place. Something lured him in here, then took its own sweet time killing him. And whatever did that is still here."

Susan shuddered suddenly, despite herself. She could hear the truth in JC's calm voice. She looked over at her grandfather. "Gramps took up ghost-hunting as a hobby when he retired. Something to keep him occupied . . . But after Grandma Lily died last year, he's been taking it all a lot more seriously."

"Am I to take it that you're not a believer?" said JC.

Susan snorted loudly, looking him over scornfully. "Of course not! I'm here to keep him company and see he doesn't get into any trouble. I've watched his back on a dozen cleansings and never seen or heard a thing. It's all empty rooms, shadows in the corners, and plumbing rattling in the walls. You know a lot about the killing; you sure you're not some kind of police?"

"How can I be sure, let me count the ways," murmured JC. "Trust me, Susan, there isn't a branch of the police that would accept any of us on a bet. Except perhaps as Bad Examples. But there was a murder here, and we are looking into it. We are concerned as to how it may have happened."

They all looked round as Graham Tiley came striding back, his footsteps echoing in the quiet. He stopped right before JC and looked at him sternly.

"I've had a look at your machines. Machines won't help you with the spirit world. Nor will official attitudes. It's all about prayer and belief and compassion. Spirits who are having trouble passing on respond best to the personal touch. Human contact, kindness, sympathy, positive attitudes. I'm here to talk and to listen, and to help if I can."

"An entirely worthy intention," said JC, getting in quickly before Melody could stop sputtering long enough to say something unhelpful. "Unfortunately . . . not all ghosts want peace. Some have to be pacified."

Suddenly, without any warning, the whole building was shaking with the deafening sounds of machines working filling the air. Huge machines slamming and grinding, overpowering. The floor vibrated heavily, shaking everyone with the brutal power and motion of unseen machinery. They all put their hands to their ears, but it wasn't the kind of sound they could keep out. The roar of the machines filled the whole factory floor, filled their heads, and rattled their bones. Susan grabbed onto her grandfather's arm with both hands, to hold him steady. They all looked around them, Tiley waving his lantern with a shaking hand; but there was nothing to see anywhere.

"I know this noise!" said Tiley, leaning in close and

shouting to be heard over the din. "Though I haven't heard it in years. This is what it sounded like on the factory floor, when all the machines were working at once. It made me deaf for a week when I first started! No ear protectors in my day . . . But they pulled all the machines out of here when they shut the place down!"

The sound stopped abruptly, and Tiley shouted his last few words into an echoing silence. The air was still, the building was steady, and the floor was calm and certain again, as though nothing had happened. But there was still something . . . in the dark, out beyond the light.

"Can you feel that?" said Happy, stepping forward reluctantly. "There's a definite presence here . . ."

"Of course there is!" snapped Tiley. "And you and your young friends have upset it, with your modern scientific attitudes! You people need to get out of here. You're making things worse. Leave me to get on with my work."

"We can't do that," said JC.

"Why not?" said Susan. "Who are you, really? And don't give me that professionals bullshit. Who wears sunglasses at night, in a deserted building? You're not from any of the official ghost-hunting groups, like FOG and PIS."

"Fog and *what*?" said Happy.

"Friends of Ghosts, and Paranormal Investigation Society," said Tiley. He stabbed an accusing finger at JC. "You're journalists, aren't you? Bloody tabloids!"

"No," said JC. "We're really not interested in publicity. The horror of ghosts, for most people, is that they're beyond all the usual methods of control. People feel helpless before them, terrified by the unknown, not knowing how to cope. But we are from the Carnacki Institute, and we know what to do with ghosts."

"Like what?" said Tiley.

"Whatever's necessary," said JC.

Again, there was something in his voice that seemed to reach the old man and calm him down. JC gave him his full attention.

"What was it like, Mr. Tiley, working here, back in the day? Was it a bad place, back then?"

"Not really," said Tiley. "Hard work, but steady. Regular work that you could rely on, year in and year out. And that meant a lot, back when I was a young man. I spent most of my working life here, man and boy."

"I don't know how you can be sentimental about it, Gramps," said Susan.

"It was work you could depend on," Tiley repeated. "And we were all grateful. Nothing much to show for it, mind. We just made parts, for other machines. We never made anything complete."

"Ah, interesting," said JC. "No sense of closure. Could be significant."

He walked slowly out across the great expanse of open space, head cocked to one side, as though listening. "Huge machines, heavy machinery, working endlessly, doing the same things over and over, tended by people doing the same things, over and over. For decades . . . A ritual, impressing itself on Time and Space, digging psychic grooves into the surroundings . . ."

"Hold on," said Melody. "Are you suggesting that this place is haunted by the ghosts of heavy machinery?"

"Think about it," said Happy. "If a man were to walk through the space where the machines manifested . . . they'd tear him apart." And then he stopped and shook his head slowly.

"No. Sorry, JC, but very definitely no. I told you, I sensed emotions—raw and harsh and wild."

"You're all talking nonsense," Tiley said firmly. "Ghosts are the restless spirits of departed people. That's it. I've read all the books, and I believe what's needed here is a lay exorcism."

"Not a bad idea," said JC, walking back to join the others. "But first, I think we should hold a séance. Summon up all the players, so to speak, so we can get a good look at them. Get some idea of what this is all about. I'll say it again. Albert Winter didn't just die here. There was more to it than that. There was purpose, and intent, to his death."

"We don't have a medium," said Tiley, concentrating on the one thing that made sense to him.

"Actually we do," said JC. "A medium is a link between the worlds of the living and the dead. And there is one member of my little team who fits the bill perfectly. Kim, dear, come forward and make yourself known, would you?"

Kim came floating out of the shadows, smiling brightly, only hovering an inch or so above the dusty floor. She allowed herself to become semi-transparent, to make it clear what she was. Graham Tiley and his grand-daughter stared at her with open mouths. Susan actually fell back a step, and Tiley had to grab her to steady her. They huddled close together, for mutual support. Kim stopped a tactful distance away and gave them both her most charming smile.

"Hi," she said. "My name is Kim, and I'm a ghost. Please. Don't be afraid. I don't bite. I'm part of the team."

Of the two, Graham Tiley seemed the most affected. He breathed heavily, his eyes fixed unblinkingly on Kim. He looked like he would have turned and run if Susan hadn't been holding on to him. He finally closed his mouth with a snap, swallowed hard, and nodded slowly to Kim.

"Dear God . . . All these years, looking for ghosts and spirits, for some actual sign that the soul survives . . . but I never saw anything. Not even sure I really believed, deep down . . . But here you are. I was right all along. You're a ghost. I can tell, I can feel it . . . Oh my dear, are you trapped here? Is something holding you to this world?"

"Yes," Kim said happily. "JC, my love, my very dear. Isn't he wonderful?"

"Get away from her, Gramps," whispered Susan. "Don't talk to her. She can't . . . She can't be . . ."

"I'm not worthy of her," said JC. "But believe me when I tell you, no-one is holding Kim anywhere against her wishes."

"Like to see anybody try," said Kim.

"How did you . . . die?" said Susan.

"I was murdered," said Kim. "But JC avenged me."

"You never believed," Graham Tiley said to Susan, a slow smile coming to his lips. "Don't worry; I always knew you were here to keep me company. So, a real live . . . real dead ghost. Right before us. What do you think of your old gramps now, eh, Susan? Not so daft in the head after all?"

"We should get out of here," said Susan. "We shouldn't be here. This isn't right! It isn't natural!"

"It's only a ghost!" said Tiley. "A person, with the body removed. Get a grip on yourself, child, and stop embarrassing me. Talk nicely to the young lady ghost. She looks to be about your age."

"What do you say to a ghost?" demanded Susan. "Hi, nice to meet you, how's your ectoplasm? Give me a break, Gramps, my whole world has just been turned upside down and inside out, and the pieces have fallen all over the carpet. You talk to her. I'm going to find a corner and mumble quietly to myself."

"Youngsters today," said Tiley. "No stamina." He smiled at Kim. "It is nice to meet you, young lady. Are you sure there's nothing keeping you from passing on? I'd be happy to help . . ."

"The only thing keeping me here is my JC," said Kim. "And I wouldn't be parted from him for all the worlds that may be. I had to die to find true love, and I won't give it up now."

"Well, well," said Tiley. "My first real encounter with a spirit. Not at all what I'd expected, but still, most exhilarating! Pardon me for asking, my dear, but if you're a ghost, why can't you speak to whatever ghosts might be haunting this place?"

"Doesn't work that way, I'm afraid," said Kim. "There are all kinds of ghosts, and all kinds of hauntings."

"But you can act as a medium, help us make contact with what's happening here?"

"I don't see why not," said JC. "Kim has a foot in both worlds, the living and the dead. What better medium could there be?"

"You have such wonderful ideas," said Kim. "Let me see what I can do."

"Hold it, hold it!" said Melody, rushing over to her equipment. "I want to record everything that happens! If only so I can clear myself of all responsibility if it all goes pear-shaped in a hurry."

JC nodded for Happy to go keep Melody company, and the telepath moved quickly over to join her—and watch her back. Once Melody was immersed in recording something, she often became blind to more immediate dangers. And Happy also knew that JC wanted him to observe everything telepathically, from a safe distance. Just in case. Kim drifted quietly out across the open factory floor, not even bothering to walk, as she concentrated on the matter at hand. She faded away some more as she gave less thought to her manifestation and more to what JC wanted of her.

Everyone looked round sharply. Nothing obvious had changed, but the sense of presence, or someone or something watching from the darkness, was suddenly that much stronger. Tiley called Susan back to him, and they huddled together, holding each other's hands. Melody bent over her instruments, rapt at what her sensors were picking up. Happy bit down hard on his lower lip, concentrating on his mental shields. All around the factory, the shadows were longer and deeper and darker. The quality of what light remained seemed subtly debased, stained, even bruised. Tension coiled on the air, gradually growing tighter. And JC . . . watched it all with an easy grin, like a ringmaster at his own private circus.

"Anything, Kim?" he said.

"Something, JC," said the ghost. "There's so much information in this place. Layers and levels, some recent and some old . . . some very old. Wait, I think I've made contact . . ."

And the machinery returned. The whole factory floor was suddenly blazing with light and packed with huge machines, all of them working, constantly moving, deafeningly loud. Parts rose and fell, other parts slammed together, and a work-force of hundreds moved around them, operating machines, darting back and forth, picking things up and conveying them away. It was terribly loud and unmistakably present, but still, somehow . . . distant. As though separated from this Time by some unimaginable direction. JC moved in close beside Tiley, so he could shout in his ear.

"This is the top layer of the stone tape, a recording, playing back. Past events soaked into their surroundings, emerging again in the Present. What you're seeing is a vision, a portrayal of what used to be here. A true vision, of real events, but not real now. We can see it but not affect it."

Graham Tiley shook his head numbly. "I remember this . . . I know these people! Men I worked with, men I knew . . . Faces I haven't thought of in years, and old friends long dead . . . Am I in there, somewhere? They all look so young! I want to go to them, and talk to them, warn them of things that are going to happen . . ."

"But you can't," said JC. "Because they're not really

here. If you walked among them, they couldn't see you . . . You'd be a ghost to them. An image, out of Time."

"Some of them are going to die young," said Tiley. "Some are going to be maimed, and killed, stupid accidents that could so easily be prevented. And I can't help them. The Past can be cruel, sometimes."

And then the huge machines, and all the work-force tending them, began to slowly fade away. The sound went first, the thunder of the machines growing steadily quieter, as though receding into the distance. Then the image itself grew thin and insubstantial and was gone. The top layer of the stone tape disappeared, as something else moved forward to take its place. New images began to form, out of the Past.

"It's the next layer of the stone tape," JC said to Graham. "The level below, from deeper in the Past. Pushing aside the more recent image to make itself known."

"It's rising," said Kim. Her gaze was far away, and her voice didn't sound entirely human. "Forcing the more recent Past aside. JC, *Something's coming . . .*"

"Who?" said JC, quietly but firmly. "Tell me, Kim. Who is it that's coming?"

"Living things, old things, summoned things," said Kim, not even looking at him. Her gaze was fixed on something only she could see. "Power. Old power. Harnessed power . . . blood and death, set to unnatural purpose . . . Something very old was called up here, to do terrible things . . . and it's still here!"

"Summoned?" said JC. "What was summoned up, Kim? And who summoned it? Why?"

"Retribution," said Kim.

JC stepped forward and took off his sunglasses. Tiley and Susan both cried out as they saw why he wore them. Something had happened to JC on a previous case. Trapped on a hell train, surrounded by demons, fighting for his life and for Kim, when all seemed lost, Something had reached down from the Higher Dimensions and touched JC briefly. Giving him the strength he needed to save them both. Much of that strength was gone now, but his eyes still shone like the sun, glowing with a strange brilliance. JC saw the world very clearly now; and when he needed to, he could See a great many things that were usually hidden from the living. All the secrets and wonders of the invisible world.

It had taken him a long time to find sunglasses dark enough and heavy enough to hide his glowing eyes.

JC glanced at Graham Tiley and Susan, and they both shrank back from his illuminated gaze.

"Don't worry," he said easily. "Think of them as psychic searchlights."

"Stop fannying around being pleased with yourself, and concentrate," snapped Melody, not looking up from her display screens. "What do you See? The readings I'm getting are all over the place, and half of them don't make a blind bit of sense. I'm getting energy spikes, electromagnetic radiation . . . I'm getting Time, I'm getting Deep Time . . . Whatever's heading our way is rising up from the bottom of the stone tape, recordings laid down centuries before. And the power readings are right off the scale . . . as though something is riding on the stone tape, using it to break out of the Past and into the Present."

"And that is never good," said Happy. "I'd run if I thought it would do any good. Something's definitely coming, JC, closing in on us, closing in . . ."

Dark shapes appeared out of nowhere, imposing their existence on reality, huge and threatening. They manifested up and down the whole length of the factory, snapping into existence in ones and twos, sticking to the shadows, keeping well away from what little light was left. Tiley held out his storm lantern, holding it high to cover himself and his grand-daughter in the soft yellow light . . . but the dark shapes ignored him, prowling round the exterior of the factory floor. They were slowly taking on shape and form, vicious and malevolent shapes, with teeth and claws and glowing blood-red eyes.

"Happy," said JC, apparently entirely unconcerned by what was happening all around him, "are you by any chance picking up anything with that amazing telepathic mind of yours? Because if so, now would be a good time to share. What are these things? What are we dealing with here?"

"I'm getting hunger, and rage, and a hell of a lot of bad attitude," said Happy, from where he was hiding behind Melody. "But you can probably tell that from looking at them. I can't seem to fix on what they actually are; I think whoever summoned them imposed a shape and form on them. Melody, what are these things? Elementals? Animal spirits? Something from the Outer Circles?"

"Beats the hell out of me," said Melody, her gaze

flashing from one display screen to the next, her fingers stabbing at her keyboards. "The readings I'm getting are . . . confused, to say the least. All I can tell you is that whatever is behind these manifestations is old. Very old. Centuries old. Hell, they might even be Pre-human in origin!"

"I'm picking up human traits along with the animal," said Happy, rubbing miserably at his head. "And not in a good way."

"Could these be sendings, from the Great Beasts?" said JC. "The Hogge, or the Screaming Hives?"

"Okay," said Happy. "I just did something in my trousers. I am leaving now. Try to keep up."

"Stand still!" snapped JC. "You want them to notice you?"

"Definitely not connected to the Great Beasts," said Melody. "No trace of the subtle energies normally associated with the Outer Abominations . . . Whatever's behind those shapes is of earthly origin. And the power source, the original summoner, is quite definitely human. People began this. Whatever it is."

"I don't understand a single thing you people are saying," said Graham Tiley.

"We do, so you don't have to," JC said breezily. "We're professionals."

"And I am only an amateur," said Graham. "But this is my factory, and my world, and I know a thing or two."

He gave Susan his lantern and strode out onto the factory floor, holding his empty hands before him. The dark shapes chasing and leaping around the factory walls seemed to slow, and take notice of him. They began to close in on him, circling. Susan looked like she wanted to go to him but couldn't move. JC went quickly over to stand beside her and make sure she didn't do or say anything that might draw the shapes' attention to her. Graham Tiley stood his ground as the dark shapes moved in. He held his hands out to them and spoke in a calm, reasonable voice.

"In the name of the Clear White Light," he said, "be at peace. Whatever you are, whoever you are, be at peace and at rest. There is nothing here to alarm you, nothing here to threaten you. We are all of us people of goodwill. We want only to help. We can help you find rest, show you the path to the better place that is waiting for all of us. Come to me. Listen to me. The Clear White Light is everywhere. You only have to open yourself to it, and it will embrace you. You don't have to stay here. There is a better place . . ."

He broke off. Several of the dark shapes were very close by then. There was power in them, and a remorseless savagery. Rage, hunger, violence beat on the air. Flashes of long, curved claws and sharp, vicious teeth. Eyes that glared with pure spite and hate. And all of them closing in on him. He tried to speak the words of help and comfort, but they wouldn't come. He could feel his old heart hammering painfully in his chest. *Not now, you old fool,* he thought. *This would be a really stupid way to die.*

JC moved swiftly forward, his bright white suit shining in the gloom, his eyes like spotlights. He put himself between Tiley and the nearest dark shapes, and as he glared about him, they all fell back, reluctant to face the light blazing from his eyes.

The shapes paused briefly, then snapped suddenly into focus as their forms finally clarified. They were all big Black Dogges, dozens of them, huge and lean and muscular, their dark bodies a good five feet and more at the shoulder. They looked like dogs but moved like wolves, with supernatural speed and grace and awful power. They padded across the open factory floor, blood-red eyes glowing fiercely, heavy claws digging deep grooves in the concrete floor. When they snarled, they showed huge mouths packed with vicious teeth. These were not creatures of the wild; they were unnatural things, from some unimaginable Past, summoned forward into the Present and shaped into the Black Dogges of legend.

"I've never liked dogs," said Happy.

"It's the old stories, come to life," said Tiley. "Only with more teeth and claws than I'd imagined . . ."

"Big, pointy teeth," said Happy. "Really big, pointy teeth. Anyone got a ball to throw?"

"No-one move," said JC, his voice carefully calm and easy. "Everyone watch everyone else's back."

"The stories say, to see the Black Dogge means you're going to die," said Tiley.

"Not on my watch," said JC. "Sometimes, stories are only stories. Happy, concentrate on finding out what they want. Melody, I need more information on what these things are when they're not being Black Dogges. And Kim . . . You can See things that are hidden from the living. Hidden even from my eyes. Try and find the ghost of the man who was killed here and started all this, Albert Winter."

"They're definitely not dogs," said Happy, sounding

almost surprised. "Not even a little bit doggy. Whoever summoned them up imposed the shape of the Black Dogges on them, to better control them. I don't know what they were before. Melody?"

"Deep Time, definitely Pre-human," said Melody. "You wouldn't believe the tachyon discharges I'm picking up. Whatever they are, they're from so far in the Past, I don't think they even exist any more. I think . . . they're trapped here."

"I've found the ghost of Albert Winter," said Kim. "He just appeared, along with the Dogges. Am I to take it that the theory of death by manifesting machines has been officially overturned?"

"It's the Dogges," said JC. "When in doubt, always go for the killer dogs with the huge claws and jaggedy teeth. Try and bring the ghost into focus, Kim. The rest of us will keep the Dogges occupied."

"You speak for yourself," said Happy. "If anyone wants me, I'll be right here, hiding under the machinery."

"You even look like touching my stuff, and I will have your balls off with a blunt spoon," Melody said immediately.

"I want to go home," said Happy.

One of the Black Dogges broke suddenly from the pack and headed straight for Melody's workstation, racing across the concrete floor. Melody produced a machine pistol from somewhere about her person and opened up on the approaching Dogge. Graham Tiley and his grand-daughter cried out, and huddled together, while JC moved quickly to stand with them. Melody swept her gun back and forth, riddling the huge Dogge with bullets, the roar of the machine pistol shockingly loud in the quiet. The Dogge didn't even try to dodge the bullets. They passed right through him, as though his huge shape was nothing but a shadow. The bullets flew on to blast holes in the wall behind. Melody kept firing until she ran out of bullets. The Dogge loomed up before her, and jumped right over her and her workstation, landing lightly on the floor behind. It ran on, then circled quickly round, to come at Melody and Happy again. Teeth showed in its great jaws as though it were laughing; but it hadn't made a single sound.

Melody lowered her empty gun and looked at Happy. "Down to you then, lover."

"What can I do?" said Happy.

"Come on . . . You took on Fenris Tenebrae, one of the Great Beasts, down in the Underground, and laughed in his face."

"I was very heavily medicated at the time!"

"Come on, do it for me," said Melody. "And there will be treats later . . ."

"Sometimes you scare me more than the ghosts," said Happy.

"You know you love it," said Melody. "Heh-heh."

They turned to face the Black Dogge, racing silently across the concrete floor towards them. Happy stepped forward and glared right into the Dogge's crimson-eyed face. He reached out with his mind, searching for whatever bound the Dogges to this place, so he could break it . . . but the sheer animal ferocity he encountered swamped him. He made a sick, pained sound, thrust the animal emotions aside, and made himself stand his

ground. Melody needed him to do this. He thrust out
a telepathic block, the psychic equivalent of throwing a
brick wall in the creature's way. And the Black Dogge
lurched to a sudden halt as it slammed right into it.
Happy advanced on the Dogge, one step at a time, and
the Dogge backed away, one step at a time. Happy
frowned till his forehead ached, hitting the Black Dogge
with one telepathic assault after another, battering it with
pure brute psychic force . . . and the Dogge kept retreat-
ing, until finally it broke, and turned, and fled back to its
pack, still circling round the factory perimeter. Happy
made a rude gesture after it and turned back to Melody,
trying to hide how much he was shaking.

"My hero," said Melody.

"You have no idea how close to the wire that came,"
said Happy. "It feels like my brains are leaking out my
ears."

"What makes you think you have any?" said Melody.

Happy glared at her. "Everyone's got ears! I think I'd
like to go home and lie down now, please!"

"Later, lover," said Melody. "I'm a bit busy right now."

The Black Dogges were still circling, still closing in
relentlessly. JC turned to the old man.

"Talk to me, Mr. Tiley. Tell me the legend of the
Black Dogges. The stories everyone tells. Including the
not-at-all-nice bits you don't normally admit to in front
of strangers."

"It goes back years," Tiley said slowly. "Long before there ever was a factory here. On this place, back in
the eighteenth century, there used to be an old manor
house. The Winter family lived in that house and owned

most of the land around. There was a quarrel, so they say, between the landed gentry Winters and a local working family, the Tileys. A quarrel, over a woman. A rape, they say, though most of the names and details are lost to us."

"I never heard any of this," said Susan. "You never told me any of this before, Gramps. Mum and Dad never said anything . . ."

"It was an old story," said Tiley. "You didn't need to be burdened with it. Sometimes, the past should stay in the past, so the rest of us can get on with our lives."

"The story," prompted JC. "The quarrel between the Winters and the Tileys. What came of it?"

"No justice then, for poor working folk," said Graham. "No law, for poor black folks. So the head of the Tiley family at that time, he used the old knowledge to curse the Winters. He used the old forbidden words, and the Black Dogges came, to harass and hound the Winters to their deaths. Don't ask me what kind of curse; that part of the story is long lost. Perhaps deliberately lost. The Dogges bedevilled the Winter family, and even people connected to the Winters. The Dogges followed people down lonely roads, late at night, speaking prophecy, always bad, always true. Other times, they chased men and women till they fell, then tore them apart. They came and went, and no-one could stand against them.

"They travelled the whole district, making the Winters' life a misery, until finally the family left the house, and the area, and spread themselves across the country. The Dogges couldn't follow, they were bound to the place of their summoning. But with no Winter left to torment, they appeared less and less, and finally vanished. The story continued, as stories do, changing down the centuries till the original details were forgotten. But we remembered. We Tileys. The manor house was torn down. The factory came much later, still owned by the Winters, from a distance.

"There were still sightings of Black Dogges, or stories of sightings, but no-one really believed in them any more. A different world, now. And then . . . he came back. The fool. Albert Winter. He was going to sell the land the factory stood on, but he wanted to see it for himself first. I wrote to him, telling him not to come, but of course I couldn't say why, only that it was dangerous . . . So he came back. To where his old family home used to stand. And the Dogges came back.

"They woke up, they rose up, and they chased him till he died of it."

"Oh, Gramps," said Susan. "You should have told me."

"I should never have brought you here, child," said Tiley. "But I never really believed, till now . . . I believed in the Clear White Light."

"You should have told me! It's my family, too! I had a right to know!"

"I wanted to protect you! The curse should have died long ago. It shouldn't still have a hold over the Winters, and the Tileys."

JC moved away, to talk quietly with Kim. She was hovering a good foot above the floor, her shape so thin and insubstantial it was barely there, just a young woman made of flickering light. JC had to say her name several times before she finally turned her head to look at him.

"Kim," said JC. "If the Dogges are still here, then the shade of Albert Winter must also still be here. Show him to me."

Kim nodded, painfully slowly, then raised one hand and pointed. JC looked, and there was Albert Winter. Running, still running, fleeing desperately from the Black Dogges that still pursued him, and always would. Ghost Dogges chasing their ghostly victim, forever. He ran and ran, staggering and lurching, running endlessly round the perimeter of the factory, and behind came the Dogges. They pressed in close, hurting and harrying him, driving him on. Sometimes he fell, and the Dogges would savage him, tearing away chunks of ghostly flesh with ghostly jaws, leaving wounds that healed immediately, so the man could be forced to his feet to be chased again. They would chase him forever, in a hunt that would never end.

Some curses are worse than others.

Graham Tiley and his grand-daughter could see it, too, now. Tiley cried out at the sight of it and had to turn his head away. Susan hugged him to her, glaring defiantly at the Black Dogges around them.

"We have to stop this," said JC. "The Past should stay in the Past . . . Albert Winter, he's the focal point! He's why the Dogges manifested again. But to put him to rest, we have to stop the Dogges. Interrupt the curse. We have to save the ghost of Albert Winter!"

"I'd quite like to save us from the Dogges as well," said Happy.

"Science can't touch them," said Melody. "I think the

Dogges are older than Science. Or whatever these things were, before they were made into Dogges."

JC looked at the old man. "You! Tiley! It's your curse. Your family summoned up the Dogges, and your curse holds them here. Release Winter's ghost from your curse, and the Dogges will be able to leave."

"I can't!" Tiley said miserably. His dark face was wet with tears. "I'd free him if I could, but I don't know how! I don't remember what words called them, no-one does any more."

"Terrific," said JC. "No, wait a minute . . . What did you say, Melody? Back before they were Dogges . . . They weren't always like this! Whoever summoned them out of the Past imposed these shapes upon them! That's the key!"

He strode right up to the nearest Black Dogge. It snarled at him, growling so low he felt it in his bones as much as heard it. Great lips pulled back to show savage teeth in powerful jaws. Claws on huge front paws dug deep into the concrete flow as the Dogge tensed, ready to spring. JC leaned forward and thrust his face right into the Dogge's, meeting the blazing blood-red eyes with his own glowing gaze; and then he spoke sharply to the Dogge.

"Bad dog!"

It looked at him. Its jaw snapped shut, and its head came up. No-one had ever spoken to the Dogge like that before. It stared at JC, fascinated. The other Dogges stopped in their tracks to stare at JC. And the ghost of Albert Winter was finally able to stop running.

"Bad dog," JC said firmly, holding the Black Dogge's gaze with his own. "This is wrong! You were never meant to be like this. You are a dog, made to take the shape and form of a dog, and a dog was always meant to be man's best friend. Some poor fool called you here and imposed this shape on you to follow the old stories; but revenge was never your true nature. You're as cursed by this as your victims. But the man who summoned you here is long gone, and his need for revenge died with him. You don't have to serve his anger any more. You don't have to be like this, any more. You're free to be . . . just dogs. Good dogs. Man's best friend."

And the Black Dogge sat down on its haunches and nodded its great head slowly. Inwardly, JC breathed a deep sigh of relief. He hadn't been entirely sure that would work. In magic, the true naming of a thing is the true nature of that thing. And so Dogge became dog. JC gestured at Graham Tiley.

"That man there is a Tiley, descendant to the man who brought you here, and bound you in this form. He is ready to release you. Isn't that right, Mr. Tiley?"

"Yes," said Graham Tiley. "The past, with all its crimes and all its revenges, should stay in the past. You're not needed here any more, so run free, noble dogs."

The great dark shapes simply faded away, gone in a moment, gone back into the Past. The ghost of Albert Winter looked slowly about him.

"Go to him," JC said to Tiley. "Forgive him. And then show him the way to leave, through the Clear White Light."

"Of course," said Tiley. "Maybe . . . he was the ghost I was looking for, all this time."

The old man walked steadily over to the ghost, and they talked quietly together, then the ghost faded away and was gone.

Kim came over to join JC, appearing entirely solid and substantial again. "I do so love a happy ending, don't you?"

"Black Dogges, haunted factories, and it all comes down to people, in the end," said JC. "Human is, as human does. For good and bad."

TWO

OUT OF THE ORDINARY

Early evening outside Chimera House, a large and solid stone-and-glass business building tucked away in the heart of London's business area. A night sky full of stars, a sliver of a new moon, and a cold breeze gusting through empty streets. No traffic, not a soul to be seen anywhere, flat amber light from the street-lamps falling on JC and Happy and Melody as they huddled resentfully together before the brightly lit windows of Chimera House. Two men, one woman, and a ghost unseen, all of them feeling distinctly hard done by.

"It's not fair," said Happy, bitterly. "We're guaranteed proper recovery time between assignments! They can't throw us right back in the deep end just because we're handy! All this extra stress is putting years on me. Of course, on me it looks good . . ."

"Pause for hollow laughter," said Melody. "What are

we doing here, JC? I'm cold, I'm hungry, and I want to go to bed. If I don't get some proper refreshment and some decent sleep soon, someone's going to pay for it, and it sure as hell isn't going to be me."

"You were all there when I got the phone call," JC said patiently. "Which means you know as much as I do. The Boss wants us here, so we're here."

"Five hours on a train, and what kind of greeting do we get when we arrive at Paddington Station?" said Melody. "Big bunch of flowers, box of chocolates, and a hearty *Well done*? An air ticket to somewhere decadent? No, we get dropped right in it again. I could spit soot . . ."

"Please don't," said Happy. "It's not a pretty sight."

"You will observe," said JC, "that our dear and much respected and even-more-feared divine Bossness is conspicuous by her absence. Which suggests that whatever we've been sent to tend to, it can't be that important. Or she'd be here, bending our ears on the matter. However, given how unusual it is for us to be directed straight to a danger site, without even a quick stop-off for a briefing, it does suggest that whatever happened here . . . was not only really bad, but decidedly recent."

"I love to hear him talk," said Melody. "Don't you love to hear him talk? He has such a way with words . . . Look, can't we at least go inside? It's bloody cold out here. I am freezing my tits off."

JC looked at her. "You really want simply to walk in there? Into an unknown situation, with unknown dangers?"

"Yes! I'm cold!"

"What exactly did the Boss say to you?" said Happy, tactfully changing the subject.

"Directions on how to get here and orders to stay put for further instructions," said JC. "And then she rang off before I could tell her to go to Hell."

Melody sniffed loudly. "You don't actually expect her to turn up in person, do you? At this ungodly hour of the morning? Far more likely she'll roust some poor unfortunate flak-catcher out of bed and send him down here for us to shout at. Hello . . . spot the expensive car."

They all turned to look at the huge silver stretch-limousine as it glided down the empty street, then eased to a halt right in front of them, with a purr of its powerful motor. A uniformed chauffeur, complete with peaked cap and supercilious expression, jumped out from behind the wheel and hurried back to open the rear door. Out stepped Robert Patterson. Tall, black, expensively dressed in the best three-piece Saville Row had to offer. A shaved head, a noble brow, and a handsome face, elegant and dignified. Robert Patterson was the public face of the Carnacki Institute, on those rare occasions when it needed to talk with other parts of the Establishment. A product of Eton and Cambridge, ex-Guards and ex-Civil Service, Patterson didn't normally lower himself to brief field agents. Certainly not out in the field. He had important paper-shuffling to be getting on with.

JC considered Patterson thoughtfully as the man stood silently, ignoring them as he gave complete concentration to checking that his cuffs were immaculate. For Patterson to appear there, in person, meant they had to be facing a very delicate situation. The kind of case in which very rich, very important, and very well-connected people were involved. So highly placed that even the Carnacki Institute had to tread carefully.

Patterson finally deigned to acknowledge the field agents, looking them over sourly. He didn't seem to be any happier about being there than they did, which cheered them up somewhat.

"Mr. Patterson," JC said smoothly. "How nice to see you. Especially when you swore you never wanted to see us again after that unfortunate incident at Her Majesty's garden party last spring. Did you ever get the stains out? No matter, no matter . . . Looking very elegant, as always, straight from your posh ride. Look at the length of it. That's not a stretch limo, that's a car with serious glandular problems. You must forgive our rather more rumpled appearance. We've just endured five hours in standard class on British Rail, direct from our last very successful assignment."

"We had to hire a mini-van!" Happy said loudly. "A bloody mini-van!"

"Hush now, Happy," murmured JC. "Grown-ups talking."

"Hell with that," said Happy. "Open up that limo and let me at the booze. I am in dire need of some medicinal brandy. Or medicinal vodka, I'm not fussy . . ."

"Damn right," said Melody. "You got any snacks in there, Patterson? I'm so hungry I could eat your upholstery. Let me at it, or I'll shoot out your tyres and key your bodywork."

"Can't take you two anywhere," said JC. "Sorry about

that, Mr. Patterson. But they aren't being entirely reasonable, after all we've been through. You can of course put it all right by saying the magic words: Extravagant Bonus."

"It's either that or we mug you for what you've got on you," said Happy. "Your choice."

Patterson made a big deal of rising above them. "Pay attention," he said, in his rich, deep, and very cultured voice. The field agents all made a point of sneering back at him, to show how unimpressed they were. Patterson pressed on. "This is a significant case, with important connections. It has to be handled carefully, with due regard for possible repercussions if it isn't handled . . . just so."

"Can't be that important," Happy said craftily. "Or the Boss herself would be here."

"Catherine Latimer is here," said Patterson. "But she's far too busy to spend valuable time talking with you. She is currently interfacing with the police and the Secret Service, making sure the whole area is evacuated, then sealed off until this is all over. Or hadn't you noticed how deserted the streets are?"

"We didn't see any Secret Service people on our way in," said Happy.

Patterson allowed himself a small smile. "Which goes to show how good they are at their job."

"I've never known London this quiet," said Melody. "Even at this god-forsaken early hour of the morning. Look, I can see empty parking spaces! That's eerie . . ."

"What are we dealing with here?" JC said bluntly. "Ghosts, demons, those evil scumbags from the Crowley Project? What?"

"Unknown," Patterson said carefully. "But almost certainly nothing you've encountered before. This whole affair is very much out of the ordinary. Even for the Institute. This entire building, Chimera House, had been officially declared *genius loci*. A bad place, psychically stained and corrupted. It has to be dealt with, quickly and efficiently. Before the vultures start gathering."

"The whole building?" said JC. "Who does it belong to? What the hell do they do there?"

"Chimera House is owned by Mutable Solutions Inc.," said Patterson. "One of the biggest drug companies, worldwide. They have branches everywhere, and annual gross sales bigger than many countries' entire budgets. In fact, they're rumoured to run certain small countries, on the quiet. This particular building is one of their private research centres. So private we didn't even know they owned it until now, and we're supposed to know things like that, given MSI's track record for working on the more extreme and dangerous edges of medical science. Chimera House pays volunteers to allow their medical staff to test new drugs on them. All very open and respectable. Good pay, civilised living conditions for the test subjects, never any problems or complaints. Until now.

"It would appear that something has gone very badly wrong inside Chimera House. Some hours ago, emergency services received an increasingly frantic phone call from the science laboratories on the third floor, calling for help. Screaming for help, to be exact. The call was abruptly terminated, right after the caller had used the word *monsters*. We're running tests on a recording of the call. There are . . . strange noises in the background. Non-human noises. Further communication with anyone inside Chimera House has proved impossible.

"Two nearby police officers responded to the emergency call. They went inside and haven't been seen since. They're not answering their radios. National Security got involved after that. They sent in a fully armed attack squad, looking for signs of industrial espionage. All communications cut off the moment they entered the building, and there's been no sign of them since, either.

"The whole building has been sealed off, but nothing else has been done . . . due to a certain amount of disagreement as to who has jurisdiction. The police are hopping mad at the loss of their officers, and the Security people want to storm the building with as many men as it takes. Neither are ready to back down to the other. MI5 and MI6 tried to stick their toes in the door, shouting *terrorists* very loudly, but since this is an MSI building, with all kinds of government connections and contracts, it got very complicated, very quickly. They'd probably still be shouting at each other if a spokesman for MSI hadn't phoned the Prime Minister, on his private line, to demand that the Carnacki Institute take control. Which is interesting for any number of reasons, not the least that they're not supposed to know we even exist. And no, the spokesman wouldn't say why MSI wanted us. So, until we figure out exactly what's going on, we have agreed to send a team in. You. Because you're the nearest A team, with the best reputation. But you are still new enough to be entirely expendable.

"Time is apparently a factor, so we can't wait for a

more experienced team. You get first shot. Go in there, work out what's going on, and stop it. And if you should happen to find out why the MSI asked for us . . . there will be honey for tea and generous bonuses all round."

"Hold everything," said Happy, raising one hand like a child at school. "We're supposed to walk into a building that's already killed a whole bunch of people? With no solid intel, no weapons, and no backup?"

"That's the job, sometimes," said JC. "And we don't know that anyone's dead yet."

"I'm not going in there without my equipment!" said Melody. "All my gear's still packed up on the freight train!"

"I have people bringing it here," said Patterson. "But you'll have to make a start without it."

"What am I supposed to do without equipment?" said Melody, sulking.

"Improvise," said Patterson. He didn't smile.

"I think we have to assume that something has gone seriously wrong with the latest drug trial," JC said quickly. "Remember that case a few years back, when they tried out what they thought was a perfectly safe drug, and half the volunteers exploded? Could be something similar. You can only learn so much from computer modelling. Sooner or later, you have to shove the stuff into somebody's vein and stand well back. Do you have any information on what MSI was testing?"

"No," said Patterson. "The MSI spokesman is only telling us what he thinks we need to know. He's currently hiding behind Proprietary Information. The Boss is putting together enough authority and influence to kick that door down, but it will take time. You should be able to find all the information you need in the building's various computers. Feel free to look at anything you feel like and make as much mess as you need. You are all officially authorised to act like utter vandals and do any damned thing you feel necessary. That's it."

"That's it?" said Happy. "What if we can't sort this out? What if we all get killed in there?"

"Don't," said Patterson.

He turned sharply and strode back to his silver limo, gleaming at the curb like an expensive ghost in the night. The waiting chauffeur opened the door for him, Patterson disappeared inside, and, within seconds, the car was gliding smoothly away. Kim emerged from the shadows to make a rude gesture after it.

"What an appalling person," she said.

"Be fair," said JC. "I can't think of anyone better suited to take on our enemies. That man could annoy anyone to death."

They all turned to look at Chimera House. It looked calmly back at them; a tall, imposing structure of steel, glass, and concrete. A building of almost staggering ugliness, with all the aesthetic considerations of a dead rat. It fit right in, in an area where form and function had taken over from pretty much everything else. Lights blazed from every window, but there was no sign that anyone was home.

"Can you see anyone moving in there?" said Happy. "I can't see anyone moving in there. Where are they?"

"If they were running drug tests, there should be people on duty at all times," said Melody. "Apart from the test subjects, there should be doctors and nurses, scientists, support staff, building security . . . They can't all be dead. Can they?"

"Kim," said JC. "What do you see?"

"Nothing," said Kim. "It's like the whole building is standing in a shadow. A dark veil for someone or something to hide behind. What do you see, JC?"

"Only a building," said JC. He turned to Happy. "Are you picking anything up, oh master of the mental miracles?"

Happy shrugged unhappily. "Just a feeling . . . That what we're looking at is an illusion. A facade. The smile on the face of the tiger."

They waited, but he had nothing more to say. He was shivering, and not only from the cold. The quiet of the empty street, and the brightly blazing building before them suddenly seemed that much more dangerous, and full of secrets.

"Keep your shields up, Happy," JC said finally. "Protect yourself in there until we've got some idea of what's going on."

"Why are you suddenly being nice to me?" said Happy, suspiciously. "That isn't like you. It's an improvement, but it's not like you."

"Because without Melody's high-tech toys, you're the only advantage we've got," JC said calmly. "Our only early-warning system, and probably our only real weapon."

"Then we are in serious trouble," said Happy. "Let's all go home and tell the Boss we couldn't find the right building."

"Brace up, man," said JC. "Be a brave little soldier, and I'll make you some of my special spag bol afterwards."

"I miss food," Kim said wistfully. "I can still enjoy the smell, but anything I put in my mouth drops straight through."

"Well, there's a mental image I wasn't expecting to take home with me," said Melody.

"Let us not go there," JC said firmly.

Melody scowled at the brightly lit building before her. "No tech, no proper briefing . . . I hate going into situations blind."

"Best way," JC said cheerfully. "No preconceptions to get in the way. Come, children, let us march into the lobby and claim it as our own."

He walked forward and darted up the stone steps to the lobby door. It was mostly glass. The others moved quickly after him. JC went right up to it and stuck his nose against the glass. His sunglasses made a loud, clinking sound. He peered carefully round the whole lobby. It was completely open to view, light blazing freely through glass windows. And it was completely empty. No sign of people, no sign of any trouble, or destruction. It looked like a stage set, waiting for the actors to make an entrance and start the scene.

"I don't see anyone," said JC, straightening up with definite creaking noises from his spine. "Not even a receptionist. I always thought they were legally obliged to go down with the ship, manning the phones to the end. I see fittings and furnishings, comfortable chairs and potted plants . . . everything as it should be. But . . ."

"Where are the bodies?" said Melody, pushing in beside him. "The police and the security men?"

"Why are you so keen that they should be dead?" said JC. "Until proved otherwise, they're missing in action. This could still turn out to be a rescue mission."

"They're dead," said Happy.

There was something in the way he said it that made everyone else look at him. JC considered him thoughtfully.

"Is that a feeling, or do you know something you really should be sharing with the rest of us?"

"I can feel death in this building," said Happy. "Like a shroud hanging over everything. And especially in this lobby. Recent death. Sudden death. I don't think they even knew what hit them until it was too late."

"Who killed them?" said JC. "Or is it What?"

"I can't put a name to it," said Happy. "It's like nothing I've seen or felt before. And I've been around."

JC looked at Kim. "Are you picking up any of this?"

"No," said Kim. "Not a thing. And that's *wrong* . . . If people died here, I should be able to see something . . . The world is full of ghosts, and fellow travellers, and images that come and go. I see all the things we share the world with. Comes with being a ghost. There are things here on the street with us right now, paying close attention to the building. But when I look into the lobby, there's nothing there. So I can only assume that someone is hiding what's happened from me. Which means, I get to go in first."

She smiled sweetly at JC and stepped through the closed door before he could stop her. She ghosted through the glass as though it weren't there, and for her, it probably wasn't. She strode into the lobby and looked quickly about her. JC tensed, his hands pressed flat against the door glass as he watched her every movement intensely. But nothing happened. Kim walked up and down the lobby, her feet bare inches above the deep pile carpet, peering interestedly at everything, until finally she turned to look back at JC and the others and shrug helplessly.

"That's it," said JC. "We're going in."

But when he tried the door-handle, it wouldn't move. Someone had locked the door from the inside. JC swore loudly and rattled the door with all his strength, like that was going to make any difference. He scowled, stepped back, and kicked the door moodily.

"Typical of Patterson. He could at least have supplied us with a set of keys."

Melody shouldered him aside and smashed the glass with one savage karate kick. She sneered at JC.

"Keys are for wimps."

JC pushed past her, stepped carefully through the door-frame, and hurried into the lobby. "Hello, ghosties! Come out, come out, wherever you are!"

"I hate it when he does that," growled Melody, following him in. Happy nodded glumly.

The Ghost Finders came together in the middle of the lobby and looked around them. Everything was still and quiet, and not in a good way. There was something wrong with the stillness. It was the stillness of anticipation, of something bad about to happen. As though an unspeakable monster was getting ready to jump out at

them from some hidden place. As though trap-doors
were about to open under their feet, to send them plum-
meting down to some unimaginable horror. As though all
the rules were about to be changed in some terrible game
they didn't even know they were playing.

"Oh, this is bad," said Happy. "This feels really bad."

"My back is crawling," said Melody. "Like someone
painted a target on it."

Kim looked at JC. "What do you feel, sweetie?"

"Like we're being watched," he said. "And I don't see
any security cameras."

"The whole place feels like fingernails dragged down
the blackboard of my soul," said Happy. "I can feel
someone sneaking up behind me, but there's no-one
there . . ."

"Yes," said Melody, trying to look in several directions at once. "Like someone's crept in and is peering
over my shoulder."

"Echoes," JC said calmly. "Psychic echoes of something that's already happened. Don't let them get to
you. Kim, are you picking up any traces of a stone tape
recording? If all these people were killed here, it might
have imprinted on the surroundings . . ."

"It's worse in here," said Kim. "It's been made worse.
Bad things happened here, on purpose. Someone walked
in blood and murder, and loved it. JC, this whole building is saturated with unnatural energies. Trying to see
what happened here is like staring into a spotlight."

Melody went straight to the reception desk, sat down
before the built-in computer, fired it up, and let out a
brief sigh of relief as her fingers tripped busily across the

keyboard, teasing and intimidating information out of the computer files.

"For a really major company, with big-time security protocols, their firewalls are strictly amateur night," she said smugly.

"Open up every file you can access," said JC. "I have questions."

"I'm in," said Melody. "Easy-peasy. What do you want to know?"

Happy looked at her. "Don't you need passwords, things like that . . . ?"

"Passwords are for wimps, too," said Melody. "You have to know how to talk to these things. Okay . . . They started the latest drug trial last evening. Code name, Zarathustra. Oh shit. That is not good. Whenever some scientist starts quoting Nietzsche, you know it is never going to be good."

"'I teach you the superman,'" JC said solemnly. "He is this thunder, he is this lighting. 'Man is something that should be overcome.'"

"Damn," said Happy. "Are you saying they were trying to make superhumans here? I thought there were a whole bunch of really serious laws against messing around with human DNA?"

"Oh there are," said JC. "Lots and lots. Which is why there are also a whole bunch of companies and governments lining up to pay serious money to the first people to come up with something useful. No questions asked. There's a quiet undeclared race on to produce something that will improve people. Superman, super-soldier, supergenius—all of them property, not people."

"There's nothing here about what this particular drug was supposed to do," said Melody. "I can't get into the science laboratories' files from down here. I need direct access. Which means we need to go further up and poke around . . . I can tell you that the new drug was administered to the volunteers around seven hours ago. So whatever went wrong, it went wrong really fast. I've got a list here, names and information on all the volunteers. Are you really a volunteer if they pay you and don't properly explain the dangers?"

"Depends how much they pay," said Happy.

"Forty thousand pounds, for two weeks, plus bed and board," said Melody.

"Chicken feed," said JC. "That's what they usually pay for testing cold cures, hand creams, allergy meds. Presumably the company didn't want to risk drawing attention to what they were doing. How many test subjects were there, Melody?"

"Twenty. Ten men and ten women, ages twenty to thirty. Of course, some of them would have been given a harmless placebo . . . Testing took place on the second floor; living quarters for the test subjects are on the first floor. Laboratories on the third . . . no information on the remaining floors."

"Something's coming," Kim said suddenly, and they all looked around.

The air was suddenly colder, painfully cold in their lungs as they breathed it in. Something was sucking all the heat out of the room. An energy drain, to power some kind of manifestation. There was a growing tension across the lobby, as though something might break, or explode. Suddenly, footsteps started down the stairs at the far end of the lobby. Slow, heavy, and quite deliberate footsteps, descending from above. Each separate sound seemed to hang on the air, unnaturally long, as though reluctant to depart. JC gestured quickly for everyone to spread out at the foot of the stairs, blocking them off. He and Kim got there first, peering eagerly up the stairs, but there was no-one to be seen yet. Melody reluctantly got up from her computer and moved across to join them. Happy stood behind her, not quite hiding. They waited at the foot of the stairs as the footsteps drew steadily nearer, louder, heavier . . . and then, at the moment when whoever was making them would have had to come round the corner at the top of the stairs, and reveal themselves, the sounds stopped. The last of the echoes died away, and there was only the quiet, and the increasingly oppressive stillness.

JC and the others waited, tense and ready for anything, but the footsteps had stopped. Nothing to hear, nothing to see. JC ran forward and sprinted up the steps to look round the corner, but there was no-one there. No sign there had ever been anyone there. JC came back down the stairs, scowling.

Then the elevator bell rang.

They all looked round sharply, and JC led the way as they raced over to the other side of the lobby, to the single elevator. The down arrow above the door was lit, and the row of numbers showed that the elevator was descending from the third floor. The laboratories . . . JC gestured urgently, and they all spread out before the elevator doors. Happy moved to not quite hide behind

Melody again, and she grabbed his arm and hauled him out beside her. They all watched the numbers descend, tantalisingly slowly. And then the bell rang again, and the elevator doors slid open, to reveal there was no-one inside. The elevator was completely empty. Happy let out a quick sigh of relief, looked away, then cried out as a uniformed police officer appeared out of nowhere, right in the middle of the lobby.

The others spun around, and looked to where Happy was pointing with a trembling hand, but none of them moved. Neither did the police officer. He stood perfectly still, unnaturally still, and stared at them all with unblinking, unwavering eyes. His uniform was perfect, not even the smallest tear or blood stain. Nothing to show how he had died. But none of them doubted for a moment that he was dead. They only had to look at his face.

"Just an ordinary police officer, a bobby on the beat," said JC. "He should never have been sent into a place like this. He never stood a chance."

"He's not breathing," Melody said quietly. "Not even showing the smallest of involuntary movements. His face is . . . empty. Nobody home. And look at his eyes . . . He sees us, but not in a human way. Whatever's watching us through those eyes isn't in any way human."

A second policeman appeared, blinking in out of nowhere, as though forced into existence by an effort of will. Again, quite definitely dead. To look at him was to know it, on an instinctive level. The two dead men stood utterly still, in the centre of the lobby. The temperature was dropping even further. JC and the others were all shivering now, despite themselves, their breath steaming on the air before them. No steam from the dead men's faces. No frost in the lobby, no ice; only the deep, deep cold.

The security men appeared next, snapping into existence one after the other, all across the lobby. Slamming in without warning, tall uniformed men in heavy flak jackets, all of them carrying guns. But the arms hung limply at their sides, as unmoving as any other part of them, gun barrels pointing at the floor. None of them moved in the least, or made any attempt to communicate. They simply stood and stared. But there was still something terribly menacing about them. As though they were waiting for the right moment to do something horrible.

It was their faces. Human faces weren't meant to look like theirs. The dead, knowing eyes . . . the complete lack of any emotion or expression . . . in faces that weren't dead enough.

"Look at the plants," Kim said quietly. "Look at the potted plants."

They all glanced at the plants, not wanting to take their eyes off the dead men for too long. The half dozen potted plants, which had been standing tall and proud when JC first led the way in were now shrivelling up and withering away. Rot and corruption set in, and curled-up leaves fell listlessly to the floor. Something had sucked the life right out of them to maintain the dead men's presence. The quality of light in the lobby had changed, too. The fierce fluorescent light now seemed strained, weakened, even infected. One of the policemen took a single step forward, his muscles stiff and awkward. Then one of the security men. And then all the dead men were advancing on JC and his team, from every direction at once, one slow step at a time. Their faces didn't change, their eyes didn't move, but there was still an awful, inexorable purpose about them.

"Stand together!" roared JC. "Back to back!"

JC and Kim moved together, as did Happy and Melody. Close enough that no-one could get between them, but not so much that they'd get in each other's way if push came to violent action. JC was grinning broadly. He was always happiest on a case when things started to happen. It meant the waiting was over, and the mission was finally under way. JC did so love to get his hands dirty, and get stuck into things. Melody had produced her machine pistol again and was waving it steadily back and forth to cover the approaching dead men. Happy was making loud, whimpering noises but stood his ground. If only because all the ways to the exits were blocked. In his own way, he, too, was happiest when things started kicking off, because at least then he knew where the danger was.

The dead men moved with ghastly, deliberate slowness, as though movement was something they only vaguely remembered. The security men still had their arms at their sides, the gun barrels pointing towards the floor, but the sense of menace and danger was even stronger. The tension on the air was so strong, JC could feel it crushing down on him, like an unbearable weight. He glared at the nearest dead man.

"Who are you? What do you want? Do you remember what happened to you here? Do you remember who you are?"

The dead man didn't react, as though words meant

nothing to him. But his unblinking eyes were fixed on JC, and there was something in his face, a strange, alien essence that made all the hairs on the back of JC's neck stand up.

"Kim," he said urgently. "Can you read them? Can you tell me anything about them?"

"There's nothing there to read!" said Kim.

"I'm not picking up anything, either!" said Happy, looking desperately back and forth. "It's like . . . there's nothing there! Except there is!"

"They're shells," Kim said suddenly. "Just shells! They're dead, they're some kind of ghost . . . but they're not surviving personalities, like me. They're what's left, after all the life and all the energy have been sucked right out. Something really bad has happened to these people. Because they're not people any more. Something else is watching us, JC, through their dead eyes."

JC nodded quickly, thinking hard. "Do they have any actual physical presence? Can they hurt us?"

"I don't know!" said Kim. "I've never seen anything like them before. They're what's left when you take the people out of people."

"Terrific," said JC. "All right, we do it the hard way, then."

He strode quickly forward, leaving his team behind, walked right up to the nearest security man, and prodded him in the flak jacket with one stiff finger. And cried out in pain and shock, as his finger sank into the dead man, disappearing from view. He yanked his finger out and staggered back, clutching his injured hand to his chest.

"It's all right!" he said quickly. "It was just so cold . . .

Like sticking my hand into the vacuum between the stars!"

"A complete absence of physical presence," said Melody. "Interesting. Not only an image but also a hole in the world . . ." She put her machine pistol away and flexed her empty hands uneasily.

"Ow!" said JC, flapping his injured hand urgently. "Pins and needles! Sensation coming back! Ow ow *ow*!"

"If they're not really there, how do we stop them?" said Happy. "They are getting terribly close now, and not in a good way, and none of them look friendly! If anyone feels like doing something dramatic and violent, I wouldn't object in the least."

"Don't let any of them touch you!" Kim said abruptly.

"What?" said Happy. "Why not?"

"I don't know," said Kim. "I'm getting a strong feeling that would be . . . bad."

"Terrific," said JC.

"We should bring a canary in a cage, for situations like this," said Melody.

"We are the canary in the cage!" said Happy.

One of the dead men surged forward, heading straight for Melody. His movements were jerky and graceless, like a puppet on unseen strings. He reached out with both hands, his unwavering gaze fixed on Melody. Happy lunged forward to stand between them. He thrust out a blocking hand, and scowled fiercely as he concentrated. The dead man exploded silently. The image flared up and was gone, as though it had never been there. All the other dead men stopped moving, frozen in their tracks, in mid movement.

"Very impressive, Happy," said JC. "Would you mind telling us what it was you did?"

"A concentrated burst of telepathically projected disbelief," said Happy, breathlessly. "My belief that he didn't exist overwhelmed Someone else's belief that he did."

"Someone else?" said JC. "What someone else?"

"Haven't a clue," said Happy.

"My brave bunny," said Melody, dropping an arm across Happy's shoulders. "There will be special treats, later."

"There are still quite a few dead men left," JC pointed out. "Any chance you could manage that trick again?"

"Not a hope in Hell," said Happy. "That one effort took pretty much everything I had."

"You just can't get good help these days," said JC. "Not to worry! Now I know those things are vulnerable, I think I might have the very thing . . ." He fished in a jacket pocket, pulled out a grenade, primed it, and tossed it neatly into the advancing dead men. "Guard your eyes, children! Flashbang!"

The grenade exploded in a blast of incandescent light. Even with their eyes closed and their heads instinctively turned away, JC and Happy and Melody all cried out as the brilliant light seared their eyes. The light snapped off, and when they could all see again, all the dead men were gone, and the lobby was completely empty.

"What the hell was *that*?" said Melody.

"The very latest in a long line of useful gadgets that I'm not supposed to have," JC said easily. "An exorcism grenade."

Melody looked at him dangerously. "An exorcism . . . Are you taking the piss?"

"The very latest improvement!" said JC. "Gets the job done in half the time! Holy light!"

"I know I'm going to regret asking this," said Happy. "But how . . ."

"You make water holy by saying the right religious words over it," said JC. "Why should light be any different?"

"It's thinking things like that that make my head hurt," said Happy.

"Wait a moment," said Kim, who hadn't been dazzled by the light at all, "How did you know that grenade wouldn't affect me?"

"Because you're with us," said JC. "One of the good guys."

"Have you ever tested that thing in the field before?" said Melody.

"Guess," said JC.

"I'm not picking up any remaining traces of the shells," said Happy. "Any chance that light destroyed them completely?"

"Not really," said JC. "More likely, the light only chased them away."

"Oh joy," said Happy.

"Deep joy," said Melody.

"Happy happy joy joy!" said Kim, pogoing up and down in mid air.

"Come along, children," said JC. "We need to get up to the next floor. We need information."

"And weapons," said Happy. "Really big weapons."

THREE

WE SHOULDN'T BE HERE

They went up the stairs to the next floor because none of them trusted the elevator. They didn't particularly trust the stairs, either, but as Happy pointed out, at least stairs don't get you half-way there and then plummet to the basement. Or turn into something nasty and swallow you up. Happy had a lot of other reasons why he didn't trust elevators in general and this one in particular, but the others were already half-way up the stairs and not listening to him. JC went bounding up the stairs two at a time, with all his usual energy and enthusiasm, Kim floating along beside him. Melody followed behind, still grumbling under her breath over what had happened to her precious equipment. Happy sighed deeply and brought up the rear, very reluctantly.

The stairs were only stairs, with no graces or comforts. The walls were bare, the single railing was as basic as health and safety regulations would allow, and the light was sharp and bright, with no shadows anywhere. Even so, there was still something distinctly uneasy about the narrow stairway, something . . . not quite right.

"I know we're going up," said Happy, after a while. "But I swear it feels like we're going down . . ."

"Steady in the ranks," said JC. "Don't let the place get to you. All right, this building has proved to be entirely spooky and mysterious, in a malevolent sort of way, full of uncanny things that we haven't encountered before, but is that any reason to be downhearted?"

"Well, yes!" said Happy.

"It makes the job that much more interesting," JC said firmly. "You're never too old to learn something new. And make a serious profit from it."

He slammed through the swinging doors at the next floor and led his team into a brightly lit corridor. He stopped abruptly to take a good look. Melody nearly ran into him. A seriously long corridor stretched away before them, barely wide enough for two people to walk down abreast. To JC's left, a series of rooms lined the corridor. All the doors were standing open. To his right was a blank wall, painted industrial off-white. With all the doors open, there was only room to walk down the corridor single file. No windows, no signs or instructions on the wall or the doors, and no signs of violence or destruction anywhere. Like the lobby, it was all very still and very quiet, with a subtle tension in the air. JC moved over to the first open door and studied it carefully.

"All right," he said. "First interesting thing. This door has a very heavy, very solid steel lock. No electronics.

Far more security than you'd need for what is, after all, a basic hotel room. Especially when beefed up by this very solid steel bolt, on the *outside* of the door. Suggesting that once the subjects were bedded in for the night, they were intended to stay put until someone came and let them out in the morning. Now why would the researchers feel the need to do that? To stop their subjects from wandering? Or because said subjects might become dangerous once they'd been dosed? Or even . . . because they might panic when the first symptoms or changes occurred and try to run?"

"Let's not get ahead of ourselves," said Melody. "The best security measure, with drug trials or anything else, is to control the supply of information. The people in the trial might have been locked in to make sure they didn't see anything they weren't supposed to. Never put down to supernatural nastiness what you can as easily put down to the fear of industrial espionage."

"A lock *and* a bolt," said Happy. "The researchers weren't taking any chances, were they?"

JC strode off down the corridor, leaving the others to catch up with him. He was doing his best to seem cool and calm and utterly at his ease, but he looked very thoroughly into every room he passed, taking it all in. The rooms were comfortable enough, if somewhat small, with all the usual luxuries. Television, computer . . .

Melody waited till they reached the third room, then she couldn't stand it any longer. She darted inside and sat down at the computer. The others stopped and came back, watching from the doorway as Melody turned on the computer and logged on.

JC sighed quietly. "So much for being in charge . . ."

"You need information," said Melody, not looking up from the many illegal things she was doing. "This is where I find information."

"Indeed," murmured JC. "I'm amazed you were able to hold yourself back this long. So, what is the computer telling you, in what I've decided to call Room Three? Because there are no numbers or other designations on any of the doors. Did any of the rest of you notice that? I always notice things like that. Happy, Melody doesn't seem to be talking to me. What about you? Do you have anything to tell me? Are you picking up anything?"

"Not really," said Happy, looking vaguely up and down the empty corridor. "No-one lived here long enough to make much of an impression. I can say there's definitely no-one alive hiding anywhere on this floor. All the rooms are empty. Still, it's odd . . . normally when I lower my shields and look around, you three all start shouting at me with your minds, and I have to fade you down before I can hear anything else. But here . . . I'm only sensing you dimly, as though from a great distance. Somewhere in this building, something is interfering with my reception."

"Are you saying someone is jamming you?" said JC.

"Wouldn't surprise me," said Happy. "Can't say I'm that bothered. It's actually quite relaxing, not having to keep all your voices out of my head for a change."

"Can you pick up any traces of the person who used to live in this room?" said JC.

Happy glared at him. "I keep telling you, I'm not that kind of psychic! I read people, and places, and that's it!

I do not read objects, channel past events, or read tea leaves! I am a telepath, and that's more than enough to deal with. I am not a miracle-worker!"

"Pity," said JC. "I could use a miracle-worker. I'm going to take a stroll further down the corridor, see what there is to see. Yell if you need anything, Melody."

And he was off and gone, with Kim drifting after him. Happy slouched sullenly in the doorway.

"We shouldn't be working this case," he said flatly. "We're supposed to deal with ghosties and ghoulies and things that go *Boo!* in the night. Whatever happened here has heavy science written all over it. We're already out of our depth, even if JC won't admit it, and way out of our comfort zone."

"You speak for yourself," said Melody, scowling thoughtfully at the monitor before her.

"I am!" said Happy. "Loudly and meaningfully, but no-one is listening! We shouldn't be here! This isn't what we do . . ."

Melody sighed loudly and turned round in her chair to look at him. "Those were ghosts, down in the lobby, weren't they?"

"Well, yes, of a sort, but . . ."

"But nothing. You heard what the annoying man from the stretch limo said—find out what's going on, and stop it. That's the job. Everything else is just details." She stopped and smiled at him almost fondly. "I know you don't like to admit it, Happy, but it's all science, all of the time. Ghosts, demons, the afterworlds—all of existence and everything beyond—it's all science. We don't always understand it yet, that's all. Now hush like a good bunny and let me get on with my work, or I'll start throwing words like *quantum* around, and you know how you hate that."

Happy shuddered briefly in the doorway and shut up, and Melody went back to work.

....

Further down the corridor, JC was looking around what he had loudly declared he was naming Room Fourteen, picking things up, examining them, and putting them down again, trying to get a feel for the last person who'd lived there. Given the number of well-thumbed magazines, like *Heat* and *OK*, he was pretty sure the occupant had been female, but he didn't say that out loud because he knew Kim would accuse him of being judgemental. There were no personal touches, no photos, no jewellery, not even any clothes. Were the test subjects supposed to go around all the time in those awful hospital gowns that only do up at the back? JC stood in the middle of the room, looking thoughtfully about him, but the room defeated him. It was deliberately bare and characterless, more like a waiting room than living quarters.

Kim threw herself onto the bed by the far wall to watch JC work, misjudged the distance, and fell halfway through the bed before she could stop herself. She quickly floated back up out of it, before JC could notice, and with precisely the right amount of concentration managed to float directly above the bed-sheets, so it looked like she was lying there. Kim wasn't alive, but she liked to pretend she could still do everyday things, as though she were an ordinary girl. For JC's sake, as well as her own.

"Anything?" she said brightly, when she was sure she could present the right image.

"Nothing useful," said JC. "No trace of any upset or disturbance here. No signs of interrupted activity. Just like all the other rooms. It's as though . . . everyone got up and left. Except, they couldn't. Because all the doors were locked and bolted shut from the outside. So someone must have come and let them all out, and given them good reason to leave . . . Even though they must have been strictly instructed not to. Which implies they knew who the person who let them out was . . . someone in a position of authority."

"Like the *Marie Celeste*," said Kim, to show she was keeping up. "The old ship found floating out at sea with everyone missing and nothing to show where they had gone."

"Yes," said JC, smiling. "Something like that." He looked over at Kim, and stopped smiling. "Kim, you're sinking again."

Her concentration had lapsed while they were talking, and she'd almost disappeared under the bed. She swore briefly and jumped up. She dropped to the floor and concentrated until her feet were as close to the carpet as she could manage without sinking through, then she walked carefully forward to stand before JC. She looked at him, almost defiantly.

"It's not easy, you know, being dead. In fact, it's really hard work. All those little things you take for granted, I have to fight for. I don't sleep, eat, or rest. I can't stand still, or sit, or lie down. Mostly, I just hover. There are strange aetheric winds that blow me this way and that, and odd impulses I don't understand . . . You don't know what it's like! I do try to be normal for you . . ."

"I know," said JC. "I know." He smiled at her, careful not to appear upset in any way. There wasn't anything useful he could say, so he settled for trying to lighten the moment. "Aren't I worth it?"

"You're the only thing that makes this bearable, JC," said Kim, with painful earnestness. "If I didn't have you, I think . . . I'd just let go."

JC stood as close before her as he could, taking off his sunglasses so he could hold her eyes with his. She was the only one who could meet his unnatural gaze these days. "You know I'd never keep you here against your will. You do know that, right? If you ever feel it would be . . . easier for you to move on . . ."

"No," Kim said immediately. "We found each other. After spending our lives alone, and thinking it would always be that way . . . Out of a whole world full of people, we found each other. How remarkable is that? I wish it could have happened while I was still alive. That I didn't have to die to find love."

"Me, too," said JC. He put his arms around her, very carefully, not quite touching her. It was difficult because he couldn't feel her, but he did his best. She put her arms around his waist, without quite touching him, and leaned her head almost on his shoulder, so their faces could be side by side. Hardly any space separated them, but it might as well have been forever. Their mouths were close, but they couldn't even feel each other breathe. Because only JC was breathing. It was tense, and it was awkward, but it was the best they could do, so they stood that way for a while.

"Are you sure you can't feel anything?" said Kim.

"Not even a ghostly chill," said JC.

"Sooner or later," said Kim, "you're going to want someone who can touch you. A lover who can hold and comfort you."

"I want you," said JC. "You're all I ever wanted, even when I didn't know you existed. I love you, Kim."

"And I love you," said Kim. "Oh JC, it's a cruel world, sometimes."

"Hey," said JC. "If it was a cruel world, we never would have found each other."

"Yes," said Kim. "There is that."

"Isn't there any upside to being a ghost?" said JC. "I mean, there are things you can do that I can't."

"Well," said Kim, "sometimes, when you're sleeping, and it's a long time till morning . . . I go flying over London. I let go of gravity and fall upwards, into the night sky, and I go soaring over the rooftops. See the bright lights turn below me like a slow Catherine wheel, see the traffic roaring back and forth like so many toys. And sometimes I fly up among the stars and look down at the Earth, like the most precious and most fragile toy of all."

"You see?" said JC. "I can't do that."

||||||||||||||||||||||||||

Back in Room Three, Melody had finally found something useful. Happy moved forward so he could peer

over her shoulder and watched very secret files appear
and disappear on the screen in response to Melody's fingers flitting over the keyboard. It was all very scientific.

"All right," said Happy, after a while. "You've got that
smug and triumphant look on your face, so what am I
missing? What have you found?"

"LD50," said Melody, sitting back in her chair so suddenly she almost head-butted Happy in the face. She
folded her arms and scowled at the screen. "And I don't
feel smug, or triumphant. This is not a good thing to
have found. LD50 is the dosage at which the new drug is
expected to kill half of the test group. Lethal Dose, Fifty
per cent. Not something you should be finding in a drug
being tested on volunteers. But this LD50 file is quite
definitely attached to the Zarathustra project. It seems to
be posing the question of what happens if the affected
subjects can't or won't die? If they insisted on surviving,
what should be a Lethal Dose?"

"Are you saying . . . the scientists deliberately gave
these people a drug so strong they *expected* it to kill
half the volunteers?" said Happy. "How the hell did they
think they would get away with that?"

"You're not listening," said Melody. "Yes, under normal circumstances, half the recipients should have died.
But what the scientists really expected was that this new
drug would keep them alive. By changing them so much
they could survive something that would quite definitely
kill normal people. LD50 was the final test, the proof
that they'd achieved what they thought they'd achieved.
I think . . . whoever was in charge of this project wasn't

too tightly wrapped. They were playing with people's lives!"

"Okay, I'm thinking *illegal*, and *unethical* and *Mad Doctors on the loose*," said Happy. "Did the company, did MSI, know they were doing this?"

"Looks like it," said Melody. "The orders and authority for this last test came straight from the top. But I would have to say, given the results these people were getting, and the scientists' reactions to what they were seeing . . . I would have to say they were all most definitely scared shitless. The changes went a lot further, and at a much faster pace, than anyone anticipated."

"Did it kill them all, in the end?" said Happy. "Is that what happened to the test volunteers? The scientists panicked, and had to dispose of the bodies?"

"Unfortunately, no," said Melody. "The test subjects survived. And changed. There's nothing here on what they became, but it couldn't have been anything good."

"Is there anything there on which patients had the placebos?" said Happy. "I mean, they wouldn't have gone through any changes. Could they still be here, somewhere?"

"There were no placebos," said Melody. "They didn't care about rigorous scientific procedures, they wanted as many affected test subjects as possible."

"But that's . . ."

"Unethical? Illegal? No-one here gave a damn about any of that, Happy. They thought the company was big enough, and powerful enough, that they didn't have to care about things like that. Which meant this was never a legal test of a legal drug, for legal purposes. MSI was after bigger fish."

"Superhumans," said Happy. "For the Military, or Intelligence, or maybe for themselves."

"Might help to explain why there was such a fight over jurisdiction once it all went wrong," said Melody. "But it doesn't explain why MSI asked for us, specifically, to come in and clean up their mess. They must have known we'd find out the truth . . ."

"Maybe they thought only people with our unique experience would be able to cope with whatever these test subjects have become," said Happy. He looked quickly about him. "And I wish I had their confidence."

They all met up again, half-way down the corridor, to share what they'd discovered. There followed a certain amount of raised voices as they tried to figure out what to do next.

"We are not equipped to deal with genetically modified madmen!" said Happy.

"Who is?" said JC. "But we are uniquely suited to dealing with things and situations that fall outside normal parameters."

"MSI lied," said Melody. "They must have had some reason for dropping us right into this mess, and I'm pretty sure it's not a reason any of us would like or approve of. More and more I'm feeling like chum thrown into the water to attract the sharks. We don't owe MSI anything."

"We're not here for them," said JC. "Patterson sent us in here on behalf of the Carnacki Institute. That means it's our ball."

"Patterson didn't know what was going on in here," said Happy. "I think we should go back out and talk to him, and the Boss, and see what they have to say."

"What makes you think we'd be allowed to leave the building?" said JC. A sudden quiet fell over the group as they all thought about that. JC looked around, making sure they'd got the implications. "We're not alone in here. The shells in the lobby were being directed by someone else. I think it's in our best interests to find out who—or what—and do something about them, before they figure out a way to do something about us."

"We can't cope with something this big on our own!" said Melody. "We need reinforcements! And my equipment!"

"And weapons," said Happy. "Really big, illegally modified weapons."

"We can't wait," said JC. "We're moving through unknown territory, and the clock is ticking."

"Clock?" said Happy. "What clock? No-one said anything about a clock!"

"There's always a deadline, in cases like this," JC said easily. "We need to understand what we're dealing with, before it comes looking for us. Those ghost shells worry me. They don't seem to have anything to do with the drug trials at all."

"Ghosts are usually some kind of reminder," said Kim. "Something from the Past, imprinting itself on the Present. Pushing reality aside to make themselves seen and heard. Either as a recording, or as a manifestation. Those shells . . . were all that remained of people. But with the personality removed, what reason did they have to remain? Why are they still here? Sorry, I'm thinking aloud . . ."

"You carry on," said JC. "You're making more sense than the rest of us."

"Somebody is keeping the shells here," said Kim, nodding thoughtfully to herself. "The men were killed to be made into ghost shells, so they could be . . . supernatural attack dogs?" She scowled prettily. Her form had become dimmer, almost transparent, as her concentration moved from manifestation to hard thinking. Her feet dipped in and out of the floor as she drifted slowly up and down. "Ghosts continue to exist, to serve some purpose. To pass on a message, to deal with unfinished business like revenge or unrequited love. All rational and emotional needs . . . but those shells were empty of anything like that. They'd been hollowed out, so someone else could use them. Which means someone—or thing—still in this building has power over life and death."

"Okay, you're scaring me now," said Happy. "Weaponised ghosts? And a hidden evil mastermind behind it all? I hate those."

"But where could it be hiding?" said Melody. "This building is supposed to be empty."

"I think . . . I don't believe anything we've been told about Chimera House," said JC. "I think someone is still here, someone—and I do believe it's a person, not the sort of Thing we sometimes deal with—with their own agenda, and their own purpose for these unethical and highly illegal drug trials. So we are going to find them, dispense vicious beatings on general principles, and then drag them out of here and find some proper legal authority to hand them over to."

"But, but, that isn't the mission!" insisted Happy. "We were sent in here to gather information, not bring evil masterminds to justice."

"Come on, Happy," JC said cheerfully. "Where's your sense of adventure?"

"I had it surgically removed," Happy said coldly. "It was endangering my life."

"It's true," said Melody. "He did. I've got it in a jar at home, on the mantelpiece."

"Our mission," said JC, in that calm and entirely reasonable tone he knew drove his companions absolutely batshit, "is to put a stop to what's happening here. That hasn't changed. Who's running this team, Happy?"

"You are," muttered Happy.

"And why is that?" said JC.

"Because no-one else wants to!" said Melody. "All right, we get it!"

"Good," said JC. "So stop arguing, suck it in, and soldier on, and I'll give you a nice sweetie to take away the nasty taste."

"I don't take sweeties from strangers," said Happy. "And God knows, no-one's stranger than you these days, JC."

"I am going to change the subject," said Melody. "Because it's either that or start hollering and hitting people, and I can always do that later. Probably while shouting *I told you so!* Have any of you noticed there aren't any security cameras? Not here in the corridor, or in any of the rooms, not even down in the entrance lobby. Rather unusual, wouldn't you say, for a company with so many important and highly illegal secrets to protect? Given that they were ready to lock in their test subjects for the night, you'd think they'd at least want to keep an eye on everyone . . ."

"Not if you don't want any official record of what you're doing," said JC. "Melody, my dear, I've been thinking . . ."

"Oh, that's always dangerous," said Happy.

"I was wondering if there was anything you could try that doesn't require any of your amazing but unfortunately not-at-all-here equipment?"

"Well," said Melody, reluctantly. "There is something I've been considering . . . Electronic Voice Phenomena. I might be able to put something together using my mobile phone and the room computer. Give me a minute."

She darted back into Room Three, and the others filled the doorway, looking in, because Melody didn't like to be crowded when she was working, and was quite capable of making that clear with a sudden back elbow or some other violent hint. She pulled the computer apart with brutal thoroughness, rooted through its guts and then linked some of them to her mobile phone. JC leaned in beside Happy, and spoke quietly in his ear.

"Do you have any idea of what she's doing?"

"Not a clue," said Happy.

"I can hear you!" said Melody, not looking up from what she was doing. "It's really quite simple . . ."

"Oh God, don't let her explain!" said Happy. "Any

time she tries to explain something scientific to me I end up with hysterical deafness for a week! In self-defence!"

"I am surrounded by Luddites," said Melody, working happily away. "Noisy ones, too."

"What are Luddites?" said Kim. "They sound sort of cuddly."

"Am I the only one who paid attention at school?" said Melody.

"Probably," said JC. "You swot, you. You could geek for the Olympics."

"And pardon me for being dead!" said Kim. "A girl can't study everything. I did extra drama classes. And flower arranging."

"Colour me surprised," said Happy.

Melody put her phone to her ear, and listened intently.

"Can you hear the sea?" Happy said helpfully.

"You slap him, JC," said Melody. "I'm busy. Wait . . . I'm getting . . . something. I can hear voices . . ."

"What's odd about that?" said Kim. "It's a phone."

"But I haven't dialled any number," said Melody. "I am very definitely hearing voices, but . . . too far away to make out. Voices, in the system. Are they always there, perhaps, hidden behind our everyday calls? Drowned out by millions of common calls and conversations?"

She fiddled with the exposed parts of the computer, and what she was hearing burst suddenly from the speakers. A sound like a never-ending wind, strange background noises like the singing of insane whales, the frantic pattering of a million angry insects. And then, slowly, human voices began to come forward, rising above the background gabble. Human voices, but far and far away, as though they'd had to cross some unimaginable distance to reach the world. It wasn't even clear what languages they were using.

"I just had an unnerving thought," said Happy. "Could we be hearing the collective unconscious? I've always wanted to listen in to that."

"You are entirely right, Happy, that is an unnerving thought," said JC. "If you have any more, feel perfectly free to keep them to yourself. And anyway, I don't believe in the human unconscious."

"Tough," said Happy. "It believes in you."

"Keep the noise down," Melody said sharply. "I'm listening . . . EVP is a new and barely understood branch of physics. Or psychics. Either way, there's a lot of theories but hardly any hard evidence you can trust . . . and then there are moments like this when it rears up and bites you on the nose, and spooks the hell out of you. You are all hearing this, right? A sea of voices, coming and going, on a dead channel. Maybe it's the voices of everyone who ever spoke on the phone network, somehow recorded and preserved, only slowly fading away . . ."

"Or it could be the dead," said Kim. Everyone looked at her, and she smiled sweetly. "Dead voices, on a dead channel. Still trying to reach out to the living, to make contact. I used to know this guy who was really into Electronic Voice Phenomena. He said it was the last great frontier of the unknown. He let me listen to some of the recordings he'd made, but I couldn't hear what he did. It was only noise . . . the audible equivalent of a Rorschach ink blot. The only shape and meaning is what we provide ourselves." She looked down her ghostly nose at Melody. "I may not have a dozen science degrees, but I do know a thing or two."

"There's far more to EVP than simple pattern recognition," said Melody, a bit defensively. "Too many people have heard the same sort of thing . . . Voices where there couldn't be voices . . . The dead trying desperately to make contact with the living, to warn them about something, something terrible and terribly important . . ."

"How come the dead never want to tell us anything nice?" JC said wistfully.

"All right," said Happy. "You're scaring me now."

And then he broke off, as all the clashing voices and deafening background noise cut off abruptly, replaced by a single voice. Slow, dragging, every word an effort. Melody threw her mobile phone away from her, and they all listened to the speakers.

Help me . . . Please, somebody, help me . . . Room Seven. Room Seven. Room Seven.

The voice stopped, and the computer speakers fell silent. There was not even a hint of hiss. Melody looked around, but the others were already off and running, heading for Room Seven.

::::::::::::::::::::::::

They hadn't got far down the corridor when they all stumbled to a halt, because the door to Room Seven was quite clearly shut. The only closed door. JC looked quickly up and down the corridor, but there was no-one about. Melody caught up with them and glared at the closed door to Room Seven as though it was a personal insult. Happy stayed at the back, looking past everyone's shoulder. Kim seemed puzzled.

"All the doors were open the last time we came this way," she said firmly. "It's not something you could miss, one shut door among so many open . . ."

"I walked right past that door to get to Room Fourteen," said JC. "And I didn't see anything. Did anyone notice anything?"

They looked at each other, but no-one was sure, one way or the other.

"Somebody has been messing with our heads," Happy said grimly. "To make us overlook Room Seven. And so subtly, so carefully, even I didn't realize it. He won't get away with that again, I'm ready for him now. And now I really want to see what's in that room. No-one craps in my head and gets away with it."

Kim stepped forward and thrust her head right through the closed door.

"Oh bloody hell!" said Happy. "I hate it when ghost girl does that! That is so not natural. That is freaking me out big-time!"

"Then don't look," said JC. "Anything, Kim?"

She pulled her head out of the door and smiled at JC. "No-one seems to be home. But it really is quite messy."

JC moved in closer and looked the door over carefully. "The lock's been smashed. And the steel bolt's been ripped right out of its socket. I'd say this door was burst open, from the inside, and whoever did it had to be really strong."

"Inhumanly strong?" said Melody.

"Seems likely," said JC.

"Suddenly, I'm not at all keen to see what's in there," said Happy. "You go ahead, I'll stand here and keep watch— *Take your hands off me!*"

"Well volunteered, that man," said JC. "God loves a volunteer!"

He pulled the door open and pushed Happy forward into the room. Happy made a whole series of loud protestations, but by then he was already inside, so he shut up and tried for quiet dignity. He sniffed at the air and shook his head.

"Smells like a zoo in here . . . Like an animal house. Wild, musky, feral . . . And I can smell blood, too. Oh yes, there it is."

By that time, they were all inside Room Seven, taking up most of the available space. The room had been trashed. The furniture and fittings had been smashed and torn apart. The carpet on the floor had been ripped and rucked up, as though trampled by wild animals. The computer had been beaten into small pieces and the pieces scattered everywhere.

"That's not easy to do," said Melody. "Somebody really had a grudge against this machine."

Everyone else was looking at the long claw marks gouged deep into the far wall. Blood was splashed thickly across walls and the ceiling. It hadn't been dried long. Great, heavy, dark red swatches of blood, and one oversized bloody handprint on the inside of the door. JC put his hand beside it, and the print was almost twice as large.

"This is where it all started," he said finally. "The first

unexpected reaction to the drug, perhaps? Did the test subject panic when the bad symptoms began? Did he cry out for help that never came and so had to smash his way out?"

"Was that his voice we heard?" said Melody. "Or was it someone who wanted us to see what someone else was hiding?"

"But look at the claw marks!" said Happy. "The size of them, and the depth of the grooves . . . think of the strength needed to do that much damage. And smell the animal stench in here! What did the Zarathustra drug do to the poor bastard?"

"Not the kind of superhuman change his minders were expecting, certainly," said JC. He turned abruptly to Kim. "What do you see here? I need to know what you see because the dead often see things that are hidden from the living."

"Of course," said Kim, calmly. "Because the living couldn't cope." She looked around, slowly. "I can't see whoever it was used to live here. It's as though all traces have been wiped clean, scoured out by the sheer intensity of what happened. No stone tape, no psychic imprinting . . . the occurrence was too powerful for that . . . But I am feeling things. Emotions. Strong, supercharged, impossibly extreme emotions, saturating the aether."

Melody sniffed. "She's making it up. No such thing as aether."

"Lot you know, girl geek," said Kim. "Emotions . . . but not human emotions."

"Animal?" said JC.

"No. More than human," said Kim. "I can feel them, but I can't understand them, or describe how they make me feel. It's like listening to a thunderstorm that's also a name that's also a howl of rage and horror and enlightenment. Emotions so big, so complicated . . . they frighten me, JC."

Happy was concentrating so hard his face was one big scowl, trying to get some feel, some sense of what Kim was experiencing, but it eluded him.

"I'm getting a word, JC," he said finally. "Yes, a word. Repeated over and over. One word. ReSet."

And then his gaze snapped past JC, caught by something behind him. Happy cried out, and pointed urgently with a quivering hand. Everyone spun round, to stare at the cracked mirror on the wall behind them. They all looked hard, but all they saw were their own startled reflections.

"What is it, Happy?" said JC. "What did you see?"

"There was a face!" Happy's face was grey, wet with sudden sweat. "There was a face in the mirror, and it wasn't one of us!"

They all looked again, but the reflection was still stubbornly only them.

"It's gone now," said Happy. "But it was there. A face. Watching us!"

"All right," said JC. "I believe you. What kind of face?"

"I don't know," said Happy. He looked confused, like an overtired child. "It wasn't human . . . not really. A face, like a human face, but . . . more so. It was like God looking out of the mirror, and judging us." He shook his head. "I can remember seeing it, but I can't remember what it looked like any more. As though my mind can't . . . hold on to it."

JC nodded slowly. For all his nervous talk, Happy was a veteran of many cases, and there wasn't much that could genuinely shake him any more. Melody moved in close beside Happy, calming him with her presence.

"ReSet?" said JC. "You're sure about that?"

"Oh yes," said Happy. "I heard it. Clear as a bell."

Then the sounds started. They all looked round sharply as they heard running feet. A great many people, all heading down the corridor, towards Room Seven. JC darted out of the room, then stopped as he saw that the corridor was empty. The sounds grew louder and more urgent, and there were voices, too, shouting and crying out, voices overlapping and drowning each other out. The sounds reached the doorway and stopped abruptly.

A new Voice filled the room, a huge, overpowering Voice, like God crying out from a mountaintop—or a cross.

Help me! Somebody, help me! What's happening to me?

A Voice that was both more and less than human, full of over- and undertones, too subtle for the human mind to comprehend. It shuddered through flesh and bone, shaking them with a deep atavistic terror. Even Kim cried out. She might be dead, but she was still human. And the Voice wasn't.

And then the Voice was gone, and everything was still and quiet again.

"Okay," said JC, shakily. "That bit out in the corridor

was a stone tape, extreme events imprinting themselves on the surroundings, and playing back . . . but the Voice . . . was a hell of a lot more than that. Something really bad happened in here."

"Or started here," said Melody. "Whatever it was, it isn't finished yet. We need to go up to the next floor, to the science labs, and get some answers."

"I'm not sure I want to know," said Happy. "They might have gone looking for a supersoldier, but I think they ended up with a lot more than they bargained for."

FOUR

SCALPEL, SCALPEL, SHINING BRIGHT

They went up the next set of stairs like a military unit. Taking their time, checking the corners and the shadows, listening hard for any hint of an attack. Kim went first, flitting silently up the stairs without touching them, out in front because of all of them she was the least in danger. *You see?* she said brightly. *Being dead does have its advantages.* JC went next, pushing forward because he always did, eager to get into the next interesting thing. Melody came next, bristling with caution, alert for the smallest noise or hint of danger, so she could do nasty things to it. And Happy brought up the rear because that was what he did best. He somehow managed to hold his peace until they were more than half-way up, but finally an urgent question forced its way out.

"What, exactly, are we proposing to do if attacked?"

"I have my machine pistol," Melody said immediately.

"Not actually noted for its use against things that are already dead," said Happy.

"Be of good cheer, my children," said JC, not looking back. "I have many useful and really quite nasty and only borderline-illegal items tucked away about my person. I won't tell if you won't."

"It's true," Kim said solemnly. "He does."

"I can't believe we're still going on," Happy said miserably. "We're ghost finders! This is a job for the psychic commandos of the SAS!"

"Well, for mass destruction, general bloodshed, and scorched-earth policies, they do have their uses," said JC. "But I think even they would admit that subtlety is not their favoured suit. There is a mystery here, questions that need answering, secrets that must be dug up, and that is what we do best. You are, of course, free to walk away at any time, Happy. But you know the rules—you walk out on an active investigation, and your time with the Institute is over."

"You say that like it's a bad thing," growled Happy.

"You make it sound like we volunteered to be ghost finders," said Melody.

"Didn't you?" JC said innocently. "I positively jumped at the chance."

"Yes, but you're weird," said Happy. He looked back down the stairs. "I'm pretty sure that leaving is no longer a viable option . . . Whatever's in here with us, it won't give up on us that easily. The higher we go, the more doors close behind us. We are climbing up into the belly of the beast . . ."

"Then try not to think too much about the eventual way out," JC said briskly.

They'd reached the next set of swing doors, giving out onto the next floor. Huddling together before the doors, they listened carefully, but all they could hear was their own massed breathing. The atmosphere was so still, it almost had a presence of its own. JC put his head right next to the door, straining for even the slightest sound or trace of movement. He bit his lower lip thoughtfully, straightened up, and looked back at Happy.

"Can you sense *anything*?"

"Not from out here," said Happy. "I swear something in this building is interfering with my talent. And I mean deliberately, not as a side effect. Something is targeting me. All right, yes, I feel like that most of the time, but this time I have evidence. There's a psychic weight in the atmosphere, an unnatural oppression . . . Trying to sense anything here is like listening for bird-song in the middle of a thunderstorm."

"A simple no would have sufficed," murmured JC. "You're sure it couldn't be some kind of basic phenomenon, a result of the drug trials?"

"No," said Happy. "Something's doing this to me."

"Or someone," said Melody.

"Oh right," said Happy. "Thanks a whole bunch. Cheer me up, why don't you?"

"I have tried being cautious and sensible, and a fat lot of good it has done me," announced JC. "I am therefore kicking that plan in the head and reverting to standard operating procedure." He slammed through the doors and strode arrogantly onto the next floor, shouting *"Anybody here? Anything weird and unnatural and quite probably illegal, make yourself known! We are here to solve mysteries, whether they like it or not, and dispense beatings to the ungodly!"*

"I really hate it when he does that," said Melody, following JC in.

"If he wants to be a target, let him," growled Happy, bringing up the rear.

"No-one ever holds the door open for me any more," said Kim, ghosting through the closing doors.

The whole of the second floor had been made over into one long science laboratory, with shining white walls and surfaces, and tables weighed down with impressive equipment, all of it stretching away into the distance. Fierce fluorescent lighting picked out every detail with almost painful clarity, with not a single shadow to be seen anywhere. The odd partition rose up here and there, presumably to close off the more dangerous procedures; but otherwise, everything was open to view. Work-benches, workstations, computers here there and everywhere, and equipment so complicated the eye seemed to slide right off it, unable to get a hold. Melody pressed forward, grinning widely and making cooing noises, her eyes sparkling as she took in the wonders before her.

"This is fantastic! I mean, look at all this techy goodness! Some of this equipment is so advanced, even I can't be sure what it is! This is way beyond state of the art, JC. I've only ever seen some of this stuff in really specialised trade magazines, usually in the *We're still running tests and crossing our fingers so don't expect to see this anytime soon* department. Available somewhen in the next decade, if you're lucky, along with the flying cars and personal jet packs. Okay—once we are finished with this case, I get dibs on everything. We are hiring several trucks and taking it all with us. I claim salvage."

"I don't think it works like that, Melody," said JC.

"It does if I say it does," said Melody. "I have a gun. Finders keepers, losers can sue me. The scientists working here clearly didn't appreciate what they had, or they wouldn't have gone off and left it. Which means it's all mine on moral grounds." And then she stopped and looked about her thoughtfully. "Odd . . . Everything here appears to be still turned on, still working . . . as though people just stopped in the middle of what they were doing and walked away."

"See!" said Kim. "I told you! Exactly like the *Marie Celeste*!"

"It's not normal to be that enthusiastic all the time," said Happy. "If I didn't know she was dead, I'd swear she was on more pills than me."

"But where are the scientists?" said Melody. "Seriously, why would they just walk, leaving everything still running?"

"Probably legged it once they saw the trial was going seriously wrong," said Happy. "As any sane or sensible person would."

"Getting bored with that song," said JC. "Not listening, not listening . . ."

"They're not gone," said Kim. "They're still here." She nodded to herself, then realised the others were looking at her. She shrugged. "Just a feeling . . ."

"Melody," said JC. "Find another computer and bully some answers out of it. Starting with exactly what is ReSet, and what is it supposed to do? And, in particular, what were the researchers expecting or hoping to achieve with this latest drug trial?"

Melody was already sitting before the nearest computer, which was still humming busily, its screen filled with an image of Stonehenge at dawn. She hammered away at the keyboard, and the computer made a series of important-sounding noises as it replaced the Stonehenge screen saver with a series of scientific files. Happy looked over her shoulder, was quickly baffled, and went back to wandering around the floor-length laboratory.

"I'm picking up something, JC, but it's hard to pin down anything distinct. There are a lot of emotions still hanging in the air. All of them quite definitely human. Fear, panic, anger, guilt, and a whole lot of *get the hell out of here*. Pretty much what you'd expect, for when everything's gone tits up big-time. But it's all . . . vague. Group feelings, rather than individual residues. Odd . . ."

"Found something!" Kim said happily. "JC, come and look! I think it's a company brochure."

She was trying to pick it up, but her insubstantial fingers kept passing through it and the desk beneath. She said a few baby swear words and stepped back. JC picked it up. He leafed through the heavy glossy pages, doing his best to ignore Kim hovering behind him.

"This would appear to be an in-house organ," he said. "Not meant for outside eyes. Basically, preaching to the company faithful. Lots of *Good times are on their way, bonuses for all, your names will go down in history so work hard for the company good.* All the usual corporate bullshit, to keep the little drones happy and hard at work. The bottom line seems to be that the company was promising a cure for pretty much everything, through the wonders of genetic manipulation. But, of course, not quite yet. All jam tomorrow . . ."

"What?" said Happy. "Is this like when I was a kid, and my mum would make me take a pill with a spoonful of jam? I miss that."

"It's from *Through the Looking Glass*," said Kim. "You know—jam tomorrow, jam yesterday, but never jam today. You must know it—it's a children's classic by Lewis Carroll."

"I have a hard time believing Happy was ever a child," said JC. "I think he was born nervous, sweaty, and trying to cadge free medications off the midwife."

"I never read any Carroll," said Happy. "I did try, but it scared the crap out of me. I was a sensitive child."

JC flipped quickly through to the end of the brochure. "Reading between the lines, what I see here is mostly qualified apologies. The theories are sound, but they don't have the funding to produce real results. Nothing here about ReSet."

"Found it!" said Melody. "Drop your linen and start your grinning, Auntie Melody has found the mother lode!" She beat a brief victory tattoo on the desk with both hands. "Not a single decent firewall in this thing. It's almost like these files wanted to be found. Anyway, gather round while I dispense wisdom and wonders."

They all did so, and she continued, her attention still riveted on the monitor. "The scientists here at MSI stumbled onto something impressive while looking for something else, which is always the way. But you were right, JC, they had to go outside the company to get the extra funding to make it work. And if I'm reading this right, I mean absolute shed-loads of money. The people on this floor needed some pretty expensive items, a lot of it quite blatantly illegal. And even immoral. We're talking half a ton of human stem cells, and even more human organs. Along with equipment so cutting-edge they must have boosted it right out of the testing labs. Oh, this can't be right, I'm looking at invoices for hundreds of human hearts, kidneys, livers, bone marrow . . . you name it, and it's here somewhere. Where could they possibly have got it all?"

"I'd guess third-world countries, executed Chinese prisoners, any number of civil-war zones," said JC. "Trafficking in human organs is the second biggest illegal trade, right after human slavery. Sometimes I think we're going after the wrong monsters. What were they doing with all those organs? And the stem cells?"

"Strip-mining them for something specific they needed," said Melody, frowning. "To make ReSet."

"Who exactly was it that supplied the extra funding?" said JC.

"No names," Melody said immediately. "Whoever it was went to a lot of trouble to remain strictly anonymous."

"Could it be Crowley Project?" said Happy. "I mean, this is the kind of nasty shit they'd get off on."

"None of the usual signifiers," said Melody. "But everything was kept carefully compartmentalised, so most of the scientists didn't know what the guy on the next bench was working on. It was all on a strictly need-to-know basis. Perhaps so no-one would know enough to feel properly guilty. This goes far beyond proprietary information, JC. We have to contact the Boss, get them to pry open the company records." She stopped and looked up from the monitor. "You know, I have to wonder, even if we succeed, if we'll be allowed to walk away from this case, knowing what we know."

"Welcome to my paranoid world," said Happy. "Cold, isn't it?"

"We don't know nearly enough yet," said JC. "And anyway, I'd like to see MSI come up with anything that could stop us."

"Don't say things like that!" said Happy. "You'll be saying *What could possibly go wrong* next!"

"Face front, brave little soldier," said JC. "If we can survive what's going on here, we can survive anything."

"Did you have to say *if*?" said Happy.

"What else have you got, Melody?" said JC.

"The extra funding did the trick," said Melody, scrolling quickly through the files. "They came up with a real miracle drug. They called it ReSet. According to this, it was a completely new wonder drug that could actually repair all damage to the human body by forcing it to reset itself to factory conditions. The miracle cure that all Humanity's been waiting for—a single drug that would fix whatever was wrong by putting everything back the way it should be. From broken bones to tumours, from viruses to organ failure. No more medicines, no more surgeries, no more transplants. Hell, ReSet could even cure the common cold! But then they tried it on actual test subjects . . . and it looks like ReSet did far more than was expected."

"I really don't like where this is going," said Happy.

"You're not alone," said Melody. "Listen . . . what's happened here is the result of the first actual drug trial on human test subjects. Everything else had been strictly computer models and simulations or experiments with the organs and cells they'd acquired. They didn't do any animal testing—apparently whoever was supplying the funding was in a hurry. The order was to go straight to human testing, and no-one here had the authority to say no. And the researchers were given very strict instructions on how the drug was to be administered. The test subjects, the volunteers, had no idea what they were getting. Poor bastards were told it was an allergy test. They were all given injections of ReSet, right here in the laboratory, and then watched closely for twenty-four hours. Nothing happened.

"I'm looking at the clinical notes. Round-the-clock observation, all life signs carefully monitored, regular blood tests . . . Nothing. Since there were no obvious reactions, and no biological changes, the test subjects were allowed to return to their living quarters, on the floor below. So the scientists could get into a real screaming match over whose fault it was that nothing had happened. They thought the drug trial was a failure because there should have been immediate signs. After twenty-four hours of sod all, they were tearing each other's hair out."

"LD50," said JC. "They expected half the test subjects to die, or nearly die, then recover, thanks to ReSet."

"Exactly," said Melody. "But the test subjects had barely been gone an hour when the first emergency call came through, from Room Seven. Things really went horribly wrong. Jesus, JC, some of this makes seriously scary reading. A lot of it is notes, made on the run by scientists half out of their minds, meant to be fleshed out later. Anyway, the scientists went down to Room Seven, accompanied by building security staff. That's probably what we heard, in the corridor. And then . . . a lot of people were killed, in and around Room Seven. There was a struggle. First the researchers attempted to restrain the occupant of Room Seven, who was freaking out big-time, then the security people waded in. They couldn't control him. Says here they used Tasers, and that was when the killing started. The man in Room Seven just . . . tore them apart, and kept on killing until the survivors turned and ran. And then . . . he killed himself. Maybe because he couldn't stand what he was turning into. What he was becoming." She paused, clearly shaken by what she was reading.

"By then, the same sort of thing was happening in all the rooms, all hell was breaking loose. The test subjects were all changing. The scientists had given up trying to control the situation, they were trying to get out alive. Two of the test subjects killed one another. Eight of the subjects went mad, apparently from simple proximity to

what was happening. They didn't, or wouldn't, change.
So the others killed them.

"It was a massacre, JC, a slaughterhouse. When they
weren't attacking each other, the test subjects turned on
the security men and the scientists. Only a handful got
out alive. They just weren't equipped to deal with what
ReSet had made out of the test subjects."

"Hold it," said JC. "Not that I'm doubting you, Melody, but . . . a slaughterhouse? There were no blood
stains in the corridor, no signs of violence. Only what
we saw in Room Seven."

"I know!" said Melody. "But according to these reports, there was blood and guts and bodies all over the
place!"

"We weren't allowed to see what Room Seven was
really like, until our mysterious hidden enemy was ready
for us to see it," said Happy. "Maybe . . . we only saw
what we were supposed to see, down there."

"Okay," said JC. "That is seriously spooky. Could
someone be messing with our minds so thoroughly without you being able to detect it?"

"I don't know," said Happy. "I wouldn't have thought
so, but I've never encountered anything like the conditions in this place. I keep telling you—we are way out of
our depths!"

"That's practically our job description," said JC. "Don't
panic yet, Happy, or you'll have nothing left when things
get really bad. Anything else of note in the computer files,
Melody?"

"The last few are short on detail," said Melody. "But
the people who made them were quite clearly trauma-

tised by what they'd seen. It was chaos down there. A lot of people died, in brutal and unpleasant ways. One researcher managed to make a distress call. We know how that worked out. Eventually, the entire building was sealed off." She half turned. "That's where we came in. Literally."

JC nodded. It was clear to all of them that they had been sent into Chimera House without proper briefing. "Anything else, Melody?" he said.

She turned back to the monitor. "Ah yes, this is interesting . . . Let me . . . Yes. It seems one of the surviving test subjects made his way up here and made a short vid recording. Look at this."

They all leaned in close around Melody as she called it up and put it on the screen. At first, it just showed a series of shifting views of the laboratory. There was no-one in front of the camera, only shouts and disturbances in the background, smashing sounds and strained human voices. Something flashed past, right at the edge of the screen, leaving a thick trail of blood behind it. It was moving too quickly to be identified, and though it was big enough to be human, it didn't move like anything human. Someone was crying, somewhere off camera, sobbing like all hope was gone. Not far away, someone else was laughing breathlessly. It wasn't a good sound. The background shouting grew louder, thick with rage and pain and horror. And then someone screamed, a vile, triumphant sound that went on and on, far past the point that a human throat should have been able to sustain it.

"What is that?" said Happy. *"What the hell is that?"*

Abruptly, the sound shut off. As though all the throats

had been cut at once. Suddenly, someone was sitting in front of the camera, staring at the screen. As though he'd always been there, and they'd only just noticed. The image was a man's head and shoulders, blocking any view of what might have been happening behind him. A man's face, gaunt with shock and horror . . . and something else none of them could identify—a strange, almost alien aspect. It took JC a moment to realise that the man wasn't blinking though tears ran jerkily down his twitching cheeks. When he started speaking, his voice was harsh and strained, actually painful to listen to, as though he'd damaged it from too much screaming.

"The world is over. The world we know is over. Wave it good-bye, we shall not see its like again. I have seen God. Or his angels. And they are not what we thought they were. We . . . are not what we thought we were. What is Man, but a poor unfinished thing . . . I have seen the future, and it is beautiful and glorious, but we have no place in it. I can see what's coming, and I can't bear it . . ."

His hands came up to his face and without the slightest hesitation he tore out both his eyes. He threw the eyeballs away, blood streaming thickly down his face. He turned his bloody head this way and that, the dark empty eye-sockets red and jagged where he'd torn the eyelids away, too. And then he laughed, bitterly, painfully, and screamed, *"I can still see!"*

Something hit the camera and knocked it over on its side. The screaming man disappeared, and all that could be seen was an area of blood-spattered floor. The scream rose and rose, beyond all human limits and meaning, then the screen went blank.

"That's all there is," said Melody. "I don't . . . that's all there is."

"What did he see?" said Happy. "What could make a man do that?"

"He must be dead, now," said Melody. "He must be dead, mustn't he?"

"Poor soul," said Kim. "What do you think he was seeing there, at the end?"

"Don't let it get to you," JC said firmly. "Look around you. We just saw this laboratory, this whole floor, being wrecked. People screaming and dying. But look around you . . . there's no evidence any of that happened. Do you see any blood, any bodies, or wreckage? Happy, are all our minds being interfered with, to stop us seeing the real lab?"

"No," Happy said immediately. "I've got my mental shields hammered down so tight God Herself couldn't see inside my mind. And I'm seeing the same lab as the rest of you."

"So what did happen here?" said Melody. "Did someone . . . clean it all up? Or was the recording a fake?"

"What we saw on the screen was real," JC said slowly. "I've no doubt about that. But there was no time stamp on the screen. So who's to say when it happened? I mean, it must have been after the drug trial, but . . . not enough time has passed to clean up the mess we saw. We're getting conflicting information here, people. I can't believe that's an accident. Someone wants to keep us off-balance."

"I've found something else," said Melody. Her voice

was still shaking from what she'd seen, but her manner was as calm and efficient as ever. It took a lot to throw Melody. "More notes on the drug testing, from one of the doctors involved. He's putting himself on record as being opposed to the LD50, but only after it had been administered. There's a lot of mea culpa here, some of it almost hysterical, but . . . Yes. Here, he's talking about ReSet, and how it didn't just re-establish the human body's factory settings. It went much further than that. You've all heard about junk DNA, right? All the DNA in the human genome that's been there forever, but we haven't got a clue what it does. What it's for. ReSet awakened, or activated, all of the human junk DNA and set it to work making it do what it was originally supposed to do. To make us . . . into what we were supposed to be. There's another vid file. Do you want to see it?"

"Not really," said Happy. "But we have to. We need to know what's going on."

"Good soldier," said JC.

"Shut up, or I will slap you," said Happy.

This time, the doctor's head and shoulders immediately filled the screen. Middle-aged, balding, in a white lab coat too small for him. There was a spray of fresh blood across the left side of his neck and shoulder, clearly not his. His face was deathly pale from shock, his eyes wide, his mouth trembling. He looked quickly about him, as though not sure he was alone, but there were none of the unnerving background sounds from the first vid file. The doctor squirmed in his chair and took a deep breath, visibly bracing himself. He stared into the camera and started talking, no name, no introduction, no build-up. Just the stumbling words of a man desperate to be heard.

"ReSet never was what they told us it was. Curing problems in the human body was only the first step. The bait in the trap, to get us interested. We weren't told what it would do next, what it was always meant to do. ReSet had another purpose. He knew. He knew that all along. That's why he funded us. ReSet was intended to make us all that we could be. All we were meant to be. We were never meant to be human. Not merely human. Somehow, part of our DNA got shut down, suppressed, frozen in place. So instead of becoming what we were meant to be, we got stuck part of the way. What we know as Humanity was only meant to be a stepping-stone on the way to something else. But now ReSet has helped finish the job! Taken the test subjects all the way to the end of the line! They're not human any more. They're the New People. That's what they are. Not superhuman, not more than human . . . Something else. Gods. And monsters."

He stopped to laugh briefly, a sad and bitter sound. "*That* is what we were meant to be. Gods *and* monsters? Intelligent design, or evolution's last laugh? Who knows . . . All of our knowledge and civilisation was a mistake, because what we were supposed to be would never have needed them."

He started laughing again, and this time he couldn't stop. He rocked back and forth in his chair and laughed his sanity away.

Melody shut the screen down. "There is more . . . but I don't think we need to see it. I doubt he had anything else to say."

"So," said JC. "ReSet rewrote the test subjects, from the bottom up, transforming the ones that didn't die into New People. Whatever they are. And they're still here, presumably somewhere above us. Those that survived the process . . . I think we need to go up and have a nice little chat with them."

"I just knew he was going to say that," said Happy. "Didn't you just know he was going to say that?"

"And what do you mean we, Pale Face?" said Melody. "You heard the mad doctor, gods *and* monsters, all in the same package. That does not sound like someone you can stroll up to and have a nice little chat with! Give me one good reason why we need to go up and talk with these very scary New People?"

"Because they're behind everything that's happening here," said JC. "That's why it's been so easy for us to get answers. They wanted us to know. Be honest, Melody— would you have been able to open up those files so easily under normal conditions?"

"No," said Melody, reluctantly. "I'm good, but I'm not that good."

"I don't think we're going to be allowed to leave until we've seen this through," said JC. "We're here for a purpose. I think . . . these New People want something from us."

"Why us?" said Happy, plaintively. "Why is it always us?"

"They might want us dead," said Melody. "Have you considered that?"

"If they'd wanted you dead, you'd be dead by now,"

said Kim. Everyone looked at her. She shrugged. "That's what I'm feeling."

"Anything else you'd like to share?" snapped Happy.

Melody leaned in close to him. "Don't upset the dead girl," she murmured. "You really want a ghost mad at you?"

Kim surprised them all by seriously considering Happy's question, her eyes far away. "Someone is hiding from us. Close by."

They all looked quickly around, but the long laboratory stretched away before them, open and still and quiet and completely empty.

"Is that it?" said JC.

"For now, yes," said Kim. "I'm not like Happy. I don't see or hear things like he does. I just get feelings."

"I feel things," protested Happy.

"Of course you do," said Melody. "In your own special way."

"Meanwhile, back at the theorising," JC said determinedly. "Someone was running those ghost shells, down in the lobby. Could that have been the New People? And if so, were they responsible for their deaths?"

"Seems like they killed all the scientists and doctors, and even some of their own," said Melody. "What's a few policemen and security men, after that?"

"Hold everything," said Happy. "Kim's right—someone else is here with us."

They all looked round again. Still nothing. The open planning and the bright fluorescent light left nowhere to hide.

"They're here," Happy insisted, his eyes wide and

scared. "Lots of them. Getting closer all the while. And they don't feel at all friendly."

JC looked at Kim, and she nodded quickly. "They're coming from a direction I don't understand. From . . . outside reality."

"Human?" said JC.

"I don't think so," said Happy.

"Not any more," said Kim. "They feel . . . awful. Like something human turned inside out, so all the bad things show. JC, I'm scared."

"Dead people, come back as something other than people," said Happy, frowning suddenly. He might have been talking to himself. "Some ghosts are stronger than others. Some are only images, trapped in a repeating moment of Time like insects in amber. Some are recordings, stone tapes playing back. Some are what remains after death. Things that won't stay dead, or all the way dead, because they're driven by some overwhelming purpose. And some ghosts are predators . . . leeching energy from the living to maintain their half-life existence in the waking world.

"It's getting cold, just like in the lobby. Something is sucking all the life energy out of this place, so the ghosts can bleed in from whatever bolt-hole they've found to manifest here, with the living."

"Who is it, Happy?" JC said quietly. "Who is it that's coming?"

"The Doctors," said Happy. "Slaughtered and butchered here by their own creations, driven insane just by being here when it happened."

"Are you saying that simply being around these New People is enough to drive humans crazy?" said Melody.

"They're too much for us," said Happy, dreamily. "We can't cope. Witnessing the change was enough to blow all the Doctors' fuses. That's what we've got here—the flotsam and jetsam of a radical experiment, the fall-out and debris from the creation of a new thing. Mad Doctor ghosts, riding the coat-tails of the New People, soaking up the energies released to maintain their insane existence after death."

"Happy?" said JC. "Happy, can you hear me? You've gone too far; you need to come back to us."

"I see you," said Happy, staring down the long laboratory at something only he could see. "I see you . . ."

Melody stepped in front of him, blocking his view. She raised both hands to cup his face tenderly, meeting his gaze with her own.

"Come back to us, Happy. Come back to me. Don't leave me here alone, in the light."

His eyes snapped back into focus, and he smiled at her. "I never knew your voice could reach so far. All right, I'm back. I don't like it, but I'm back. What's happening, and is it too late to head for the exit?"

"The Doctor . . . is in," said a voice, seeming to float down the long, open floor towards them. A foul, desiccated voice, dripping with ill will.

The whole floor was changing. The very structure and constituents of the long laboratory became warped and twisted, wrenched out of shape by unnatural forces. Advance harbingers of the Mad Doctor ghosts, altering the world into something more to their liking, something more able to support their awful existence. Making the world over into a reflection of their own insane needs and wishes. Solid surfaces slumped, flowing and re-forming. Metal ran away in lumpy streams, like melting wax, while scientific equipment heaved and turned, taking on new shapes and meanings. The walls bowed slowly inwards, and the ceiling drooped. The light intensified, becoming painfully bright—perhaps because the Mad Doctors wanted what was happening to be clearly seen, and appreciated. Or perhaps to make the hunting easier.

The computer Melody had been working on swelled up suddenly. The monitor screen burst stickily and vomited its contents onto the floor. The pool spread, as bits of silicon and steel grew legs and scuttled across the floor like maddened insects. All across the laboratory, machines unfolded like blossoming flowers, becoming strange enigmatic things with too many angles. The glass windows all along the far wall disappeared. Where they should have been was *nothing*—an absence in the world, something the eye couldn't even acknowledge.

"Scalpel, scalpel, shining bright, in the horror of the night," said the voice. "What unnatural hand and eye can undo thy yielding flesh?"

"I am getting serious operating-theatre vibes," said Happy. "And not in a good way."

"Look," said Melody, pointing down the long floor. "The Mad Doctors are here."

They came scuttling and crawling, around and over and in between the warped and twisted structures that now filled the laboratory. They moved in sudden darts, like white-coated spiders, sometimes on two legs and sometimes on more. Mad Doctors in pristine white gowns and blood-spattered surgical masks, ghostly hands clutching scalpels and bone-saws and sharp steel probes. Their eyes were cool and vicious and full of a terrible, hot insanity. They had left their humanity behind them when they died and become something else, with new thoughts in their twisted minds, and dark foul emotions.

There was no way of telling how many Mad Doctor ghosts there were. They were here and there and everywhere, blinking in and out, never still.

"We can see what's wrong with you," said the voice. It didn't seem to come from any one ghost in particular. "We can see what's bad in you. We're going to cut it out and play with it, and make it ours. And oh what fun we'll have—while you last."

"Happy," JC said quietly. "Are they really there? I mean—*physically* there?"

"Oh yes," said Happy. "Very, very definitely solid and real . . . These are powerful manifestations, JC. Dead, but not departed. I think . . . they exist in the spaces between spaces, in the odd little gaps and lacunae of reality, hiding like trap-door spiders. Think of them as a by-product of the process that made the New People. Or think of them as aetheric parasites. Remaking the laboratory was them putting on something more comfortable. They want to terrify us. I think they feed on fear."

"They're still ghosts," said JC. "And we deal with ghosts."

"They're predators," said Kim, her nose wrinkled

with disgust. "And they're hungry. I can see them more clearly than you can. They're not human any more. I don't have words for what they've made themselves into, for what they really are. They're insane, JC, and their madness is contagious. It's affecting the world."

"Can we destroy them?" said JC.

"They're dead," said Kim. "But not all the way. You might say . . . they're clinging on to existence by their fingernails. Their madness lets them do impossible things, but that very madness is what makes their grip on reality so precarious. Pry them loose, JC."

"Sounds like a plan to me," said JC, rubbing his hands together in a brisk and hearty fashion.

"But what are we going to *do*?" said Happy. "I don't see our usual bag of tricks working with these ghosts. And those scalpels look really sharp."

"We'll do what we always do," JC said grandly. "Experiment, with extreme prejudice."

"How do I get out of this chicken-shit outfit?" said Happy.

The Mad Doctor ghosts came charging forward. Some ran, some scuttled, some hopped and leapt like white-coated bugs. Some swarmed over the crazily outcropping structures they'd created. Some walked jerkily, in sudden strobelike motions, as though they couldn't be bothered to cross all the space they travelled through but rather jumped from bit to bit. They brandished their cutting tools with horrible glee, laughing the vague but confident laugh of the utterly insane. Their eyes were deep and dark, horrifyingly empty of anything a sane man could hope to understand.

Melody stepped forward and opened fire with her machine pistol. She swept it back and forth with cool precision, raking the ranks of the Mad Doctor ghosts with a steady stream of bullets. But she couldn't seem to hit any of them. Some of the ghosts darted back and forth with inhuman speed, easily avoiding the gunfire. Others simply weren't there when the bullets arrived. And some simply stood and laughed at her as the bullets went straight through them. Bullets ricocheted from warped structures or sank into moist spongy surfaces. The Mad Doctor ghosts laughed their hateful laughs and kept on coming.

JC glanced at Happy. "Even in the midst of all this, I have to ask—where does she keep that gun when she's not using it?"

"I've never dared ask," said Happy.

"Which part of *they're already dead* did you miss, Melody?" said Kim. "You're not going to take them out with a bullet. You'd have more luck clubbing them over the head with the barrel."

"Can't blame a girl for trying," Melody said airily, making her machine pistol disappear again. "I am now officially open to fresh ideas. Preferably very soon because those bastards are getting really close."

A Mad Doctor ghost appeared out of nowhere, leaping in from the extended blind spot where the windows used to be. He threw himself at Kim and passed straight through her. She cried out, in shock and horror. The Mad Doctor ghost howled and shrieked and jumped up to run about on the ceiling, slashing at the air with his scalpel. JC moved in close beside Kim, half reaching out to hold her.

"Are you all right, Kim?"

"It wasn't only his body that went through me," said Kim. "It was his mind, too. Or what was left of it. His thoughts don't make sense any more, JC."

JC nodded quickly, pulled another of his holy-light grenades out of an inner pocket, primed it, and tossed it into the midst of the Mad Doctor ghosts. But it never got there. While it was still in mid air, the ghost standing on the ceiling caught it easily with one hand, then dropped down to squat on a massive steel shape. The Mad Doctor ghost shook its head violently back and forth as it ate the grenade, biting large chunks off it. The bloody surgical mask split like a crimson smile to allow the ghost to chew on the grenade like a toffee apple. Holy light burst out of the grenade in sudden fierce blasts, and the Mad Doctor ghost sucked it all up.

"Close your mouth, JC," Kim said quietly. "And tell me you've got something else up your sleeve apart from your arm."

"Of course," JC said quickly. "It's just that . . . I rather had my hopes set on those grenades."

"I'm picking up something!" said Happy. "There's someone else on this floor, apart from us and those bloody things! I think someone's running the Mad Doctor ghosts, the same way they ran the shells in the lobby! Someone or something is connecting them, supporting them!"

"I told you they were barely hanging on," said Kim.

A Mad Doctor ghost slipped and slid across the floor towards them, grinning with malicious intent, moving faster and faster as though gravity and friction were things he didn't need to bother with any more. He brandished a gleaming bone-saw with horrid glee. JC went forward to meet it, and the bone-saw lashed out with supernatural speed. JC only had time to get his arm up to protect his throat, and then the jagged razor-sharp edge slashed through his sleeve and arm. Blood spread quickly across the ice-cream white sleeve. He didn't cry out with pain, only glanced at the stain on his sleeve and roared with rage.

"Look at what you've done to my best suit, you bastard!" JC grabbed the nearest half-melted chair and brought it down on the ghost's head with all his strength. And perhaps because the Mad Doctor ghost had made the things in the laboratory part of its world, the chair smashed the ghost to the ground. JC hit the ghost with the chair again and again, rage fuelling his strength, and the ghost scuttled away across the floor with JC close behind.

Half a dozen Mad Doctor ghosts hit Melody and Happy from every side at once, forcing them apart. Melody spun and danced, punched and kicked, and held the ghosts at bay through sheer ferocity, for a while. Scalpels and bone-saws cut viciously at her from every side, and every cut came that much closer to getting through. Melody's fists and feet shot out with deadly skill and furious energy, but none of it did her any good. Sometimes her hands connected with something like flesh and bone, but more often they glanced stickily from a grinning face or sailed right through. The ghosts were only as solid as they chose to be. They faded in and out, even passing through each other as they crowded round Melody. She began to get the feeling that the fight was only continuing because they liked to see her dance.

Happy made a run for it, first chance he got, and the giggling ghosts chased him in and out of the distorted surroundings, cutting at him with their sharp blades, to keep him moving. Every now and again, a ghost would appear suddenly to block his path, and Happy would hit it with a concentrated blast of telepathic disbelief. The Mad Doctor ghost would burst apart in an explosion of ectoplasmic strings, then pull itself back together as Happy ran on. After a while, he noticed that while the ghosts scrambled around and over the maze of enigmatic structures that filled the whole floor, they never ran through any of it. They had entered the physical world and made it theirs, so now they had to follow at least some of its rules. Happy sprinted down a narrow chan-nel, thinking fiercely, and when he got to the end, he stopped and spun around and gave the following Mad Doctor ghosts the finger. They howled with rage and came leaping and skittering after him. He threw his whole weight against the nearest towering structure and forced it over, to fall on top of the ghosts. The sheer weight slammed them to the floor and held them there, and Happy did his special victory dance—only to stop abruptly in mid step as the ghosts began to slowly ooze up through the heavy weight.

Happy looked quickly around him, then froze in place as he realised the far end of the laboratory floor had dis-appeared. In its place, strange lights flared and flickered in an off-kilter honeycomb of caves and depressions, held together with shimmering ectoplasmic strands. Thick fluids dripped, lubricants for the cells of the honeycomb as they turned and revolved around each other. As Happy watched, new cells slowly formed at the edge of the honeycomb, forcing their way further into the world. Happy stared at it, studying it with more than his eyes, and knew it for what it was. The world the Mad Doctor ghosts had made for themselves, located in the spaces between spaces, so they could hide like rats in the walls of reality. The ghosts had brought their world with them, and it was making itself at home.

A Mad Doctor ghost appeared suddenly before Happy, and he reacted instinctively by kicking it good and hard in the balls. The ghost dropped its bone-saw and crashed to its knees. Happy kicked it in the head, and it fell over backwards.

"The longer they stay in our world, the more bound by its rules they become," said Kim, drifting up by the ceiling. "That's what they want—to become real again. They don't know they're dead."

Happy nodded quickly, and picked up the ghost's bone-saw. It was cold and fragile in his hand at first, hard to get a hold on, but the longer he hung on to it, the heavier and more real it felt. The ghost reared up before Happy, screaming and howling as it reached for its weapon. And Happy cut its head off with one hard blow. The head fell to the floor and shattered slowly, like a smashed egg in slow motion. The headless body drifted apart, like smoke on the wind. The bone-saw disappeared from Happy's hand.

He looked back down the laboratory, in time to see the Mad Doctor ghosts pull Melody down and swarm all over her. Scalpels flashed brightly. Happy yelled her name and sprinted back the way he'd come. Melody fought as hard as she could, but she was only human, and her attackers weren't, any more. They held her down with their cold hands, while one of them pressed a scalpel against her belly.

"It's all got to come out," said a familiar voice. "The insides are the best part. Flesh is wasted on the living."

Happy hit the ghosts like a cannon ball, scattering them with his sudden appearance and a telepathic blast of sheer rage and fury. The ghosts were blown away by his fierce concentration and ran madly this way and that, flailing their arms, light glinting fiercely from their surgical weapons. Happy hauled Melody to her feet, and they stood back to back as the Mad Doctor ghosts remembered their purpose and circled them slowly.

"You hurt?" Happy asked Melody.

"I'll live," said Melody. "Any chance you can do that again?"

"Not for a while," said Happy. "That kind of thing takes a lot out of you."

"Any other ideas?"

"Not really."

"Terrific," said Melody.

JC had found Kim. "Is there anything you can do to help? Anything you can see here that we can't?"

Kim nodded slowly, her head bobbing directly below the ceiling. "The ghosts all look the same to me. They're all Mad Doctor ghosts—no trace of individuality. It's like they've all been overwritten by something stronger. Whatever they were exposed to didn't only make them crazy, it made them all crazy in exactly the same way. Someone has taken advantage of that to graft on purpose and intent. Driving them on, like it did the shells. These Mad Doctor ghosts are really just more of the building's attack dogs, another layer of the New People's defences."

She broke off abruptly as one of the Mad Doctor ghosts came dancing along the ceiling towards her. It shot past her, scalpel flashing as it lashed out at her, and Kim cried out in shock and horror as the vicious blade cut deep into her ghostly flesh. Blood-tinged ectoplasm ran down her arm and dripped from her fingertips.

"Paper cuts scissors, doctor cuts patient," said the Mad Doctor ghost, pirouetting unnaturally slowly in place. "You're all grist to the mill to us, the living and the dead. Suffering is such sweet sorrow, and we eat it up with spoons. We will cut you all up and put you back together, remake you in our own fashion, to serve our special needs and pleasures. And you will last forever, and your torment will never end."

"JC?" said Kim. "Please do something. I'm really not ready for a fate worse than death."

"JC!" yelled Happy. "We're surrounded! And their world is invading ours! Any suggestions would be gratefully received!"

"Kim says they're all linked!" JC yelled back. "Can you find that link and break it?"

"Now I know what to look for . . ." said Happy. He concentrated, and his face lightened a little. "Yes! It's there! Like a signal, connecting and commanding them. So if I interrupt that signal, like this . . ."

The Mad Doctor ghosts cried out and lurched in every direction at once, like puppets whose strings had been yanked out of them. Lost, without purpose or identity, they flailed madly, striking at each other and the empty air. They were still dangerous, still foul and malignant, but for the first time they seemed vulnerable.

"Time to go old school, I think," said JC. He took a phial of holy water from inside his jacket, unscrewed the cap, and poured the blessed water carefully over each of his hands in turn. And then he walked quite deliberately into the midst of the Mad Doctor ghosts and laid those hands on them one at a time, speaking the powerful old Words of Exorcism. The ghosts crumbled and dissolved under his blessed touch, as the Words broke their connection with this world. One by one they vanished, driven out of reality, sent on to whatever was waiting for them. None of them ran, or fought, or tried to avoid his touch. They stood trembling where they were, like rabbits staring into approaching headlights. Until he came at last to the final ghost who held up one hand for him to pause for a moment. It dropped its scalpel, which disappeared before it hit the floor, and pulled down its blood-spattered surgical mask, to reveal a surprisingly human face. The eyes were still tormented but no loner insane.

"Go up," he said. "Go all the way up. The New People are waiting. But beware. We looked into the Medusa's gaze. Don't you make the same mistake."

JC laid his hand on the ghost's head, and it faded away, as though it had only been hanging on to say those last few words.

JC nodded slowly and went back to join the others. Kim dropped down from the ceiling to drift along at his side. Happy and Melody were leaning on each other, breathing hard. The laboratory had returned to its original shape and purpose, and the bad world at the end of the floor was gone. JC started to say something, then stopped and looked at the tear in the sleeve of his jacket. The crimson stain was still there, from where the ghost's scalpel had cut him, but when JC pushed the edges apart, the sleeve was cut and bloodied; but the flesh beneath that was untouched.

"My arm doesn't hurt any more," he said. "And I don't mean it's healed—more like it was never cut at all."

"Same here," said Melody. Happy was too busy checking himself in all sorts of important places to speak.

"And I'm fine, too!" said Kim. "Though I still don't know how he was able to touch me . . ."

"Belief," Happy said finally. "It's all about belief. They were imposing their world-view on us, so if they thought they could cut us, they could."

"You're right," said JC.

"Someone take a photo," said Happy. "Moments like this don't happen very often."

"You were right when you said this isn't what we signed up for," said JC. He looked slowly around him. "This is above and beyond the call of our pay grade. We're investigators, not soldiers. But . . . someone has to stop these New People, and we're all there is."

"You heard the loony ghost," Happy said reluctantly. "The New People want to see us, and they're not going to let us out of here till they get what they want."

"But are they the ones running the shells, and the Mad Doctor ghosts, or is there another unseen party, operating from the shadows?" said Melody.

"Wonderful," said Happy. "More complications."

JC looked around at the high tech scattered across the laboratory. A lot of it had been smashed or knocked about, but some still seemed more or less intact. He looked at Melody.

"Any chance you could use something here to get a message out to Patterson, or the Boss? Tell them what's going on, get them to send in some serious reinforcements?"

"You really think the New People would let us talk to the outside?" said Melody. "I mean, I'll try if you like, but . . ."

JC looked at Happy, who shook his head immediately. "I've been mentally yelling for help for ages. Screaming at the top of my mental voice. No response."

JC scowled, folded his arms, and thought hard. "We know a lot more than when we started," he said finally. "But I don't think we've got anything like the full picture yet. If these New People really are everything they're supposed to be, why are they waiting around for us? No . . . something else is going on, and we need to find out what. So let's go up and take a walk through the other floors and see what there is to see, before we go have our nice little chat with the New People."

"I just knew he was going to say that, again," said Happy.

"You must be psychic!" Kim said sweetly.

FIVE

SOMETHING OFFAL

There comes a point in every investigation into the unnatural when it's easier to go on than to go back. When
you're in so deep you have to pull up your waders and
press forward, and let the Devil take the hindmost.
Though no-one had ever really been able to convince
Happy of that. But JC drove him up the next set of stairs
with kind words and curses, and soon enough they came
to the next set of doors, the next floor, and the next chance
to find a few answers. JC didn't bother with listening at
the closed doors. He barged right through and into what
proved to be another long open-plan laboratory. More
workstations, more computers, and more high tech he
couldn't even name, let alone understand. The only difference he could see was that on this floor there was a
tall standing partition, some two-thirds of the way down.

JC strolled through the place liked he owned it, hands stuffed deep in his trouser pockets, smiling cheerfully around, defying anything to jump out at him. Kim strode along beside him, head held high, and only the truly unkind would have pointed out that her feet weren't quite making contact with the floor. Melody followed, stopping and starting as she was distracted by some new shiny machine she hadn't seen before. Happy settled for sulking in the rear, glowering suspiciously in all directions.

Surprisingly, it was Kim who stopped first and looked unhappily about her. "I'm getting a really bad feeling from this place," she said slowly. "But nothing like what we experienced downstairs. The scientists were working on something different here, something completely unconnected with the ReSet drug. I think this . . . is where they made monsters."

"What?" Happy snapped. "Monsters? Could you perhaps be a little more specific?"

"No," said Kim. "You're the telepath. You tell me."

Happy shuffled his feet and avoided everyone's eyes. "It's like . . . the closer we get to the New People, up above, the more their sheer presence overwhelms everything else. I feel like I'm trying to peer through a thick fog, but even so, I'm not picking up any thoughts here." He stopped, and sighed. "Melody, put that down. You don't know where it's been."

"I was only looking at it!" said Melody.

"No you weren't," JC said sternly. "You're like a little kid—you can't look without touching. And I would have to say that you weren't just touching that . . . whatever it is—you were caressing it in a quite disturbing way. Don't think I haven't got my eye on you, young lady."

"But they've got things here I've only heard about in nerd and geek chat rooms!" said Melody. "Tech so advanced Stephen Hawking would get a hard on from just looking at it! I am having this, JC. If it doesn't all go bad like the tech on the lower floor did, I am having all of it. It belongs to me on a moral level."

"Melody . . ." said JC.

"I found it! It's mine!"

"Concentrate on the job," said JC. "And we can talk about a little quiet looting when it's all over."

"It's not even close to being over," said Happy. "Heads up, people, we are not alone here. Still not getting any thoughts, but something's in here with us. Not human as such . . . I can sense its presence, but I'm damned if I can get my head round what it is."

They all stood close together, staring quickly about them. Fierce fluorescent lighting picked out everything in sharp detail, with hardly a decent shadow anywhere. No sound, nothing moved, and there wasn't a sign of a living soul anywhere. The atmosphere was cold and tense, but the Ghost Finders were getting used to that. They all still jumped when Melody abruptly broke from the group to pick up and study some papers on a nearby desk. They watched as she speed-read through them.

"Well?" JC said politely, after a while. "Anything interesting, or indeed, you know, useful?"

"Oh, you will not believe what they were up to here," said Melody, skimming through the last few pages.

"What happened on this floor is officially banned in every civilised country, and even a few others who have problems with the basic concept of civilisation. The scientists here were working with stem cells, because they can be made to function as any kind of cell, and they've been using them up by the truckload. Remember the invoices I found below? You can't legally get your hands on this amount . . . You know stem cells are derived from aborted human embryos, right?"

"I thought I read somewhere that scientists can get stem cells out of the human placentas, these days." said JC.

Melody sniffed. "Some scientists don't like to change their ways. As long as something works, they tend to stick with it. But what's really nasty is what these people were using them for. They had their very own Bio Reactor, basically a machine that can build living materials from a basic set-up. So—stem cells, artificially strengthened through genetic modification, then persuaded to form complete individual human organs. For the transplant trade. And they didn't stop there. They weren't only making hearts and kidneys and lungs to order—they were working to strengthen and improve these organs, to make them more suitable for transplantation. Superorgans. Very expensive, for very illegal black-market transplants."

"JC," said Happy. "We really have to get the word out about what's going on here. You can bet that Mutable Solutions will make all this evidence disappear long before the proper authorities can get involved. These bastards can't be allowed to get away with this."

"I'm sorry," said Kim, "but I don't understand. More

organs, for transplant? Better organs? That's a good thing, isn't it?"

"Depends how much you charge," said JC. "People are supposed to receive organs based on how badly they need them. This is an expensive way to queue-jump. This whole floor is a crime scene."

"We have to make contact with the outside world!" said Happy. "People have to hear the truth, before MSI can bury it!"

"I'm not disagreeing with you, Happy," said JC. "I just don't see how. No phones, no e-mail, no telepathy. Everything's being jammed."

"Then one of us has to get the hell out of here and deliver the bad news in person," Happy said firmly.

"Of course," said JC. "A volunteer is what's needed here. Would I be right in thinking that you have such a person in mind?"

"I'll go!" said Happy. "Be glad to see the back of this place. Really!"

JC considered him thoughtfully. "You're really willing to go back down all those stairs, on your own, past all those very dangerous floors, and through a lobby probably still booby-trapped with things even worse than shell ghosts? In the hope that, if by some chance you should actually reach the exit door, you would be allowed to leave the building alive?"

"Well," said Happy, "When you put it like that . . . Not as such, no."

"There is a short cut," said Melody.

"Where?" said Happy immediately. "Point me at it. Oh wait a minute—the elevator? I don't think so."

"I was thinking more about the window," said Melody. She pointed at the glass windows that made up most of the opposite wall. "I mean, I'm sure they're all heavily reinforced security glass, but one good burst from my machine pistol should take care of that. Then all you have to do is climb down the outside of the building, thus avoiding all the nasty floors and unpleasant surprises in the lobby, and hurry off to summon the cavalry."

"Climb?" said Happy. "The word *plummet* comes more forcefully to mind! You know I hate heights."

"Sounds like a plan to me," JC said cheerfully.

"You're all against me," said Happy.

"Cheer up, lover," said Melody. "I was only kidding. I won't let the nasty team leader throw you out the window."

"Thank you," said Happy.

"Not as long as there's any other option."

Happy glared at her. "I don't know why I put up with you."

"Because I can do that incredibly disgusting thing with my tongue," said Melody. "And you love it when I . . ."

"Not listening, not listening!" JC said loudly. "Far too much information. Let's leave the topic of throwing Happy out the window for the time being. Truth is, I don't think whatever is in here is going to let any of us out, through the doors or the windows, anytime soon. Melody, if you'd be so good . . ."

"I know, I know, find a computer. Got one right here."

"Then boot it up and get me some answers," JC said

brusquely. "In particular—why this whole floor feels so *bad* . . ."

Melody sat down before the computer, and it turned itself on before she could even touch it. She scowled at the glowing monitor for a moment, then stabbed at the keyboard. Files came and went on the screen. Melody sniffed loudly. "No firewalls, not even basic security protocols, just like before . . . Someone is definitely going out of their way to make this easy for me." She glared up at the ceiling. "I do not need any help! I am a genius, dammit! I do not need my hand held!"

"Never mind the mysterious helper," said JC. "What appalling and completely illegal things were these scientists up to?"

"It confirms what was in the papers I found," said Melody. "None of the work on this floor had anything to do with ReSet. The work here was MSI's original research, before the extra funding diverted them. The company kept this research going in the background, just in case . . . The scientists were trying to develop improved human organs, to be better than the originals. Organs that would be far more resistant to damage and could actually supercharge the human body."

"I told you," said Kim. "Monsters. They were making monsters here."

"They were working with individual organs, not creating Frankenstein creatures," Melody said dryly. "And according to this, they weren't having much success. Stem cells to organs to superorgans—a lot can go wrong along the way. But something happened on this floor when the New People were created below. Strange energies were released. They sleeted through the whole building, changing everything they touched. It affected the organs being produced by the Bio Reactor. It made things. New things. The scientists took one look and ran screaming."

"Took one look at what?" said Happy.

"I don't know," said Melody. "But I'm pretty sure whatever these things were, they're still here."

She shut down the computer and stood up abruptly, glaring about her. The others huddled together unconsciously, checking out every possible hiding place with a hard look, and still they couldn't see anything. The atmosphere had moved beyond tense to actually oppressive. They all felt like they were being watched, studied, by cold, unseen eyes. Happy sniffed the air.

"Is it only me, or can you smell something?"

"Yes," said JC. "A ripe, spoiled sort of smell. Meat that's gone off. Blood, too. Other things of that nature, none of them good."

"It's getting stronger," said Happy. "It's leaving a really nasty taste in the back of my mouth."

"Hush," said Melody. "I can hear something . . ."

They all stood very still, straining their ears against the quiet, and slowly they began to hear soft, approaching sounds. Dragging sounds, of something heavy hauling itself along the floor, through sheer will-power. Wet, slapping sounds, slipping and sliding, coming from a dozen different directions at once.

"Oh no," said Happy. "I know it's going to be some

horrible human shape of patched-together organs, probably all red and blobby with no proper exterior, so you can see things moving inside, with dozens of eyes bobbing about at the top. Dripping blood and bile and leaving a smoking trail of acid behind it . . ."

He stopped as he realised they were all looking at him.

"You've been watching those Japanese manga movies again, haven't you?" said JC.

Happy wrapped his dignity around him, and stared back. "*Legend of the Overfiend* is a classic! Though it does practically define the phrase *guilty pleasure*."

"Take a few of your little chemical helpers, and get yourself together," said JC. "You're no use to me if you can't keep your head in the game."

"I am trying to cope without them," said Happy. "Ever since my piss started turning funny colours. Better living through chemistry is all very well, but in practice it doesn't half take it out on your liver."

"And because you can't get it up when you're trashed," said Melody.

"Why do you keep putting mental images into my head that I know I'm going to have to scour out with wire wool?" said JC.

"Heh-heh," said Melody.

Kim drifted in beside her. "Maybe we should make time for some girlie talk, later," she said. "It's not easy having a love life when you're dead."

They all looked round sharply. The heavy, dragging sounds were definitely closer. Wet, slippery sounds accompanied them, sounds that grated on the nerves and upset the stomach. All of them heading straight for the group, with definite purpose.

"I suppose a big transplant Frankenstein thing isn't entirely out of the question," said Melody. "But the noises don't seem right for that."

"Definitely organic," said Kim. "And kind of squishy."

"They were only developing organs," JC said firmly. "Not building actual people."

"Who knows what happened after the new energies changed things?" said Melody.

"Hell with this," JC said briskly. "I'm not built for standing around and waiting."

He strode down the long, open floor, towards the sounds. It took him a while to realise that none of the others were following him. Not even Kim. JC stopped and looked back.

"Oh come on! This is definitely time for *Go team go!*"

"Not even for a substantial raise and a stretch limo all my own," said Happy. "I know my limitations. And they very definitely include squishy things."

"Right," said Melody. "I have a really bad feeling about this. I say we skip this floor and go straight up to face the New People. I could cope with New People. Strange, invisible, squishy things is something else entirely."

"What is the matter with you people?" said JC. "Big Black Dogges with mouthfuls of huge jaggedy teeth didn't even slow you down!"

"Don't like strange squelchy things," Kim said firmly. "Especially ones I can't see."

"Right," said Happy.

"Damn right," said Melody.

JC looked round suddenly. Something was moving about very near him. He spun round and round, glaring in every direction, and then, finally, he looked down. And said, *"Oh shit."*

"What?" said Happy. *"What?"*

But JC was already sprinting back to join the group. He stumbled to a halt before them and put a hand on Melody's and Happy's shoulders to support himself while he got his breath back. His face was slack with shock. The others stared wildly back to where he'd been, but they still couldn't see anything.

"Damn, JC," said Melody. "I don't think I've ever seen you move that fast before."

"Should we be leaving?" said Happy, practical as ever.

"JC, talk to me, sweetie," said Kim. "What was it? What did you see?"

"Should we be running?" said Happy. "JC, what did you see?"

"They're coming," said JC.

"What's coming?" said Melody.

"We were looking in the wrong places," said JC, straightening up and regaining his composure. He glared back the way he'd come. "We should have been looking down. At the floor."

He pointed, and they all looked, just in time to see the first attackers hump and slide into view. The things were crawling across the floor, humping along like massively oversized worms or slugs, leaving long smeared trails of blood and filth and steaming acid behind them. They were red and purple and black, lumpy and distorted, though their basic shapes were still recognisable—and they were all much larger than they should have been. More of them came crawling across the walls, leaving streaky viscous trails behind them, and even more hung from the ceiling. Hundreds of modified, improved, augmented human organs, made strong and self-sufficient by the Bio Reactor and unknown energies, set loose to move independently, with implacable progress and intent.

They were all covered in networks of dark, pulsing veins, their outer membranes sweating strange acidic fluids. They heaved and pulsed, the size of heads or basketballs or dogs. But oversized and distorted as they were, they were still quite clearly hearts and lungs, kidneys and livers, and even tangles of living intestines. They had no eyes, no apparent sensory apparatus at all, but they obviously knew where JC and his team were, and they headed straight for them.

"You have got to be fucking kidding," said Melody.

"Oh, that is gross," said Happy. "Seriously gross, with a whole side order of disgusting. Human insides should stay on the inside, where they belong. But they're still an improvement on the Frankenstein blobby thing I was expecting, I suppose. I mean, those things are *wrong*, on so many levels, but they're not exactly dangerous, are they? Just big lumps of meat, humping across the floor. What are they going to do—hump our legs to death?"

"You don't get it," said JC. "When you're up close like I was, you can sense what they're thinking, what they want. Though it's not so much thought—it's more like brute, basic instinct, turned up to eleven. They want something from us . . ."

"What?" said Melody. "What does a living organ want?"

"They know they can't survive for long like this," said JC. "They were built to survive, but they're not self-sufficient. So they want in, where it's safe. Don't you get it? *They want to get inside us!*"

"I am leaving now," said Happy. "Women and children should try and keep up."

"Too late," said Kim.

They all looked at her, and she pointed behind them. While they'd been discussing the situation, the living organs had quietly surrounded them. They were crawling across the walls and the windows, and hanging from the ceiling, and rows of the red and purple things had moved to block the way back to the exit doors. And all of them were slowly closing in on the group, with blind, unstoppable purpose.

"Now can I use my machine pistol?" said Melody.

"Be my guest," said JC. "Go for it."

The machine pistol was already in Melody's hand. She smiled tightly as she opened fire on the living organs. Hearts and livers the size of heads exploded messily, spattering the surrounding organs with rich red blood. The membranous surfaces drank it all up thirstily. Melody raked her gun back and forth, blasting away organ after organ; and then she ran out of bullets. She looked at the gun and shook it angrily, like that might help. She swore briefly and looked at the others.

"You have used up a lot of ammo recently," said Happy. "Dare I inquire whether you have any more? Only I think we really should— *Oh shit!*"

"Don't let it touch you!" yelled Kim, as Happy retreated quickly from a rapidly pulsing heart. "It could be really bad if it touches you!"

"Blunt-instrument time, people!" said JC, grabbing up a very large, very heavy microscope from a nearby table. The others quickly armed themselves with similar items, except for Kim, who drew up her legs and hovered, sitting in mid air. The living organs hunched up and launched themselves through the air at their targets. They flew at impossible speed, on the unseen wings of unknown energies. JC lashed out with his improvised weapon and caught a pulsating heart in mid air. His hands and arms vibrated painfully from the impact. It was like striking something really hard and solid, and he remembered that a heart is basically one big muscle. But the sheer impact smashed the oversized organ apart, scattering bloody pieces like a rain of offal. More organs launched themselves, and the group stood together, guarding each other's backs, lashing out with their blunt instruments, sending blood and bloody pieces flying through the air every time they connected. It was hard work, every impact shaking the group to their bones, and they were soon sweating profusely and gasping for breath. And still the living organs came, driven by brute basic instinct to get back where they belonged, inside a human body. Happy cried out with disgust every time he hit something, and Kim moaned in terror as the things drew steadily closer.

An oversized liver, dark purple like a veined balloon, shot straight for Melody's face. It came at her from an unexpected angle, and she only got an arm up in time to block it. The heavy organ clamped onto her arm, wrapping around it, and the sheer weight was almost enough to pull her over. The heavy muscles in the liver ground against her arm, trying to crawl up the arm to reach her face, her mouth. Melody dropped her weapon and grabbed at the organ with her hand. Her fingers skidded helplessly from the tough, leathery exterior. Secreted acids stung her palm and fingers.

"Don't let it near your mouth!" yelled Kim. "It wants to crawl inside you!"

"I know!" yelled Melody.

She stopped grabbing at the liver, pulled back her head, and head-butted the ugly thing. The impact sent her staggering backwards, but the liver lost its grip on her arm and fell away. It hit the floor hard but didn't break. Melody picked up the nearest chair and clubbed the organ to death.

Happy tried to stop the advancing organs with a telepathic blast, summoning all his mental strength to force an attack past the deadening oppression that weighed on his mind, but even his concentrated disbelief couldn't affect things that had no minds, no sense of self, only the brute will to survive. A heart the size of a pit bull terrier came flying in out of nowhere and slammed against his chest, driving him back several steps. It clung to him, pulsing in rhythm to his own heart, sweating heavy acids as it tried to burn its way through his chest, to burn out his heart and replace it. Happy didn't know whether he'd survive such a process and didn't want to find out the hard way. The heart snuggled against his chest with horrid familiarity. It wanted in. It wanted to be in him. Happy tried to pry the thing loose, crying out with horror and disgust.

Kim floated this way and that, her face screwed up with indecision, not knowing what to do for the best. JC seemed to be holding his own, and Melody was doing bloody business with her chair. Happy seemed to be the most in trouble, so she dropped her feet to the floor again, strode forward, and grabbed at the heart on Happy's chest with her ghostly hands. Her fingers plunged deep inside, and the huge heart convulsed, turned grey, withered, and fell away. It was dead before it hit the floor. Happy clawed at his acid-holed shirt with both hands, making mindless noises of distress.

"That's it!" said JC. "They can't stand contact with you, Kim! Because you're dead, because the energies that manifest you clash with the energies that motivate them . . . Something like that. I don't know! Maybe you just scare them to death! Everyone crowd around Kim!"

He and Happy and Melody formed a tight circle around Kim. The living organs surrounded them, but stopped dead when they got too close, as though there was some invisible barrier they couldn't cross. They obviously couldn't stand to get too close to the dead girl.

"All right," said Melody. "Now what? They can't get to us, but we still appear to be trapped."

"I'm thinking," said JC.

"Think faster!" said Happy.

"The Bio Reactor!" said JC. "All of these things were born of the Bio Reactor, which I'm guessing is tucked away behind that far partition. Happy, can you see any connection between the living organs and the Reactor?"

"Yes . . . something!" said Happy. "Don't ask me what it is, but it's there!"

"Kim, head straight for it," said JC. "Walk slowly and carefully, and we'll all stick close to you."

"Very close," said Happy.

Kim stepped forward, and the others moved with her. The organs fell back, as though panicked by something they couldn't stand or understand. Kim and JC, Happy and Melody made their way down the long length of the open-plan floor, and the organs moved along with them, still surrounding them but maintaining a more-than-respectful distance. A few let go of the ceiling overhead and dropped on the group, but JC and Melody were always ready to beat them aside. Happy would have, too, but he was so completely unsettled, he was never ready in time. He was breathing painfully hard, and his eyes were wide and wild.

They finally eased past the partition wall, and there was the Bio Reactor, waiting for them. It didn't look like much—a great metal kiln some ten feet tall, its top brushing against the ceiling tiles, maybe eight feet wide around the base. A single hatch faced them, closed, with a wild flaring light rising and falling behind it. The glowing hatch glared at them all like a single unblinking eye.

"I'm still not picking up a single intelligent thought," said Happy, his voice definitely a little higher than it should have been. "But I am getting a sense of *presence* . . . From the Bio Reactor, not the organs. It knows we're here. It knows we're the enemy. It's planning something . . ."

The metal hatch slammed open, and a huge leathery tentacle shot out. It was made up of organ and muscle tissue, bonded together, to make a single gripping organism. It lunged at the group, and they scattered despite themselves. Kim cried out as she was left alone, and the tentacle shot straight at her. It whipped right through her, and immediately the whole tentacle withered and shrivelled up, all the life going out of it as it fell limply to the floor.

"That's it!" said JC. "Kim, walk right into the Bio Reactor! All the way in and out the other side!"

He stepped forward to encourage her, and the tentacle came to life again. It still had one end inside the Bio Reactor, and new life pulsed down the length of it. It snapped around JC and pulled him down. He cried out as the muscle tissue constricted around him like a snake. Melody and Happy rushed forward, grabbed at the tentacle and tried to pry it off, but it was stronger than all three of them put together. Kim hesitated, and JC yelled at her.

"Never mind me! Walk through the Reactor! It can't hurt you!"

"I can't leave you!" said Kim.

"You have to! Now move! Move!"

Kim ran forward, plunging through the open hatch and inside the Bio Reactor. The moment she entered the huge device, the fierce light snapped off, and the tentacle dropped down, dead. JC wriggled his way out of its grasp with help from Happy and Melody. They put him back on his feet and let him lean inconspicuously on them until his legs were firm again. Kim came out from behind the lifeless machine and floated back to glare at JC.

"I can't believe you made me do that!"

"It was necessary," said JC, only a little breathless. "And part of the job. We all play to our strengths. I was almost sure it couldn't hurt you."

"Almost?" Kim's glare was very cold. "We will have words about this later, JC."

She turned her back on him, and moved quickly back down the long floor. The others followed after her. Over-sized organs lay everywhere, dead and already rotting . . Those stuck to the walls and the ceiling were falling off, in ones and twos, to splatter and fall apart on the cold, hard floor. The smell was appalling.

"You know," said JC. "I could really go for a good fry-up, right now."

"Animal," said Kim, not looking back.

SIX

GHOSTLIGHT

"I am getting really fed up with climbing stairs," said Happy, in a more than usually fed-up voice. "It's not like they ever take us anywhere nice. And it still *feels* like we're going down, rather than up. Like we're descending into Hell, step by step by step . . ."

"If you were any gloomier, you'd walk around under your own personal thunderstorm," said Melody.

"If the New People really are superhumans, or perhaps more properly posthuman," said JC, "it should feel like we're ascending towards Heaven. Or at the very least towards Olympus, to commune with the gods."

"And yet it doesn't," said Happy. "Funny, that . . ."

"Not talking to you, when you're in this kind of mood," said JC. "Melody, you're the one with all the information at her fingertips. What's supposed to be next?"

"Could be anything," said Melody. "There was nothing at all about this floor on any of the computers. Could be empty."

"We're not that lucky," said Happy.

"Not listening to Mr. Moody," said JC. "Hardly seems likely, does it? A whole floor left empty, in such a high-rent area?"

"Nothing about this building makes sense," said Melody. "I don't think MSI knew half of what was really going on here. Someone's been playing games, and we're the latest contestants."

"You mean, whoever it was that supplied the extra funding for ReSet?" said Happy, to show he wasn't being left out of anything.

"Who can say?" said JC. "Upwards and onwards, my children . . ."

"Oh God, he's getting enthusiastic again," said Happy. "That's always dangerous."

"Shut up, Happy," said Melody.

They stopped at the swing doors, listened briefly, then walked right in, on the grounds that being cautious hadn't got them anywhere before. JC stopped the others with an upraised hand the moment they were inside. The whole of the floor was full of thick, curling mists, a pearlescent grey fog that stretched away for as far as the eye could see. Like a great grey ocean, greater than any building could hope to contain. There was a definite sense of being *outside*, and that the fog stretched away forever. Strange lights came and went in the pearl grey reaches of the fog, which moved constantly, slowly, as though troubled by some unfelt gusting breeze. The mists curled and roiled, churning in slow vortices, and the lights came and went, came and went . . .

"Okay," said JC. "This is new. You don't normally get fog inside a building."

"Unless something's gone seriously wrong with reality," said Melody. "Which is always possible, given everything that's happened here recently."

"I like fog," said Happy. "Fog is nice. Fog is not dangerous, or threatening, or liable to jump on you without warning. I can live with fog."

"I'm more worried about what might be hiding in the fog," said JC.

"You see." said Happy. "You had to go and spoil it, didn't you?"

"Everyone stay right where you are," said JC. "Don't get out of sight of each other, or of the doors. Lose track of where you are, and you might never get out of here."

"Life was so much easier when I was paranoid," Happy said wistfully. "When I was delusional, and the world really wasn't out to get me."

"It's not simply fog," said Kim. They all looked at her, but she had nothing else to say.

"I think the creation of the New People damaged the state of reality itself, inside this building," said JC. "Or at least, I hope the changes are confined to this building . . . Either way, their arrival has placed an unnatural strain upon the local environment. You've heard of sick building syndrome, where the building itself can affect people's health in unfortunate ways? That's low-level *genius loci* at work. But there is also haunted building syndrome, a building that's gone bad, that either creates ghosts or calls ghosts to it. The whole of Chimera House has been adversely affected, psychically stained, by recent events, an imprinting that will take decades, maybe even centuries, to clean up and make right. Things that would normally be improbable, or wildly unlikely, become more possible in places like this. Even inevitable . . ."

"Like the Bio Reactor's mobile organs?" said Kim.

"Exactly," said Melody. "You don't normally get to see things like that outside of a Cronenberg film."

"*They Came from Within*!" said Happy. "Oh, that's a classic! I had to sleep with the lights on for days, and I never felt the same about swimming pools."

"Strange little man," said Kim. "I've never cared much for horror movies."

"Did you join the wrong team!" said Happy.

"Shut up, Happy," said JC. He stared thoughtfully at the curling fog. "When this is all over, we may have to destroy the entire building. Blow it up, tear it down, crush the rubble, and scatter it at sea."

"Chimera House has become a strange attractor," said Melody. "Attracting, pulling ghosts to it."

"Like moths to a candle," said Happy.

"Oh dear," said Kim. "You mean proper ghosts? People ghosts? I've always found them rather unnerving."

"But you are one!" said Happy.

"But I still think I'm human," said Kim. "I still feel human. Even though I do sometimes see or hear things that only the dead can know."

"Like what?" said Happy.

She stared at him very seriously. "You really don't want to know, Happy."

"I'm a Class Eleven Telepath!" said Happy. "I see things every day that would make grown men rip their own heads off!"

"But I'm dead," said Kim.

"You're right," said Happy. "That does trump a hell of a lot of things."

"I don't know much about ghosts," said Kim. "Despite being one. It's one of the reasons I joined this team. I don't understand ghosts. They scare me as much as they do you."

"I am going to change the subject," said Happy. "Because this one is creeping the hell out of me. Given that the computers didn't have anything to say about this floor, and so therefore it couldn't possibly contain anything important or significant, why don't we skip it and move on up?"

"Doesn't the fog fascinate you?" said JC.

"Let me think about that for a moment no not at all," said Happy. "I have officially decided I can take it or leave it."

"We are staying," JC said firmly. "Because we need all the information we can gather as to what went down here before we have to meet the New People. In a situation like this, information is ammunition. And . . . we really don't want to overlook anything that might come sneaking after us and creep up on us from behind. Do we?"

"Very good point there," said Happy. "God, it's coming to something when you're the paranoid one on this team."

They all went back to staring into the great grey expanse before them. JC stepped cautiously forward and swept one hand through the fog. It felt cold and damp, as though it had blown in off some ancient unknown ocean. He shuddered suddenly, not from the cold. Whichever way he looked, endless shades of grey filled his sight, with no trace of the floor they were supposed to be on anywhere. Lights flickered and flared, glowing and fading in the grey deeps, like taunting will-o'-the-wisps. JC squinted. The fog was hard on the eye, the featureless grey almost painful to look at for too long. He strained his altered eyes against the fog. He couldn't shake off a very definite feeling that somewhere deep in the fog, something was staring back at him.

JC turned to Happy. "Time to do your thing, team telepath. What do you sense about this fog?"

"Nothing specific," said Happy, scowling in concentration. "No thoughts, no intent, no emotions . . . Just this *diffused* sense of presence."

Kim nodded immediately, looking nervously this way and that. Melody stuck both thumbs in her belt and tapped one foot ominously on the floor. She felt frustrated and left out, with nothing to contribute. She felt naked without her equipment. With all her usual toys at her disposal, she could have analysed the hell out of the fog by then, broken it down into its various components, and come up with half a dozen different solutions to the problem. But there wasn't even a computer she could use in the room. She said as much, and JC nodded soberly.

"We have been relying on the building's computers, rather a lot. And I'm starting to wonder if we can trust what they've been telling us. You said yourself someone was making it too easy for you to access information. Maybe they only meant for us to know what they wanted us to know."

"Someone was definitely sending messages through the computers," said Melody. "And they've all been spot on useful, so far."

"Quite," said JC. "Convenient, that. Perhaps a little too convenient."

"Then why not tell us what's going on here?" said Happy.

"Maybe they don't know," said JC. "A sign, perhaps, that our mysterious benefactor isn't all-knowing."

He took off his sunglasses and unleashed his brightly glowing eyes on the fog. Happy and Melody turned their heads away, unable to look at him directly. It wasn't that they were afraid of what they might see if they were to look directly into JC's golden eyes, it was that they found the light too fierce, too unrelenting, for human eyes.

"What does it look like, JC?" said Happy. "When you see the world through those eyes?"

"Everything seems so clear, so simple," said JC. "As though . . . everything finally makes sense."

"I don't know why you two keep looking away," said Kim. "It doesn't bother me. They look like eyes to me. Nice colour, too."

JC took another step forward, concentrating on the fog. He couldn't see anything new, but wherever he turned his gaze, the fog reacted. It seemed to recoil from him, churning and roiling violently, as though disturbed or agitated. When he swept his hand through it, there was no reaction, but he got the sense that the fog didn't like his golden gaze at all. That perhaps . . . the fog was frightened of it.

"The fog!" Kim said suddenly. "*It's* the presence!"

JC nodded slowly. "Yes. It is. I've heard of this phenomenon though I've never encountered it before. Don't know anyone who has. But I know what this is, what it has to be. It's rare, very rare. Takes a lot of energy to produce and maintain, to make it even possible . . . This is ghostlight. Undifferentiated ghosts. This is what will become ghosts, in time. As the building calls the dead to it, they will form out of this fog, taking on shape and nature and purpose."

"Okay," said Melody. "That's all very fine and groovy, but what is it exactly? Are we talking ectoplasm of some kind?"

"Spookier than that," said JC. "What we're looking at isn't really water droplets suspended in the air. Our eyes interpret this as fog because that's as close as our minds can get to understanding it. This . . . is pure potential, the raw chaos from which order unfolds itself."

"Oh crap," said Melody.

Dim dark shapes began to form in the grey depths of the fog. Row upon row of them, standing unnaturally still, stretching out wider and further back than the building should have been able to accommodate. Most of the shapes were human, or at least humanish. Others were larger, bulkier, distorted. And some were only abstract shapes, impressions of people, like nightmares given shape and form in the waking world. JC looked back and forth, trying to get some sense of numbers, and failing. So many ghosts, drawn there by the birth of the New People, and what had been done to Chimera House. Standing in ranks, as though waiting for something. For some voice, perhaps, to tell them what to do.

"Have you noticed?" Happy said quietly. "They all seem to be looking at you, JC. They're not even glancing at the rest of us. Which is not necessarily a bad thing, of course, but it is interesting, and possibly even significant."

"The eyes have it," said Melody. "They're attracted to the light."

"No," said Kim. "It's more than that. I think it's because JC has been touched by the Outside, the afterworlds. They recognise that and respond to it."

"Yes . . ." said Happy. "I'm picking up all kinds of things now. Fear, and fascination, and . . . a whole bunch of other things I don't even recognise, let alone understand. These ghosts might once have been human, but they don't feel like people. I'm not picking up even the most fundamental sense of identity, or individuality. It's almost like . . . looking at them from far, far away. And it's almost as though they think of JC . . . as one of them, only more so."

JC looked at Happy, who flinched away from the golden gaze in spite of himself. "How can they be ghosts and not people?" said JC. "What are ghosts, except memories of people?"

"I don't know! It's as though they're . . . becoming people! The ghostlight is using the memories of ghosts to make forms rather than the other way round! These are . . . copies of ghosts, created by the fog, to do . . . something!"

"The ghosts of London," said Kim. "From the Past, the Present, and maybe even the Future. Memories of the London dead, drawn to this place, to be made again out of the ghostlight. I never knew there could be so many kinds of ghosts. I don't think some of the things rising out of the ghostlight are even human, or ever were."

Happy moved in close beside JC though still careful not to look at him. "Come on, JC, this is where we usually rely on you to pull a rabbit out of the hat, and by that I mean produce some really nasty weapon out of your capacious pockets. Tell me you've got something really destructive about your person that can deal with this."

"Well," said JC. "I have a brass knuckle-duster, a silver dagger, and several phials of holy water to sanctify them with. I have various useful herbs and charms, in small sealed bags to keep them fresh. I've even got an amulet, somewhere. And I have—something else."

"What?" said Melody. "

"It's not something I should have, so I'd better not tell anyone," said JC. "And it may be a bit too much for this particular situation. It's not exactly fine-tuned. If I use it, I'm not sure what might happen. We might end up in pieces, end up scattered all over the Moon."

"I vote we don't use it, then," said Happy.

"Unless we absolutely have to," said JC.

"Well, of course," said Happy. "That goes without saying."

"What?" said Kim. "Under what circumstances could having your bodily parts scattered over the craters of the Moon possibly be considered a viable option?"

"There are times when death is the kinder option," said Melody.

"You had to say that, didn't you?" said Happy.

"Children," said JC, "the ghosts are becoming restless."

Some were swaying in place, others were turning their heads to orientate on the Ghost Finders in general, and JC in particular. Some stepped slowly forward, advancing through the mists, heading towards the group. JC gave them the benefit of his best golden glare, but it didn't seem to bother them in the least. And as they drew closer, emerging out of the fog, they began to reveal more of themselves. Some were suicides, with bloody wounds at their wrists and rope marks at their throats, or sullen faces distorted by gas or poison. Some were broken and shattered, pieces of splintered bone protruding through dead white flesh—jumpers, probably. Some were murder victims, still displaying their death wounds from knives and guns. Some were only children, with cold dark eyes, abused and murdered by those they had every reason to trust.

People who die peacefully don't make ghosts.

Not all of the figures were entirely human. Some were like animals, and some were like machines, and some . . . were simply monsters. Because you can't hide your true nature after you're dead. JC considered them all carefully and noticed that the dead weren't looking just at him. Some were fixing on Kim. She'd noticed, too, and wavered uncertainly this way and that, trying to escape their gaze. When she found she couldn't, she moved in close beside JC. He gave her his best reassuring smile. The ghosts were coming out of the fog, slowly, deliberately, more solid and more real.

"They're just images," Melody said loudly, though whether she was trying to convince herself or the others was open to question. "They don't have any physical form. They can't . . . They can't hurt us!"

"Try saying it louder," said Happy. "You might convince some of them. They looked solid enough to me . . ."

"They're drawing strength from the ghostlight," said JC. "Which, in turn . . . is drawing strength from the altered reality of the building. And, possibly, from the New People . . ."

"Don't you have anything good to say?" demanded Happy.

"Not often," JC admitted. "Comes with the job, and the territory."

Happy scowled. "They feel real. More like individuals, now. Though all I'm picking up from them is . . . bad intent."

The first rank of ghosts was almost upon them, dead hands reaching out for Kim. They smiled at her, devouring her with dark, unblinking eyes. She cried out and shrank away. JC moved forward, to stand between her and the approaching ghosts. He took out his silver dagger, and quite deliberately cut his palm with the razor-sharp edge. He closed his fist, and blood dripped thickly from it.

"Spilled blood has a voice," said JC, almost casually. "It calls to the dead. Leave her alone, you bastards! Concentrate on me!"

When he cut himself, the ghosts had stopped. When he spoke, all their heads turned at once, towards JC, and when they started moving again, they all headed straight for him.

"All right," said JC. "Now I've got their attention, a plan would probably be a good idea. Anyone got any ideas? Because I think I'm going to be very busy in a moment."

"I don't know what to do!" said Melody. "I don't have my tech, my gun's no use . . . What can you do, against an army of ghosts?"

"The fog keeps making more of them," said Happy. "The ghostlight's the source of their power, but how do you fight fog . . ."

"The fog!" said JC. "That's the answer! It shouldn't be here, inside the building! It's an unnatural condition, which makes it physically precarious. Which means vulnerable! Melody, run back down to the previous floor, log on to the computer, and access the building's internal systems. Override the air-conditioning, throw it into reverse, and have it suck the fog right out of here!"

"I thought you said it wasn't really fog?" said Happy.

"The more real it becomes, to make the ghosts real, the more real its physical properties become," said JC. "Don't argue with me, I'm a doctor!"

"No you're not!"

"I might be. You don't know. Melody . . ."

But Melody was already off and running, through the doors and back down the stairs. Happy started to go after her.

"Happy, stay right where you are!" JC said urgently. "I need you here. You have to look after Kim while I'm busy."

Happy hesitated, looked longingly at the doors, then looked at Kim, cringing miserably back against the far wall. He sighed, heavily.

"What do you need me to do?"

"Good man," said JC.

"I've always thought so," said Kim, trying hard to smile bravely.

"I know I'm going to regret this," said Happy. "What's the plan, JC?"

"Well, I plan to keep them occupied, while you keep Kim safe, and Melody hopefully saves the day," said JC.

"That's it, is it?" said Happy.

"Everything else is just details," said JC.

The first ghost to emerge fully from the fog seemed utterly real and solid, and very dangerous. The fog itself seemed to be thinning, as more and more ghosts walked out of it. Up close, they were a horrid sight. Road-crash victims, dragging broken bones and twisted necks. Victims of domestic abuse, with wild, feral eyes. Victims of gang wars and honour killings. Old men and women who died alone and weren't found for months. All of London's dark, dead secrets, given shape and form and purpose by the ghostlight.

A tall, spindly figure in the rotting remains of an evening dress, with a dead white face and outstretched hands like claws, loomed suddenly up before Kim, coming at her from out of nowhere. Kim shrieked, and Happy thrust himself between Kim and the ghost, and hit it with a concentrated blast of disbelief. The ghost blew apart in slow motion, falling away in bits and pieces, dissipating back into the fog.

"Thank you, Happy," said Kim.

"You have no idea how much that takes out of me," said Happy, trying for a companionable grin and almost bringing it off. "JC! They really are getting awfully close now!"

"I'm on it!" said JC. "Time to go old school again . . ."

He slipped the brass knuckle-duster onto his left hand with the ease of long practice, transferred the silver dagger to that hand, then produced a phial of holy water from inside his jacket. He carefully unscrewed the metal cap, poured a generous amount over the brass and the silver, drank the rest to be on the safe side, and tossed the empty phial aside. He grinned nastily at the ghosts before him and went to work.

He strode right into the first rank of ghosts, cut them up and knocked them down. Being dead, they shouldn't have taken any damage or felt any hurt, but because they believed they had bodies, they did, with all their inherited limitations. JC punched them in the head with his blessed brass knuckles and cut their throats with his silver dagger, and the dead figures fell apart before him, dispersing back into the fog before they could even fall to the floor. But even as JC turned to new opponents, the old ones were already re-forming, re-created by the power of the ghostlight. JC fought on, not because he thought he could win, but because while the ghosts were concentrating on him, they would leave Kim alone.

And, hopefully, forget all about Melody.

But no matter how hard he fought, no matter how much he roared and struck about him, he couldn't hold them all. Some ghosts ignored him completely, heading straight for Kim, perhaps because she was dead but still acted as though she were alive. She still had the spark of life within her. She stared, horrified, at the ghosts advancing on her. She tried to back away, to pass through the wall behind her, and found she couldn't. The ghost-light was in control of local conditions. JC saw what was happening and tried to get back to her, but the ghosts surrounded him, reaching out to him with cold, dead hands. It was all he could do to keep them at bay.

"Happy!" he yelled. "Don't let them touch her!"

"Can't you exorcise them?" said Happy.

"Do these creeps even look like they believe in God?" said JC.

The ghosts swarmed all over him, even as he lashed wildly about him, the silver dagger tearing through ghostly flesh and the brass knuckles smashing ghostly bone. They laid their hands upon him, and he cried out despite himself. Cold, dead hands, drawing the living warmth right out of him, to feed their endless hunger for what they had lost. A terrible cold shuddered through JC, a physical and spiritual cold, which numbed his thoughts as well as his body. Frost formed on his clothes, then on his flesh. He struck out at the ghosts, with slow, sluggish movements, though there was hardly any feeling left in his hands any more. He was trying to force the ghosts back, so he could get to Kim. But they crowded in around him, pressing him from every direction at once, and all he could see were dead, hateful faces, hideous grins that showed teeth but no human emotion, and all he could feel were the cold, dead hands, falling on him from everywhere at once, leaching the living warmth out of him.

The golden light from his eyes didn't bother the dead at all. They sucked it right up.

Happy did his best to protect Kim, but the ghosts were closing in on both of them. He scowled till his head ached, concentrating on projecting a telepathic defence, a simple circle of sheer will-power, a line the ghosts could not cross, because he believed in the line more than they believed they could cross it. Happy truly was a powerful telepath, perhaps even more so than he allowed himself to know, but even so, he was only one man, and the ghosts were so many. The circle around Kim and Happy shrank, inch by inch, forced back by the pressure of so many dead minds, as the ghosts pushed remorselessly forward, wanting in. Happy stood between Kim and the ghosts, defying them to get past him, to her. Putting everything he had into her defence, and to hell with what that would do to him later. Cold, dead fingers reached out, and the defensive line shrank back before them, and Happy shivered, deep in his soul, from their proximity.

But he made them work for it, one step at a time. Because JC was trusting him to protect Kim, and though he would never admit it, Happy would fall in his tracks before he'd let JC down.

Kim looked at Happy, and at JC, both of them fighting with everything they had, both of them dying by inches, all for her. She became so furious she forgot how frightened she was. She moved forward, through Happy, who smiled unexpectedly at a sudden feeling of peace and happiness and the smell of elderflowers, and then Kim went on, right into the midst of the ghosts. She blazed with a sudden light, fierce and incandescent, like a living star. It was the same golden glow that shone from JC's eyes, only taken up to the next level. The blazing light stopped the ghosts in their tracks and forced the curling fog back on itself. The dead withered, and retreated, turning their faces away from her, away from the proud, shining light, lurching back into the protection of the ghostlight, which in turn fell back, back . . . The ghosts abandoned Happy and JC, who stood utterly still, mesmerised, in awe of what Kim had become. JC stretched slowly, as the living warmth welled up in him again, and crusted frost cracked and fell away from him. He stumbled back to join Happy.

"I never knew she had so much life left in her," said JC. "Where is all that energy coming from?"

"My love for you, darling!" said Kim, not looking back as she drove the dead before her, blazing with the light of worlds beyond ours.

JC smiled and nodded, and waved encouragingly to Kim; but he wasn't sure he believed that. When forces from the afterworld reached down to touch him, had they perhaps also touched Kim? And if so, for what purpose?

Kim was blazing so very brightly, and the ghosts had all disappeared back into the fog. But the ghostlight was no match for Kim's unearthly glow.

"That can't be good for her," said Happy.

"She's strong," said JC. "Stronger than she realises."

Suddenly, the air-conditioners kicked in, sucking the fog out of the room. The air began to clear immediately, and, without the ghostlight to draw on, the ghosts quickly faded away and were gone, becoming shadows, and less than shadows. In a few moments, the fog had lifted, sucked entirely away, leaving behind a perfectly ordinary-looking, entirely empty floor. JC strode forward to join Kim. She was still glowing, but not as fiercely. She turned to meet him—a man with glowing eyes and a woman who glowed. Happy had to look away. It was too much for him, too much for any human to look upon. Or at least, that was what he told himself. He glanced back sharply as Melody came charging through the swing doors. She took one look at JC and Kim, staring into each other's glowing eyes, and looked away.

"Nice work with the air-conditioning," said Happy.

"No problem," said Melody. "I'm not entirely sure where the fog's gone, but that's a problem for another day."

"And hopefully another team," said Happy. "Because once I'm out of this building, they will not see my twitching arse for dust."

Melody glanced quickly at the glowing couple. "Did I miss something?"

"Something," Happy agreed.

They glanced cautiously at JC and Kim, surrounded by a golden glow, with glowing eyes only for each other.

"Makes you wonder if this is how we'll all feel, when we finally meet the New People," said Happy.

SEVEN

....

LET LOOSE THE BEAST

They took their time, going up the stairs to the next floor. The mission and the building had taken a lot out of them. JC led from the front, as always, but even he had trouble maintaining his usual enthusiasm. He stopped little more than half-way up the stairs and sat down abruptly. The others immediately seized the opportunity to do the same. Kim hovered uncertainly beside JC, looking him over worriedly, and he gave her the best reassuring smile he could before leaning tiredly against the cold stone of the stairway wall. He looked down at Happy and Melody, sitting side by side some steps below, shoulder pressed against shoulder, their two heads tilted together. They looked even more tired than he felt. But they were all tired, battered, injured. They'd all spilled some blood. No time to rest and recharge their batteries, no time out to get their heads round everything that had happened.

No-one said anything because there was still work to be done, so . . . what was the point? Even Happy had cut back on his usual whingeing, if only because he had more pride than to vent without good reason. Wasting a good moan on minor occasions would cheapen it. So he sat quietly with Melody, trembling and twitching occasionally from the psychic distress of his surroundings, while JC looked down at him and felt obscurely guilty for dragging him into a case like this.

JC probably could have kept going, but he made a point of taking a rest anyway because he knew the others would stay on their feet as long as he did, for pride's sake. So he sat down and took a breather, taking one for the team. And it did feel good . . . to sit, relax, breathe steadily, and take a short break from all the madness.

JC smiled down at Happy. "What's the matter with you, Happy? You're sitting slumped on that step like an old man."

"I feel like an old man," growled Happy.

"Don't you move, lover," said Melody. "I'll get you one."

They all managed some kind of smile, but none of them had the energy to laugh. JC adjusted the sunglasses over his glowing eyes, to make sure none of the light was escaping. The glasses weren't in any way magical, or scientifically augmented, and shouldn't have made any difference to the glow in JC's eyes, but they did. They toned things down, made the glare bearable to those around him, and helped him see the world more clearly. JC assumed it was a psychological thing and made a point of never testing it. No-one should have to see the world too clearly for too long. He nodded to Kim.

"That was some display you put on back there, sweetie. I didn't know you could glow like that."

"Neither did I," said Kim. "Until I had to. It disappeared the moment the ghostlight disappeared. I haven't tried to call it back. I'm not sure that would be safe. I'm not blind to how it affected Happy and Melody. Besides, it made me feel . . . uncomfortable."

"Did it hurt you?" said JC.

"No," said Kim. "Quite the opposite."

There was a long pause as they all considered the implications of that, in their various ways. There was something of an uncomfortable gap now, between JC and Kim, Happy and Melody. Even if none of them were ready to acknowledge it yet. Between those who glowed, and those who didn't. Happy finally broke the quiet, if only because silence bothered him more than uncomfortable truths.

"It does feel good, to sit and rest," he said. "A little downtime, between all the ghosts and ghoulies. I only hope there aren't any long-leggity beasties up ahead. I've never liked things with too many legs. Don't like the way they move . . . All very well for you to smile, JC, the rest of us haven't got your energy."

JC nodded slowly. "Say it, Happy. It's all right. Say what's bothering you."

"How am I supposed to know what you're thinking? I'm just the team telepath. And you, it would seem, are so much more now. Certainly more than me. I can't do the things you do. Are you the team psychic now?"

"I don't know," said JC. "Most of the time I'm me, same as I always was."

"And sometimes your eyes blaze like the sun," said Melody. "And the monsters run screaming from you."

"You're different," Happy said bluntly. "Ever since you got those eyes. It's like you can do anything."

"Trust me, that's not the case," JC said carefully. "It might seem that way, but I'm as vulnerable to the bad things as you. In case you didn't notice, I was taking the same beating as you from those cold-hands ghosts. I could have died back there if Melody hadn't taken control of the air-conditioning and saved the day."

"It's me, isn't it?" said Kim, sitting in mid air now, hugging her knees to her chest. "You're afraid of me, aren't you? Please don't be afraid of me. I may be a ghost, but I'm a nice ghost. Like Casper, in the cartoons."

"Casper the dead baby?" said Happy, smiling a bit. "I always thought that was a really creepy concept."

"I don't know where that light came from, or why it chose me," said Kim, peering at him from over her knees. "And I don't think I want it to happen again. What use is a gift you can't control?"

"You were changed, along with JC, down in the depths of Oxford Circus Tube Station," Melody said stubbornly. "And it's not fair! Happy and I were down there, too, fighting the good fight, and we didn't get anything!"

"We got each other," Happy said diffidently.

"Don't interrupt me when I'm on a roll!"

"Sorry, dear."

"I've got a pair of trousers I could lend you," JC said solemnly. "Since you don't seem to be wearing them at the moment."

"Are you kidding?" said Happy. "She scares the crap out of me!"

"I thought you two were having lots and lots of sex?" said Kim.

"What's that got to do with anything?" said Happy.

"Stop trying to distract me from feeling unappreciated and hard done by!" snapped Melody. "Why didn't we get a special gift?"

"We are not worthy," Happy said solemnly.

"I will slap you in a minute, and it will hurt," said Melody.

"Trust me—if you want this gift, you're welcome to it," said JC. "I can see the world more clearly than I ever did before, but that's not always a good thing. You wouldn't believe some of the things we share this world with. We walk in dreams and nightmares, in beauty and horror, and the sheer pressure of it all is more than my eyes can bear. And did you know, I can't see colours any more? Except when I take my shades off? When I wear my sunglasses, which is most of the time, for my own sanity . . . all I see is black and white. Makes me wonder what else I've lost, as the price for this special gift."

"I really would like to run some tests on you, JC," said Melody. "Put you under a microscope and see what's become of you. For your own sake, as well as my curiosity. Glowing that fiercely can't be good for you."

"Hold everything, go previous," said Happy. "Are you talking radiation? Kim was glowing all over me, back there! Am I going to be sterile now? Are you going to make me get my ya-yas out in your laboratory, Melody, and poke them with sticks?"

"You know you love it when I wear the nurse costume," said Melody. "Now behave yourself. The glow isn't any form of radiation I'm familiar with. I have done some research. It's not even light, as such, it's the indication of an Outside force coming into contact with our lesser world."

"Not really any wiser," said Happy.

"That's why I won't let you run any more tests," said JC. "I have enough worries as it is, without you adding to them." He looked at Happy. "Nothing's changed, Happy. Not really. I'm still me, in every way that matters. I never envied you your telepathy, I always knew what it did to you. Do you think this is any different?"

"God, we're one hell of a team," said Happy. "The psychically walking wounded."

"Speak for yourself," said Melody.

"I am, I am," said Happy.

"So, are we still a team?" said JC.

"Of course we're a team!" said Melody. "Who else would put up with the likes of us?"

"Yay!" said Kim, uncurling in mid air. "We totally bonded! Yay for us!"

"Oh God, now she's getting enthusiastic, too," growled Happy. "Bad enough when JC does it. I warn you all now, there is only so much sweetness and light I can put up with before the projectile vomiting starts."

"Since we are all clearly back to our usual selves, make yourself useful, Happy," said JC. "Scan the surroundings. See if you can pick up any hint of what we might be heading into."

"Way ahead of you, as always," said Happy. "I've been trying to force a scan through the general psychic jamming all the way up here, but it's useless. The entire building's affected, and it's only getting worse the higher we go. The closer we get to the New People. It's like they've psychically pissed in all the wells, poisoning the whole building's ambience. If I didn't know better, I'd say Chimera House is possessed. It's like normal reality has been overwritten by something far more powerful."

"The New People," said JC, thinking. "We are going to have to do something about them."

"When we finally get to meet these all-powerful, god-like people, don't stand anywhere near me," said Melody. "I plan to be right at the back saying, *He's nothing to do with me.*"

"I don't know," said Happy, frowning. "It might be them, whatever they are now, or . . . I keep getting this feeling that someone's playing games here. And that maybe the New People are pawns who only think they've become queens and kings."

"How very eloquent," said Melody. "I'm impressed. Really. I told you hanging out with me would be good for you."

"Some of you must be rubbing off on me," Happy said solemnly.

"If not, it's not for want of trying," said Melody.

"I swear to God, your entire life is a double entendre," said JC. "And far too much for my innocent ears. Let us get up and let us go; the job isn't anywhere near finished yet."

They strode up the remaining stairs two steps at a time, burst through the usual swing doors, then stopped right where they were. All the lights were turned off. It was hard to see anything. The only illumination came from outside, amber shafts of street lighting falling through the glass windows that made up most of the far wall. The situation reminded JC of the abandoned factory, and not in a good way. Most of the light was soaked up by a thick, heavy darkness that gave every indication of being very real and very solid. JC gestured sharply for the others to stay exactly where they were. The whole floor felt *wrong* to him, in so many ways.

"What's that smell?" Happy said quietly. "Can all of you smell that? It's hot and wet and . . . swampy. I'm getting rotting vegetation, murky jungle, and something quiet definitely animal. Like being inside an enclosure at the zoo. Damn, that smells bad . . ."

"The air is hot and damp," said Melody. "Beyond damp—saturated with moisture. I was in the Amazon rain forest, as a student, and this is a lot like that . . . but inside a building? At least the ghostlight was only supposed to be fog. This feels very much like the real thing."

"The ghostlight was created," said JC. "So was this. You were right, Happy, someone's been messing with reality, playing games with the building and everyone in it. Someone or something has overwritten local conditions to make new worlds, inside the building. Test runs, perhaps? Tread carefully, children. We are in unknown territory."

"Let me try the light switches," said Melody. "Shed some illumination on what's going down here."

"Don't," said a Voice, from deep in the darkness. "We like it this way."

JC strained his vision against the dark, searching for the source of the Voice. The sound of it had been harsh and brutal and inhumanly deep. Like a beast from the most savage part of the jungle that had taught itself to speak, the better to terrify its prey. Something moved, in the shadows. Huge and broad, radiating animal grace and power, and hard brute force. Old, old instincts yammered at the back of JC's mind, screaming for him to run. He shook himself hard and slapped all the light switches beside the door.

Half a dozen fluorescent lights flickered into life up on the ceiling, enough to reveal a vast tract of tropical jungle spread out before him, where the rest of the floor should have been. It seemed to stretch away forever, as though the end of the floor had become a gateway to another world. Massive trees with huge, dark trunks, and long branches drooping under the weight of heavy foliage. Dark green leaves with heavy veins and serrated edges. Hanging vines and creepers, and great pools of dark, steaming water. Thick, unfamiliar vegetation, filling in the gaps between the trees. Technicolor flowers with huge pulpy petals. The harsh buzzing of insects and the shrill cries of unknown birds.

A crimson light suffused the massive jungle, blazing blood-red from some hidden source, pointing out all the savage details of a setting that had no business inside a London office building. The rich red light made it appear like a living slaughterhouse, where red in tooth and claw was business as usual. The blood-red jungle was a place of death and suffering, and didn't care who knew it.

"They made this for us," said the Voice, from deep in the bloody shadows. "The New People. Wasn't that nice of them? They called it all into being with the wave of a hand. So to speak. They can do things like that—play with the structure and substance of the world like a child building sand-castles."

Every word was clear, the meaning obvious, but still the Voice grated on the ear and on the soul, vicious and savage and brutal as any beast. For all its human speech, there was nothing human in it. JC stepped forward, making a point of looking down his nose at the jungle, his whole posture suggesting he was entirely unimpressed.

"Come out where I can see you," he said. "I don't talk to people who hide in the shadows."

There was a pause, then a slow roll of laughter, a cruel and utterly malicious sound. "Don't be in such a hurry. We're not to everyone's taste, these days. Once I was a man, like you, but I got better. ReSet saw to that. But . . . not all of us blessed by the drug became New People. We all took the same drug, but ReSet only woke up part of our junk DNA. Perhaps it was damaged in us, or it mutated, down the millennia. Either way, we were cheated of our inheritance. We only got part of the package. Not enough to take us all the way, to what we were meant to be. We didn't get to become more than human, to become New People. No—we became monsters. Not fit to associate with the glorious and wonderful New People, up on the top floor. We are Outcasts."

"How many of you are there?" said JC. "Maybe there's something we can do to help."

"Help?" said the Voice. "What makes you think we want help, little man? There are two of us here, now. Male and female, as it should be. There were others, but we killed them. They were superfluous." The Voice laughed again, a dark and nasty sound that sent shivers up and down JC's spine. "Only room for one alpha male and alpha female. The best of the best. The beast of the beast. So we killed the others and ate their bodies. Delicious . . . There's still some left if you're interested."

JC gestured surreptitiously for Happy to ease in behind him. Without looking back, JC murmured over his shoulder, "What are you picking up, Happy? Are there really only two of them here?"

"I can't see or hear a damned thing," Happy said quietly. "The jamming's so oppressive in here, I have to keep all my mental shields nailed down tight to stop my brains leaking out my ears. Sorry, JC, you're on your own. I'm going to go back and hide behind Melody now."

A single dark figure moved slowly forward to the edge of the jungle, emerging from the blood-red light and the dark shadows. It was nine, ten feet tall, with broad shoulders and a vast barrel chest. It was careful to stay a silhouette against the blood-red light. Its powerful arms hung down past its knees, and the ground trembled with every step it took. It stood still, and another figure suddenly appeared beside it. Just as tall, just as massive, but something about it suggested female, to the first figure's male. They stood easily together, as though they be-

longed in each other's company and no-one else's, in the
bloody jungle the New People had made.

"Take off your sunglasses," said the Voice. "We want
to see your eyes."

JC did so, with his very best dramatic flourish, as
though he'd meant to do it all along. His eyes glowed
fiercely bright, but the golden glow didn't travel far and
made no impact at all on the blood-red light. JC's eyes
didn't affect the jungle or the two figures in the least. JC's
breath caught in his chest as he saw them clearly for the
first time. The larger figure laughed its slow, awful laugh.

"Yes . . . You have more in common with the New
People than we do. You have their eyes . . ."

JC swallowed hard and fought to keep his voice steady.
This would be a really bad time to sound nervous or uncertain. "Come with us. We represent an organisation
that is used to dealing with strange and unnatural things.
We have all kinds of specialists. We can help you."

"Can you?" said a second Voice, the female Voice. It
was just as savage, just as brutal, but there were emotional
undertones that somehow made it even worse. "I don't
think you understand, you Good Samaritan. Can you
undo what has been done to us? Make us human again? I
don't think so . . . We've moved on from being human."

"What makes you think we'd want to go back?" said
the first Voice. "To being merely human? That's your
limited thinking getting in the way there. If you could
only see us, and our world, the way we do . . . without
your petty human preconceptions getting in the way . . .
This is a glorious world, and we glory in it."

"I can See you," said JC. "I can See everything you are. Step forward into the light, and show yourselves if you're not ashamed to be seen."

He put his sunglasses back on and gestured for the rest of his team to come forward and stand beside him. They did so, some more readily than others. There was a pause, and the two dark shapes moved smoothly forward into the blood-red light at the edge of the jungle. They straightened up, to show themselves off, and JC could feel the rest of his team fighting not to look away. The two figures were physically and spiritually monstrous, a blunt assault on the senses. The triumph of the beast over man. Like demons from the Pit taking on the shape of man to mock and befoul the human figure. They were both a good ten feet tall, and half as broad across the shoulders. Swelling chests, muscular arms and legs, all of it covered with thick dark fur matted with blood and shit and other things. Their hands had claws, their mouths held massive teeth, and sharp, pointed horns thrust up from their broad foreheads.

The male and female had grossly exaggerated sexual characteristics, as inhuman as every other part of them. They moved like animals, held themselves like animals, and they stank of blood and musk, of slaughter and sex. They were everything that humanity was supposed to have left behind and risen above. To look at them was to know there was nothing left in them of human reason, or human concerns. They would do what they would do because they could, and because they wanted to. They had left Humanity behind, or perhaps thrown it off, for the freedom that provided. Their faces still had human lines, but there was nothing of man or woman in them. And if the eyes are the window to the soul, only the Beast looked out.

"Oh God, JC," said Kim. "Do you see what I'm seeing? They did this to themselves! ReSet changed them, but these shapes came from urges and needs hidden deep within them. Horrid dreams, bestial nightmares, all the things we're not supposed to want or believe in . . ."

"Monsters from the id," murmured Happy.

"We could have been anything that we wanted to be," said the male. "But if we couldn't rise to be New People, what was the point? So we let the Beast out. Followed the alternative path our partially awakened DNA showed us, the way we could have been if Humanity hadn't got in the way. We didn't have to give up much to become so much more. Meet the progenitors of a new race. All the power of the Beast, and the intellect of man, with none of the drawbacks. I am Gog. This is Magog. You may kneel and worship us, if you like."

"Are we not glorious?" said the female, Magog. "We're what happens when you strip away all the human limitations, physical and mental and spiritual . . . When you let the Beast out, and adore it. It's amazing what you can do, what you can achieve, without conscience or ethics or control to get in the way. We can do anything."

"And we have," said Gog. "And we will. Oh, the things we'll do . . ."

"What about the New People?" said JC. His mouth had gone dry, and he had to fight to keep his voice calm and apparently effortless. "You really think they're going to let you run wild?"

"You think they care about the world?" said Gog. "They're up there deciding what to do with it."

"Making their minds up about what to make of it," said Magog. "And when they're finished with the world, we won't recognise it at all."

"They have no use for civilisation," said Gog. "They don't need it."

"I really think we need to get out of here," Melody said quietly. "We are not equipped for big-game hunting."

"Look at the size of those brutes," said Happy, very quietly. "They'd run us down before we got anywhere near the doors. Keep them talking, JC. Give us time to think of something that doesn't involve wetting ourselves."

"My plan exactly," said JC. "Think hard. And quickly." He raised his voice to address Gog and Magog again. "Do you know what the New People are planning? What their intentions are?"

"No," said Gog. "I don't understand them, any more than you could. They don't think like people any more. They've risen above that. Perhaps they don't think at all. Perhaps they do something better than mere thinking . . ." He rolled his head slowly across his broad shoulders. And then he smiled, to better show off his teeth. "They're up there, at the top of the building, deciding the fate of the world . . . But whatever they finally settle on, you can be sure neither your kind nor mine will have any part in it. They don't need machines, or tools, to change their world, or a civilisation to protect them from it. They're the gods we were all supposed to become, before something went wrong in our DNA, and we all had to settle for being human."

"Whatever kind of world the gods choose to live in," said Magog, "odds are, we won't understand any part of it."

"So what are you doing here?" said JC.

"A world within a world," said Gog. "A playground for the cute little doggies to romp in."

"The jungle is where we belong," said Magog. "The New People set us here, to wait for you. Oh yes—they knew you were coming. They've always known. I don't think Time works the same way for them. They put us here to keep you from bothering them. Because we make such excellent guard dogs."

"I don't believe you," said JC.

"You think we care?" said Gog. "We don't care about anything. We don't have to, any more."

JC turned his head slightly to look back at the others. "Anyone got any good ideas yet?"

"I vote for running," said Happy. "Everything forward and trust in the Lord, separate and hope they don't get us all, and even I don't think this is a good idea."

"Normally, I'd say we should at least go out fighting," said Melody. "But look at the size of those things! They look like they could bench-press a blue whale."

"They are the three-headed Cerberus, guarding the gates to Heaven and Hell," said Kim. "We have to get past them to get to the New People. That's why the New People put them here. To test us, to see if we're worth talking to."

"Don't suppose you feel like glowing?" Melody said to Kim.

"I've been trying to bring it on from the moment I saw those awful things," said Kim. "Not even a glimmer."

"Terrific," said Happy. "We can't run, and we can't fight. What does that leave? Hoping we choke them when they eat us?"

JC turned back to Gog and Magog. "What do you want? What do you want, with us?"

"Maybe we just want to play with you," said Gog. "Play tag, in and out of the jungle. You're It."

"We're Outcasts," said Magog. "No place for us in the glorious new world that's coming. So we might as well enjoy ourselves in the time that's left to us. And take out our frustrations on you."

"You're good people," said Gog. "We can tell. You stink of it. We will make you scream and suffer."

"For our pleasure," said Magog.

"Told you," said Happy. "Beasts, in body and soul. Hey wait a minute . . . Something's changed. Something just changed."

"What?" said Kim, looking quickly about her. "Are there more of them?"

"It's not them," said Happy. "It's the jungle. Look at the jungle . . ."

"Oh my God . . ." said Kim.

"What?" said JC. "What about the jungle?"

"It's growing," said Melody. "Look at that . . . the jungle's moving forward."

They all looked. The hot and steamy jungle world was closer than it had been. The blood-red edge was crawling forward, foot by foot. Vines and creepers hung down from the nearby ceiling, turning slowly, twitching at the group, as though stirred by dreaming thoughts. The buzz of insects was louder, the bird cries closer, and the heavy stench of rotting vegetation and corruption was all around them. The blood-red world had consumed all the rest of the floor, creeping up on the group like a silent predator, while their attention had been fixed on Gog and Magog. The two beasts laughed silently together.

"It's in my head!" Happy said suddenly. "The jungle's in my head!"

JC shook his head slowly, sickly. He could feel the pressure of the wild, of the Beast, closing in around him. The smell of it in his nose and mouth, the damp sweat of it on his skin, and the deep, dark, atavistic temptation of it, in his head and in his heart. To let go of being human, to let the Beast loose . . . to be free of all restraint and conscience . . . JC shook his head hard, refusing to give in. His hands clenched into fists, and his teeth clenched so hard his jaw hurt. JC did not give in, whether the pressure came from outside or within. He didn't do that.

He looked back to see how the others were doing. Happy and Melody were both crouching, almost on all fours. Happy's face was wet with sweat. Melody saw JC looking at her and growled at him, from deep in her throat. Happy beat his knuckles against the floor.

"It's changing us, JC! Changing us inside and out . . . The jungle . . . is its own world, with its own rules. You can't be in the jungle and not be a part of it. Whatever you're going to do, JC, do it now. Or Gog and Magog won't be the only beasts here."

Kim looked desperately at JC. She hadn't changed because she was dead, and the call of life had no hold over her. JC gave her his best reassuring smile. From the look on her face, it wasn't that successful. JC looked back at Gog and Magog.

"So," he said. "You have a weapon. The jungle. Unfortunately for you, I have a better weapon. Ever seen anything like—this, before?"

He took a small withered object out of an inner pocket and held it up so they could all see it. A monkey's paw, made into a Hand of Glory. The thin fingers had been soaked in wax from a dead man, and the fingertips made into wicks. Words had been spoken over the paw, and dread Power invested in it, and its presence alone was like a hammer-blow on the air, its very existence a rotten weight on the surface of the world. Gog and Magog stared at it, fascinated.

"Bloody hell!" said Happy, straightening up suddenly without even realising.

"I don't like it," said Kim. "It's nasty. It's looking at me . . ."

"Those things are strictly forbidden!" said Happy. "Even the Crowley Project won't let its people use one of those in the field!"

"Only because their leaders are scared their field agents might use it against them," said JC. "All right, I'll admit having it is against all the rules, but if we were the kind of people who gave a damn about rules, we wouldn't be field agents, would we?"

"Come on, JC," said Happy. "Those things are seriously forbidden. Lots of places they'd hang you just for knowing such things were possible. Hell, they'd hang you for knowing someone who knew things like that were possible."

"With good reason," said Melody. "Some things should be forbidden. Because they're too powerful."

"They have their uses," JC said easily. "The sight of it pushed the jungle right out of you, didn't it?"

Happy and Melody looked at each other. They were both standing like people again.

"Where did you get it?" said Melody.

"eBay," said JC. "You can find all kinds of stuff on eBay. Now hush, children, daddy's working."

He stepped forward, showing the monkey's paw Hand of Glory to Gog and Magog, and the edge of the blood-red jungle retreated before him. The two beasts stirred uneasily. They couldn't look at him or the Hand directly.

"A Hand of Glory can find any door, unlock any lock, reveal anything hidden," said JC. "And a monkey's paw can force a change on reality, on a small scale. So put those two things together, and I have the power to find what ReSet did to you and undo it."

Gog and Magog looked at each other, then back at JC. Gog growled at him. "We can't go back. We won't go back. Not now we've tasted real freedom. We were never meant to be human! We might not be New People, but this is better than the small, insignificant things we were."

"I'm sorry," said JC, and part of him really was. "But I have no choice."

Gog and Magog charged forward, crossing the intervening space with inhuman speed, claws outstretched for throat and heart. JC said a single activating Word, and flames blossomed at the paw's fingertips. There was a flash of brilliant light, and when it subsided, the blood-red jungle was gone. Fluorescent light filled the whole empty floor, stretching away before JC. And at his feet, a naked man and woman lay very still. JC blew out the candle fingers, very carefully, and put the withered paw away. He knelt beside the man and woman and checked for pulses. He looked up at the others and shook his head.

"They're dead," he said shortly. He stood up slowly, brushing himself down here and there, checking that his marvellous ice-cream suit was hanging properly. A style is a style, after all. And it kept him from having to think things he didn't want to think.

"Did the Hand kill them?" said Kim.

"Indirectly, perhaps," said JC. "But you heard them. They didn't want to live as people, any more."

"Maybe they couldn't," said Happy. "After all the things they'd done as beasts."

"They didn't feel guilty," said JC. "They just didn't want to give it up."

Happy looked at him, meaningfully. "If you had that awful thing with you all along, why didn't you use it before? Did you really think it was that dangerous to us?"

"I had some concerns. But mostly—well, you don't use a backpack nuke to crack a nut," said JC. "Anytime you use something this powerful, it attracts attention. The wrong kind of attention. I've already been touched by forces of Good from Outside. I really don't want to be noticed by the other side."

"You have got to let me run some tests on that when we get back," said Melody.

"Wouldn't do you any good," said JC. "As far as science is concerned, it's only a preserved monkey's paw. And you don't want to try investigating it from the other side."

"Why not?" Melody said immediately. "Knowledge is knowledge."

"Because you don't want to attract attention to yourself, either," said JC. "Bad enough if Outside forces take an interest—can you imagine what the Boss would have to say if she found out? At best, she'd take it away. At worst . . ."

"There are still places where they hang you for knowing such things exist," said Happy.

"Right," said JC.

Happy shook his head. "Who looks at a monkey's paw and thinks—*That isn't dangerous enough? I must make it into something even nastier?*" He stopped abruptly and looked at JC. "Something this powerful . . . It worked against the Beasts. Would it work against the New People?"

"Only one way to find out," said JC.

EIGHT

HUMAN IS

"No more stops, no more investigations, no more distractions," JC said firmly. "I think we've all had more than enough of taking it floor by floor, and I don't see that there's anything more we need to know or learn. So, to hell with whatever may or may not be lurking on the remaining floors. I say we go straight to the top of this benighted building and cut to the damned chase. We need some serious face-to-face time with the New People."

"Assuming they have faces," Happy said gloomily. "If they're as far above us as the Beasts were below . . ."

"You always have to look on the glum side," said Melody. "Look at it this way—the sooner we crash the party on the top floor and put our case to the New People, the sooner we can all go home, and I can get back to doing disgusting things to you in the bedroom. We're not even half-way through that book I showed you."

"I'm quite looking forward to meeting the New People," said Kim. "I'll bet they're all sparkly and glamorous and . . . and all the colours of the rainbow!"

Melody sniffed. "Somebody read far too many flower fairy books when they were little . . ."

"Oh I loved those!"

"Later, Kim," said JC. "I think we need to prepare ourselves for the possibility that these New People aren't going to be anything we expect . . . or can accept."

"What if they're not superhuman?" Happy said doggedly. "What if they're posthuman? What if they are gods?"

"Good question," said JC. "In which case, presumably some kind of sacrifice will be required, and I will nominate you."

"Are you really planning on using that Hand of Glory thing against the New People?" said Melody.

"Not if there's any other option," said JC. "The Hand is very definitely a last resort. If you see me draw it, start running."

"Way ahead of you there," said Happy.

"No-one said anything about taking on gods and monsters when I joined up with the Institute," said Melody.

"Should have read the small print," said JC. "Onwards and upwards, my children."

‚‚‚‚‚‚‚‚‚‚‚‚‚‚‚‚‚‚‚‚‚‚‚‚‚‚‚‚‚

They made their way slowly up the last remaining stairs, taking their time. They were all really tired, physically, mentally, and emotionally. They paused to glance at each set of swing doors they passed, straining their ears against the quiet, but they never saw or heard anything on any of the other floors. The only sounds were their feet scuffing on the steps and their own harsh and laboured breathing.

But the higher up the building they went, the heavier the atmosphere became. Every floor they passed brought them that much closer to the territory of the New People and added an extra weight to the body and the soul. JC struggled on, every step that little bit harder, calling for more strength, more nerve, more concentrated will. As though he was fighting a part of himself that didn't want to go any further. That didn't want to know who or what these New People might be. It is a terrible thing, to contemplate placing yourself in the hands of living gods. But JC lowered his head and bulled on because he was damned if he'd give in to any pressure, from outside or inside. He had a job to do, and he was going to do it. It was perhaps the only thing he really believed in.

"Can't shake off a feeling we're being watched," said Melody. "Is anyone else feeling it?"

"We're heading towards Something," said Kim. "I can feel that."

"They know we're coming," said JC. "The New People. They're waiting for us. Smug bastards . . ."

"I am definitely not standing anywhere near you when we meet them," said Happy. "What do you think they'll look like?"

"Probably a lot like us," said Melody. "I mean, come on—whatever changes or improvements ReSet has worked in these people, they're mostly likely to be on the mental and psychic level. Even the Beasts, Gog and Magog, were still basically human in shape. Their mind-sets had been affected the most, making them what they were. I think we're building these New People up into far more than they can reasonably be."

JC stopped abruptly, leaned heavily on the railing to get his breath, and looked back down the steps at the others. "If I've been counting off the floors correctly, and I have, the stairs around the corner above us will lead to the final set of doors, and the final floor of this building. Happy, are you picking up *anything*?"

"Something big and scary," said Happy. He leaned heavily on Melody's shoulder, his face wet with sweat, flushed a really unhealthy colour. "It's taking all my shields to keep it outside my head. Don't ask me what it is, JC. Or what's causing it. I think . . . it's the presence of the New People, weighing down on reality, over-whelming everything else. Just by being here, by exist-ing . . . they're the most important thing there is."

JC frowned. "You haven't started taking your little pills again?"

"I wish," said Happy. "I would love to be able to float off on a soft pink cloud of medication. But I daren't. I daren't be that open, that vulnerable. Operating at any-thing less than one hundred per cent in this situation will get us all killed. You can put good money on it."

"My little boy is growing up," said JC. "I am so proud."

"Up your arse with a bent banana," said Happy.

Suddenly, a voice spoke to them from above. A very human, very familiar voice.

"Well done, thou good and faithful servants. I really wasn't sure you'd get this far."

They all stared intently at the corner above them, as

slow and steady footsteps descended towards them. And
then he came round the corner, and there he was, standing at the top of the stairs, smiling urbanely. Robert Patterson, sharp and immaculate as ever in his smart city
suit, looking very pleased with himself. Tall, black, a
shaven head and a noble brow, handsome features and a
condescending smile—a high-up functionary in the Carnacki Institute who very definitely should not have been
there. JC looked at him for a long moment.

"What the hell are you doing here, Patterson?"

"You'd forgotten all about me, hadn't you?" said Patterson, extending one perfect white cuff and flicking an
invisible piece of lint off his sleeve. "That's all right. Everyone does. For all my high-ranking duties in the Institute, I'm really nothing more than a glorified messenger
boy, sent here and there at the Boss's whim, to carry out
all the dreary day-to-day business that our dear Catherine
Latimer can't be bothered with. All the soul-destroying
shitwork that makes the Institute run smoothly—Patterson
will take care of that. But, unfortunately for all concerned,
that hasn't been true for some time. I don't answer to the
Carnacki Institute, or Catherine bloody Latimer, any more.
I'm part of something bigger and far more important, now.
An organisation, a cause, greater than anything you could
hope to understand."

Happy looked at JC triumphantly. "You see? You see!
I told you there was something going on behind the
scenes! I told you there were secret enemy forces, operating in the shadows, working to undermine us, while we
were all kept distracted with everyday missions . . ."

"Try not to sound quite so pleased about it," said Melody. "If I'm reading the situation right, Patterson's presence here means we are in even deeper doo-doo than we thought . . ."

"Oh yes, you are all screwed," said Patterson. "You are all quite monumentally screwed and shafted. You were out of your depth the moment you walked through the lobby doors."

"How did you get up here ahead of us?" said JC. "I saw you leave, in that hideously overstretched limo."

"I never really left," said Patterson. "I had the driver stop the car once we were safely out of sight round the far corner, got out, came back here, and entered through the back door. Yes, I know you were told there wasn't one. How remiss of me. And then . . . I used the elevator. That is what it's for . . . I've been ahead of you all along."

"Whom do you represent?" said JC.

"Like I'm going to tell you," said Patterson. "You don't need to know. You can all die like you've lived, in ignorance."

"If you're not going to hit him, make way for someone who will," said Melody.

"Stay right where you are!" said JC, not looking back. His gaze was still fixed on Patterson, who didn't seem that bothered by the golden glare behind JC's sunglasses. JC chose his words carefully. "If you and your organisation, whatever it is, are responsible for funding the ReSet drug, then you're responsible for everything that's happened here." His voice was cold and harsh enough to wipe the smile off Patterson's dark face. JC moved up a step. "All the deaths and all the horror and all the things that might still happen. All down to you. Plus the deaths of the policemen and the security men called to investigate. Am I right?"

"Of course," said Patterson, pulling his arrogance around him like a shield. "It wasn't difficult. They all trusted an obvious authority figure like me, right up to the moment when it became clear that they really shouldn't have. I killed them all because they were in the way, disposed of the bodies, and held their ghosts here, or what was left of them, to guard the lobby. I knew our revered Boss would be sending a team in soon. I should have known it would be you. You do have a reputation for crashing in where you're not wanted."

"Hold it," said Happy. "The Boss wanted us here? I thought MSI insisted we be sent in?"

"Oh please," said Patterson. "MSI haven't a clue about what's been going on in their building. Haven't known for ages. ReSet was our very own cuckoo's egg, set in place to force everything else out of the nest. I only told you MSI insisted on your presence to throw you off the scent."

"Are you also the one who's been feeding us information through the building's computers?" said Melody.

"Smart girl," he said. "I've been telling you what you needed to know, or what I wanted you to know, so you wouldn't go looking in places I didn't want you looking. I've been leading you round by the nose, all along."

"All right," said JC. "ReSet was your baby. Let's jump to the big question. Why?"

"Human is as human does," said Patterson. "And

frankly, that's not good enough. What we've done with the world so far has been very disappointing. So events were arranged here to lead to the creation of something more than human, better than human. Something that would surpass Humanity and achieve all the things our limited and self-centred species has so signally failed to achieve. Remember poor misunderstood Nietzsche—Man is something to be overcome."

"How come secret organisations never want to do anything nice?" Kim said wistfully.

"The clue is in the description," said Happy.

"We've been planning this for a very long time," said Patterson. "And we're not about to let you butt in and screw it up now. The greatest minds of this generation have been considering a single fundamental question—What if Man was a mistake? What if we were supposed to be so much more, but we fell short of our true potential? We were never meant to be something as small and limited as Man! We were supposed to fly like angels! We were all supposed to be living gods and walk this world in majesty and glory! And it's not too late. We can all blaze like suns. We can all shine like the stars!"

"Is this like the sixties?" said Happy. "When people thought that taking lots and lots of LSD would turn them into superheroes? The mind's true liberation, through frequent frying of your neurons? Trust me—that really didn't work out too well."

"You think so small," Patterson said coldly. "Little man. Touched with the gift to see the world clearly, and all you've ever done is complain about it. Wake up and smell the gravitas! We weren't supposed to be like this!

We weren't supposed to suffer, to get ill, to get old and die! ReSet will set us free from all that. We will go on and live lifetimes and become what we were always supposed to be!"

JC considered him thoughtfully. "What if these New People you've brought about aren't human? What if they don't look like us, think like us, feel like us?"

Patterson smiled. "Would that really be such a bad thing? Would the complete replacement of Humanity be such a great loss?"

"Okay, someone's taken the train to freaky town," murmured Happy.

"Why are you here now?" said JC, moving up another step towards Patterson. "Why show yourself to us? You've been conspicuous by your absence, until now."

"You were never really meant to get this far," said Patterson. "I let you in because . . . we had to let somebody in. We needed someone to clear up the mess. All the unpleasant side effects to our glorious creation. But now it falls to me to stop you here. To stop you interfering with things you're incapable of understanding or appreciating. My organisation has plans for the New People. And we can't have you upsetting them with your unwanted presence."

"Given everything we've overcome and dealt with to get this far," said JC, "how do you plan to stop us?"

Patterson actually smirked, he was so pleased with himself. "You think you're the only one to quietly remove useful and highly dangerous items from the Carnacki Institute Armoury? Look what I've got here . . ."

He extended one hand, so they could all see what was

nestling on his palm. A small black box, gleaming and glistening, covered with rows of curling brass sigils. Everyone looked at the box, then looked at Patterson.

"I have to say," said Melody, "I have eaten things that looked more interesting than that."

"Hell," said Happy. "I've crapped more interesting things than that."

"Typical," said Patterson. "I show you a wonder of the world, and all you can manage is vulgarity. This . . . is a Boojum. Because it makes things softly and silently vanish away. I say the Word, and whatever I point the box at . . . isn't, any more. You're all going to disappear, right here, and no-one will ever know what happened to you. You'll be a small part of the great Chimera House Mystery—all the people who worked here, or walked in one night and were never seen again."

"Cut the crap, Patterson," said Melody. "I hate it when people give cute names to machines. Boojum, my arse. Lewis Carroll has a lot to answer for. That box is nothing more than a simple dimensional frequency adjustor. Took me a moment to recognise it, it's so primitive. I built one of those when I was sixteen! Out of bits and pieces I ordered from the back pages of the *Fortean Times*!" She looked at JC and the others because they were all looking at her. "We all have our own basic frequencies, that tell us which dimension of reality we belong to. Or possibly vice versa. That box changes people's frequencies, so that they drop out of this reality and into another one."

"And you built one when you were sixteen?" said Happy.

"Well," said Melody, "I didn't say it actually worked . . . But the theory was sound."

"So," said JC, "that box is still basically a Boojum, for all practical intents and purposes, in that it can make us all disappear. Do you have any defence against it, Melody?"

"If I had my equipment with me . . ."

"I'm going to take that as a no," said JC. "So hush now, children, while daddy negotiates." He smiled engagingly at Patterson. "Let's start with a basic *Why?* shall we . . . ? Why did you, or your unseen lords and masters, set out to create the ReSet drug in the first place? Did you know it would create New People?"

"Let's just say we had hopes," said Patterson.

"But Gog and Magog, in their own Beastly way, were quite convinced the New People are going to destroy the world," said JC. "Tear down human civilisation because they don't need it. Remake the entire world, and perhaps even reality itself, in their not-at-all-human image. How will your organisation profit from that?"

"Oh, I don't think things will get that far," said Patterson. "There are checks and balances in place . . . things going on behind the scenes, behind the scenery of reality, to ensure nothing too bad happens. Pieces have been moved into place to take advantage of the situation. But I think I've said quite enough. You don't need to know any more. It's time for you to go."

He held up the Boojum, and JC produced his Hand of Glory. The two men said their activating Words, pretty much in unison . . . And the small black box and the small withered paw both vanished, gone in a moment, blinking out of existence simultaneously as two great powers cancelled each other out. Both men looked at their empty hands, and it was all very still and very quiet in the stairwell.

JC launched himself up the intervening steps and threw himself at Patterson. They slammed together and wrestled fiercely in the confined space. Happy and Melody charged up the stairs, while Kim shouted fierce encouragement to JC. Patterson forced JC off him, with a great effort, and swung wildly at his attacker, who ducked aside at the last moment. Patterson's strength and momentum carried him right past JC and over the stairwell's railing, and out into the void. He grabbed the railing with a last desperate effort, and hung on to it with one hand, dangling over the long, long drop. He looked down, then up at JC. Happy and Melody crowded in on either side of JC, and the three of them looked at Patterson. Kim hovered above them all.

None of them moved to help Patterson. Great beads of sweat appeared on his dark face as he hung helplessly, unable to pull himself back up. He glared up at them but said nothing. He wouldn't beg. JC regarded him dispassionately, and when he finally spoke, his voice was so cold it actually shocked the others.

"For all the people who died here, because of you. For all the lives you ruined, through the ReSet drug. For killing the policemen and the security men. For creating the New People and endangering the whole world . . . For being a traitor to the Carnacki Institute, and the whole of Humanity . . . It falls to me to pass judgement on you."

"JC?" said Kim. "What are you doing, JC? You can't just kill him . . ."

"Yes, I can," said JC. "For all he's done and all he's made possible—yes, I can kill him."

"Hold it, hold it, take it easy," Happy said quickly. "JC, I can see where you're going with this, but don't. We can't kill the man. He knows things, JC. We need to know who he's working for, if there are other traitors inside the Institute, and everything these people are planning!"

"I'll never tell," said Patterson. He swung slowly from his single handhold, making no attempt to pull himself up. "I'd rather die than have them angry at me. There really are fates worth than death."

"You aren't actually going to kill him, are you, JC?" said Kim.

"For God's sake, JC," said Melody.

"'Vengeance is mine, saith the Lord,'" said JC. "But he isn't here right now, and I am."

He slammed his fist down on Patterson's hand. The dark fingers sprang open under the impact, and Patterson lost his grip. He fell like a stone, screaming all the way down. JC watched him fall and wouldn't let himself look away until he lost sight of the man in the gloom of the stairwell. The scream cut off abruptly, and JC finally turned away.

"Damn, JC," said Happy. "That was . . . hardcore. I'm not saying you were wrong, necessarily, but . . ."

"You killed him," said Kim, looking at JC as though she'd never seen him before.

"It's part of the job, sometimes," said Melody. "We're

trained to kill the bad guys, if necessary. If there's no other way."

"Yeah," said Happy. "But there's a difference between taking out a threat in the heat of the moment and a cold-blooded execution. I mean, I never liked Patterson, but he was one of us. Still a part of the Carnacki Institute."

"Yes," said JC. "One of us. That's why I did it."

He led the way up the last remaining set of steps, and one by one the others followed him up, all of them watching him thoughtfully, in their own ways.

::::::::::::::::::::::::

All too soon they ran out of stairs and stood together looking at the last set of closed swing doors. None of them made any move, for quite a while. JC finally reached out a hand to the doors, then snatched it away again as a great Voice was heard, filling the stairwell, filling their heads. Not a human Voice, not even human words, but still it seemed to JC and the others that Something called to them, summoned them, to come to the final floor and account for themselves.

"What the hell was that?" Melody said hoarsely. "It was inside my head . . ."

"It went right through all my shields and barriers as though they weren't even there," said Happy. "And no, JC, I'm still not picking up anything else. That wasn't telepathy. It didn't feel anything like telepathy."

"The power," said Kim. "The sheer power . . ."

"If they're that powerful, we'd better not keep them waiting," said JC. "In we go, children. Best foot forward and try not to show me up."

He pushed the doors open and strode straight in, and the others followed right after him.

JC kept walking, even though he wasn't sure where he was any more. He could feel the pressure, the sheer presence of the New People, even before he could see them. An overwhelming impact, as though their simple existence had stamped itself onto reality so completely, it was hard to feel anything else. He finally stumbled to a halt, stopped in his tracks by the sheer alien strangeness of the situation. A fierce, unnatural light with no obvious source suffused everything, a light painful even to his altered eyes, and a great Sound filled the air, without beginning or end. JC felt it in his bones and in his soul as much as heard it. He knew that he was in the presence of something unknown, and perhaps even unknowable.

The others had stopped with him. Happy and Melody and Kim huddled close together for the simple comfort of human contact. They all had their eyes screwed up against the light, and the sound and the heavy presence of a place not meant for human kind. Kim seemed as much affected as any of the living.

"We shouldn't be here," Happy whispered, like a child in a cathedral. "We don't belong in a place like this."

"Chin up, my children," said JC, as clearly and calmly as he could manage. "Yes, I would have to say that we are in the presence of things unknown . . . But that's the job, when you work for the Carnacki Institute."

"I resign," said Happy.

"Shut up, Happy," said JC.

He took off his sunglasses and looked around. In this new place his eyes hardly glowed at all. It was as though the golden light was nothing compared to the harsher light of what had been the top floor of Chimera House. JC nodded slowly, and put his shades back on.

"We have a job to do," he said flatly, "And we're going to do it together. Because it's our duty, and our responsibility, to the Institute and perhaps all Humanity. And because we're the best damn team in the Institute, and we don't back down from anything. Right?"

"Right," said Happy.

"Damned right," said Melody.

"If I weren't already dead, I think I'd be very worried," said Kim. "But yes, of course you're right. Let's do it."

They all moved slowly forward, pushing against the presence of the New People, like swimmers breasting a heavy tide.

The light seemed to fall away some as they moved on, revealing the substance and details of the place in which they found themselves. Huge abstract shapes loomed up everywhere, weird mutated structures that watched and observed. Great pyramids with massive unblinking eyes; jagged energies crackling up and down the air like slow lightning; blurred uncertain shapes that had the feel of living things. Wherever JC looked there were colours he couldn't name, objects with too many details for the human eye to encompass, and nightmare forms on the edge of his vision that shrieked of bad intent . . . And always, everywhere, the feeling of potential doors, or even trap-doors, that led Somewhere Else. Doors to let things In as well as Out . . .

The New People were waiting for them. Four of them. Standing inhumanly still in the middle of everything, untouched and untroubled by the world around them. The world they'd made, or perhaps a world that appeared to accommodate who and what they were now. Often it seemed that there were more than four of them, dozens or even hundreds, in infinite ranks, superpeople in a superposition, everywhere at once. Their number and location was constantly changing, and yet at the same time there were only four, standing before JC and his group, waiting. JC squeezed his eyes hard shut, and then opened them again, but it didn't help. He wasn't sure what he was seeing was actually happening, or whether it was his mind trying to make sense of an impossible situation.

He couldn't look at the New People directly; none of his group could. They shone too brightly, they were too real, too overpoweringly there. Stamped on this world like an identifying imprint. Each of the New People existed in more than three dimensions at once. They had length and width and breadth, and other things, too. Other dimensions, physical and spiritual dimensions.

Happy couldn't cope with what he was seeing, or experiencing, even with his shields in place. He dropped to his knees and vomited noisily. Melody crouched beside him, partly to comfort and protect him, partly so she didn't have to look at the New People any more. She didn't vomit, but she looked like she wanted to. JC understood. It hurt him to look at them, even with his blessed eyes. The New People existed in spiritual dimensions as well as spatial. The human brain wasn't equipped to deal with so much information at once.

And all the time, JC was thinking . . . *Is this what we were meant to be? What we all should have become? Or is this what we were spared?*

Kim moved in close beside JC, gazing uncertainly at the New People. "I can't see them," she whispered. "It's all just light to me. Why can't I see them?"

JC shook his head vaguely, then turned his whole body away from the New People. It didn't help. He didn't need to see them to know they were there. Their presence overlaid everything.

The longer JC and his people remained in the new place, the more they saw. Contact with the New People opened their inner eyes, opened up their minds, to the noumenon—all the adjacent levels of reality, the worlds within worlds, or surrounding worlds, the interpenetrating and overlapping worlds that most of us are mercifully unaware of. All the places and all the things that exist right next to us, blessedly hidden from normal view. Because if most of Humanity knew who and what we shared this world with, they'd go stark, staring mad. JC had seen some of it before, through his golden eyes, but never as much as this.

He shut his golden eyes and still caught glimpses of other places, other worlds, other dimensions, where life had taken on shapes and aspects far beyond the possibilities of this limited Earth. He saw two suns shining fiercely in a sick green sky, over a landscape that was always moving, never still. He saw dinosaurs with huge, distended heads stalk purposefully through stone galleries and massive tunnels, carved into the side of a mountain. He saw a dull red sun drop sullen bruised light from a mustard yellow sky, over man-sized insects that crawled all over a stone mound the size of a skyscraper, darting in and out of deep dark holes in its sides, intent on unknown missions.

JC cried out, and put his hands to his head. He thought he said, *Too much, too much*, but he couldn't be sure. His thoughts came painfully fast, idea upon idea, rushing through his mind, darting this way and that beyond his control, as he fought to understand and assimilate a dozen improbable things at once. Sudden sharp insights slammed into his head, insights into the nature of reality itself. Blindingly obvious . . . but he was never able to remember them afterwards. Or at least, not in any way that made sense. Except sometimes in dreams . . . from which he woke cold and sweating, crying out, gripped with a nameless horror.

He sat down suddenly, and Kim hovered over him uneasily. JC gritted his teeth together, and concentrated on being the master of his own mind, the captain of his soul. And slowly, piece by piece, he put his thoughts back together again. And when he opened his golden eyes, he was at last able to cope with what he saw.

And one of the first things he saw was Happy, pushing away Melody as she tried to stop him dry-swallowing a handful of pills from various containers. JC forced himself back up onto his feet and went over to Happy, who

abruptly stopped what he was doing and let more pills
fall from an open hand. He looked at JC and his eyes
were wild, almost feral.

*"Guess what, JC? You were right all along! The drugs
don't work!"*

JC still stumbled doggedly towards him, Kim floating
timidly at his side. Even with his renewed mental disci-
pline, he was still seeing things. Great inhuman faces,
with incomprehensible expressions, watching, watching.
They seemed to come from all directions at once, and
some things that weren't even directions. Strange things
moved through the air, filling up the spaces between
spaces, like the micro-organisms that roil and riot in a
drop of water. They shot this way and that, passing through
things and people and even each other. And then there
were large forms, so big JC couldn't even guess at what
they were, moving through the building and its contents
as though they were the ghosts.

JC forced them all out of his gaze and his thoughts,
and went on, step by step, refusing to be stopped or
turned aside until finally he reached Happy and Melody,
after what seemed like miles, or hours, or worse. Melody
was trying to talk to Happy, but her words couldn't reach
him. She didn't seem as bothered by the surroundings, perhaps because most of her attention was fixed on
Happy. JC lurched forward and thrust his face right in
front of Happy's. He whipped off his sunglasses, so that
his golden eyes stared right into those of the telepath,
filling his view. Happy met the golden gaze and slowly
relaxed, as though someone had thrown him a lifeline.

The golden glare kept everything else out. Happy breathed deeply, and sense returned to his eyes. He nodded jerkily, first to JC, then to Melody.

"All right. I'm back. I'm not sure where, and I don't think I like it, but I am quite definitely here. Can we go now?"

"Go where?" said JC, stepping back. "You see any way out of here? We're in the world of the New People now, and we have to start with them."

He turned to face them, and everything else disappeared. Driven away, pushed aside, by the sheer presence of the New People. Only them, and the light they stood in. Or generated. And when they finally spoke, they all spoke at once, like a thunderous cloud or choir of voices. Just four motionless figures, in all their many dimensions, but when they spoke, there might have been four hundred or four thousand, as many aspects as there were dimensions.

We've been waiting for you. The intrepid Ghost Finders of the Carnacki Institute. We knew you were coming. Clearing up the mess left by our creation. Birth is always messy.

"Do you know who's behind your creation?" said JC, forcing the words out. "Do you know about Patterson?"

Of course. He had plans for us. So did the people he represented. But they were so limited in their thinking. So human. Patterson couldn't understand us. Nor could his organisation. We are so much more than they expected. They planned our creation but couldn't deal with what they got. You are all of you incapable of under-

standing what we are, what we have become. The human mind lacks the capacity to contain what we are. And what we will do.

"What do you want?" said JC.

To make everyone like us, of course. To wake up the world, and everything in it, and set it to useful work. To do all the things that matter, instead of filling in time till death. There is so much that needs doing, matters of great scale and worth—putting the universe to rights.

"What if we don't want that?" said Happy, moving forward to stand with JC. "What if we'd rather choose our own way?"

You will want it. After you've been changed. Upgraded. Made wondrous New People, like us. When you are like us, you'll understand everything. The universe and its purpose will be clear to you. All the answers to all the questions you ever had, will be yours.

"But will we still care about those questions, and those answers, when we're not human any more?" said Melody, stepping forward to be with JC. "Will we still care about any of the things we care about now, as poor, limited, human beings?"

"Will we still love?" said Kim, stepping in beside JC. "Will he still care for me, and I for him, as man for woman? Will we still have that?"

Don't be afraid. We are more than you, not less. We have gained much and lost nothing. We are different from you now, but we still contain you.

"That isn't answering the question," said JC. "Would Kim and I, Happy and Melody, still share our simple human love for each other? Would the fundamental things still apply—care and compassion, honesty and honour, good and evil, life and death? Would they still matter to us? And if not, how could we still be us?"

Why would you want to settle for something so small?

"You see?" said JC. "You're the ones who don't understand. You'd have to destroy what makes us . . . us, to make us you. You've gone too far, progressed too far beyond us. The world isn't ready for you. Not yet. People aren't ready yet. You can't jump to the front of the queue, to the top of the evolutionary ladder. We have to get there on our own, achieve it on our own, or it won't mean anything. We have to earn it by our own efforts, one step at a time. Remember what you were. Who you were. What it felt like to be human. Small joys and small achievements are no less real for being small. Remember what you wanted out of life before chemical godhood gave it to you on a platter."

We remember . . . but only as a dream. A long nightmare from which we have at last awakened. But yes—we do remember.

"You think all our junk DNA being blocked off just . . . happened?" said JC. "No. It's there waiting, for the right time. For us to be ready for it. It'll awaken itself when conditions are right. And then, and only then . . . we'll all become like you. When the world needs us to be like you. Because by then, hopefully, we'll have earned it."

The New People paused. They seemed to be talking among themselves, but it was not speech that JC or Happy or Melody or Kim could comprehend. Finally, they spoke again.

Yes. This is not our Time. We are ghosts from the Future. That's where we belong. So that is where we will go. Now.

And they were gone. All of them, gone. The overpowering presence of the New People disappeared, snapped off, as they moved on into Future Time. Except . . . JC was always sure afterwards, that for a moment one of the New People, the terrible transformed living gods, dropped her godly mask to look back at him as the young woman she'd originally been . . . to give him just the ghost of a smile, before she left.

The four Ghost Finders, the three living people and the dead woman, looked slowly around them. They were standing in an empty floor at the top of an office building in London, and everything else they had seen there was already a fading memory. The world was back the way it should be, and full of only those things that belonged there. And the warm amber street light falling through the glass windows was like a benediction.

"That's it," said Happy. "It's all over?"

"No," said JC. "This is over, but we still don't know who or what Patterson represented. Why they wanted us, and what they hoped to achieve. Remember what those Crowley Project agents said, down under Oxford Circus Tube Station? That there are people operating behind the scenes, weakening the walls of the world, for purposes of their own . . . Nothing to do with the Project or the Carnacki Institute. We need to find out who these people are. Before they do something even worse than this."

"Could we at least take a day off, first?" said Happy. "I am so tired I feel like I could go into reverse."

"Of course!" said JC, smiling broadly on his people. "All work and no play makes Jack a pain in the arse. But still, you know, I have to wonder . . . what kind of world the New People might have made. Whether it might actually have been . . . something very like Heaven."

NINE

RIDER ON THE STORM

Some hours later, outside Chimera House

The night was almost over. The sun was fighting its way up the sky, pushing back the dark with streaks of red and gold. The shadows were no longer as deep, or as menacing, and a few of the more optimistic birds had started singing. London's morning traffic was getting under way, the muted roar barely audible in the distance. It was still bloody cold, though.

The Carnacki Institute had turned out in force to mop up the mess left behind by its latest mission. Dozens of people were running this way and that, up and down the street before Chimera House, all kinds of people, representing all kinds of specialities, all of them moving like they had a plan. Or at the very least, all trying hard to look busy so they wouldn't get shouted at. Some were inside the lobby, taking readings with an impressive array of instruments. Others were already deeper in and further up, cleaning the place thoroughly, before the local authorities were allowed in. Removing all traces of the weird and uncanny, and any and all evidence that might give lesser mortals nightmares. Scientific equipment was being removed, computers wiped clean, and certain objects were being bagged up and taken away for examination, autopsy, or a quick trip to the incinerator.

Everyone was moving quickly, hard at work, because the area had already been sealed off and isolated for far too long. People might start asking questions. Though the Carnacki Institute would have already seen to it that they wouldn't get any answers. For their own good. The best way to keep a secret is to make sure no-one knows enough to understand which questions to ask.

JC, Happy, and Melody waited patiently outside Chimera House, being looked over by the Carnacki Institute's very own medical team. Which on such short notice, and at such an ungodly hour of the morning, consisted of one paramedic ambulance, with driver, and one bleary-eyed uniformed nurse. JC had already been checked out, and declared fine. He bestowed his most gracious smile on the nurse as he pulled his ice-cream white jacket back on.

"Of course I'm fine," he said grandly. "I could have told you that. I am always fine."

"Actually, you look like something big and determined kicked the crap out of you," said Melody.

"Yes," JC said patiently. "But apart from that, I'm fine."

"Oh good," murmured Kim. "I was getting a little worried, back there."

No-one could see or hear her, for the moment. She had made herself invisible so as not to spook the late-comers—and because she was still quite shy around strangers. JC could feel her presence near him, like the smell of a wild rose or the warmth of an unfelt breath on his cheek.

Happy sat in the back of the ambulance, sipping hot chicken soup from a plastic mug bearing the legend *He's dead, Jim.* "I'm feeling better, too, if anybody cares. This is good soup. Good starter. Does anyone else feel like sending out for pizza? If we all club together and order the big size, we can get a stuffed crust . . ."

The nurse shut him up by thrusting a thermometer into his mouth. She'd already taken a blood sample and was shaking her head sadly. Happy raised an eyebrow.

"Don't believe everything you see on a chromatograph readout," he said carefully, around the thermometer. "It was an emergency situation. I don't do the pills thing any more. Well, not as much, anyway."

"It's a wonder to me you have any blood left in your chemical system," snapped the nurse. "I've seen your file. We pass it around back at base when we want to freak out the new girls. When you die, we're going to put your organs on display, as a Horrible Warning to Others. Some people don't even want to wait till you die. If I were to take your blood pressure, would I regret it?"

"I don't know," said Happy. "How good are your nerves?"

"Oh, get the hell out of my ambulance," said the nurse, whipping the thermometer out of his mouth. She studied it for a moment, winced, and threw it away. "I haven't got the patience to deal with self-harmers." She manhandled Happy out of the back of the ambulance and gestured impatiently to Melody. "Come on, science girl, get your geeky arse in here. Happy, JC, don't either of you go rushing off anywhere. I want to check you out with the Geiger counter before I sign off on you."

"Amateur," said Melody. "If I had my equipment here, I could test us for a dozen different kinds of radiation you've never even heard of."

"Speaking of which," said JC. "Look what's just turned up."

Melody looked where JC was pointing, and immediately pushed the nurse aside to sprint off down the street to where two large men were straining to push her equipment along on a trolley.

"Babies!"

The two men pushing the trolley took one look at what was heading their way, abandoned the trolley, and ran for their lives. Melody had a reputation for dealing very harshly with anyone who damaged her scientific instruments in transit. She threw herself across the piled-up equipment and hugged it all fiercely.

"It's all right, babies—mommy's here! Did any of the nasty men touch you, sweeties?"

JC looked at Happy. "There's something entirely not natural about how that woman relates to her precious toys. If she shows half that much passion in the bedroom . . ."

"Don't go there," said Happy. "Trust me—you don't want to know."

JC grinned. Then the smile faded from his face. "Look who's here," he said, quietly.

Everyone stopped what they were doing and looked around as the revered and very-much-feared Boss of the Carnacki Institute, Catherine Latimer, her very own bad self, came striding out of Chimera House. She hit the crowd at full speed and kept going, expecting everyone who mattered to keep up with her. And, of course, they all did, if they knew what was good for them. She talked in half a dozen different directions at once, giving orders, making observations, motivating people with harsh language and sharp looks. She gave new instructions to a dozen departments and sent them off on urgent errands with her voice still ringing loudly in their ears. Catherine Latimer got things done because everyone under her was too scared not to do them on her behalf. She stopped briefly, to glare back at Chimera House as though it had done all this to personally annoy her, then gave her full attention to the second field team she'd called in, standing patiently to one side.

JC had spotted them the moment they arrived and had been careful to maintain a more-than-respectful distance. It was no secret that the new team were here to search the whole building from top to bottom, in case JC and his team had missed anything. Trust, but verify, while carrying a really big stick. The Carnacki Institute got through mottos like a dog gets through fleas, but this one suited better than most. JC looked the new team over thoughtfully. He knew them. Everybody did.

Latimer wasn't taking any chances—she'd brought in
the Institute's longest-established and most successful A
team. Really big hitters, with a nasty reputation, led
by the living legend Jeremy Diego, along with his ex-
otic telepath, Monica Odini, and the tech wizard, Ivar ap
Owen. They'd solved more cases, put down more Bad
Things, and kicked more supernatural arse than all the
other field teams put together. Diego himself was efficient, glamorous, and almost unbearably arrogant. In
other words, everything JC aspired to be.

Diego looked across at JC, and his gaze was only
spared from being openly contemptuous by its basic lack
of interest. JC made a point of smiling meaninglessly
at Diego, as though he sort of recognised the face but
couldn't quite put a name to it.

Diego wandered casually over to confront JC, who
made a point of adopting an especially casual and unimpressed pose. The two team leaders nodded and smiled
politely to each other, because other people were looking, but neither of them offered to shake hands. There
were limits. Diego stuck his hands in the pockets of his
long duster coat and made a point of looking JC square
in the sunglasses.

"Anything in there we need to look out for?" he said
casually. "Anything that was a little bit too much for you
or might need another slap round the head to keep it
quiet?"

"No," said JC, smiling easily. "Nothing worth the men-
tioning. My team always takes care of business. Though
if you could bring yourselves to clean up some of the
mess . . . since you're there . . ."

"We'll run all the usual checks anyway," said Diego. "In case you missed something. Better safe than sorry, eh?"

"Of course," said JC. "It's always best to keep busy when there's nothing important left to do."

By then, both men were being so laid-back it was a wonder they hadn't toppled over. Diego and JC exchanged quietly venomous smiles before Diego turned his back on JC and wandered unhurriedly back to his own team. Happy moved in close beside JC.

"You wouldn't believe what their team telepath Monica just thought at me! Some people have far too much imagination and not nearly enough inhibitions. You haven't got a notepad, have you, JC? I need to jot something down, while the details are still fresh . . ."

"Tempted?" said JC.

"With her?" said Happy. "I'd rather stick it in a blender. I've heard stories about her. Most of them end up with emotionally distressed young men being dropped off at hospital emergency rooms. Besides, Melody would tear me limb from limb. Or even worse, ask Monica to join us for a threesome. I don't know which option scares me more."

"Heads up," said JC. "Here comes trouble . . . Melody! Stop caressing that computer and get over here! I think the Boss would like a word with us."

Melody came hurrying back to join JC and Happy. She knew the value of a united front against danger and had always been very big on safety in numbers. If only so there was someone else to hide behind when the shit started flying. The nurse saw Catherine Latimer striding forward and retreated quickly into her ambulance, locking the door behind her. JC would have joined her if he'd thought it would do any good. Meetings with the Carnacki Institute's Boss rarely went well when he and his team were involved. Somehow, JC knew she was already working on a way to blame the whole mess on him.

The Boss crashed to a halt before JC and his team, who all made a point of nodding casually to her in a totally unimpressed sort of way. Latimer considered each one of them in turn with a cold and very direct gaze. She wasn't all that impressive, physically, but her sheer force of personality more than made up for that. Medium height and sturdy, she wore a superbly tailored grey suit and smoked black Turkish cigarettes in a long ivory holder. She had to be in her seventies and looked like she'd fought for every inch of it. She was the most impressive, efficient, and downright dangerous woman JC had ever met. He spent a lot of time avoiding her, which most of the time she seemed to appreciate.

"I am here," said Catherine Latimer, the Boss, in an even more than usually harsh and clipped voice, "because the first I knew anything about this mission was when you phoned in to say it was all over. It would seem Patterson set the whole thing up himself and ran it personally from behind the scenes. I'm still having trouble accepting that Robert was a traitor. I've known him for years, man and boy. His father was one of my best field agents, back in the eighties. I trained Patterson personally, pushed him up the promotions ladder as fast as I could . . . I had such plans for him. He would have gone far, the fool."

"It's always the ambitious ones you have to look out for," Happy said wisely, as the Boss paused for a moment, lost in thought. She glared at him.

"When I want your opinion, I'll have my head examined!" She switched her glare to JC. "Was it really necessary to kill him?"

"Yes," JC said steadily. "He betrayed every one of us, put all of Humanity at risk by dealing in things he didn't understand and couldn't control. And he boasted that he and his secret backers were planning to do even worse things in the future. He had to die."

"Did you make him understand that we would have given him full immunity, and round-the-clock protection, in return for information?" said the Boss.

JC met her gaze steadily. "He was more afraid of his own people than he was of us."

"It's true," said Happy. "He said he'd rather die than betray them. He did. I was there."

The Boss looked at Melody. "Do you have anything useful to add?"

"He wasn't the man you thought he was," said Melody, as kindly as she could. "He wasn't the man any of us thought he was."

The Boss nodded slowly. "I want every bit of information you have about this secret organisation Patterson answered to. Every word he said about them. I want fully detailed reports from all three of you on my desk before the end of day." She looked back at Chimera House. "These . . . New People. Were they really living gods, or the final destiny of human evolution? I would have liked to have seen them. It's not often you get to see something completely new, in this business." She looked back at JC and his team. "You got lucky. You do realise that, don't you? This could all have gone horribly wrong, in so many appalling ways. But, still—you did good. Well done. Don't even think of asking for a raise."

She drew heavily on her ivory holder, and blew a thick cloud of aromatic smoke out onto the early-morning air. "How could something as important, as extreme as this, have got so far completely undetected by anyone in the Institute? Patterson wasn't that high up, or that connected . . . He couldn't have managed all this on his own. You're sure he didn't mention any other names . . . Of course not. You would have said."

JC could have said something there but didn't. Happy and Melody took their cues from him.

"Reports," the Boss said savagely. "Extremely detailed reports. And God have mercy on your souls if they aren't in on time."

She turned her back and strode off, to organise things and shout at people a lot. JC, Happy, and Melody all breathed a little more easily, and moved away to find somewhere quiet, and private, so they could talk. Once they were safely away from the crowds, Kim manifested again, a vague impression on the air, an outline of a young woman in pastel colours, so the others could see and hear her. She hated to be left out of things just because she was dead.

"We're going to have to be very careful about what we say in our reports," said JC. "And careful that they all agree with each other, in the things that matter. Because there's a lot we're going to have to leave out, or at the very least fudge around. We don't know how many other traitors there might be, hidden away inside the Carnacki Institute."

"Are you saying we can't even trust the Boss?" said Happy, his eyes widening at the thought of trying to keep things from the dreaded Catherine Latimer.

"She's the Boss!" said Melody. "She's in charge of everything! If she's gone over to the dark side, we are all royally screwed!"

"I think we can still trust her," JC said steadily. "If only because she's got too much pride to hide her dark side under a bushel. If she was the villain of the piece, she'd want everyone to know, and bow down to her. No—I was thinking more that whatever we tell the Boss might not stay with the Boss."

They all paused to consider the implications of that, and none of them liked what they were thinking.

"We have to go our own way now," JC said finally. "Follow the leads we've got and run our own very secret investigations into who's really who, and what's really what, inside the Carnacki Institute."

"We can't trust anyone any more, can we?" said Melody.

"Welcome to my world," said Happy. "Lonely, isn't it?"

"We only trust each other," said JC.

"Situation entirely bloody normal," said Happy. But he couldn't keep from grinning.

"Just because one conspiracy theory has turned out to be true, it doesn't mean they all are," JC said sternly.

"Let us all please concentrate on the matter at hand. The Carnacki Institute is far too important to the world to remain compromised in this way."

"What is this other secret organisation?" said Melody. "We don't have a name, or a statement of intent."

"They have got to be big," said Happy. "And I mean really, really big to have the connections and resources to pull off something like this, right under the Boss's radar."

"So how come no-one even heard a whisper?" said Melody. "You can't put something like ReSet together without making serious waves."

"We did hear a whisper," said JC. "Those agents from the Crowley Project, Natasha Chang and Erik Grossman. They said there were forces at work bigger than either the Institute or the Project. But we didn't believe them because Project agents lie like they breathe. They live to spread lies and paranoia. But now . . ."

"We have one end of the string," said Happy. "I say we tug on it and see what unravels."

"You are enjoying this entirely too much," said Melody.

"My entire paranoid existence has been justified," said Happy. "I am a deeply satisfied man."

"We're not going to solve this mess overnight," said JC. "We have to be in this for the long haul . . . all the way to the end. So we carry on taking cases, going on missions, as though everything were still normal. People . . . some people . . . are going to be watching us very carefully."

"But . . . wouldn't it be safer to let it go?" said Kim.

"I mean, what can the four of us do, against a secret society this big, this dangerous?"

"We go on," said JC. "Because we have to. Because it's part of the job. And because no-one plays us and gets away with it."

"Right," said Happy.

"Damn right," said Melody.

"Oh well, if you put it like that," said Kim. "Kill them all, and let God sort them out."

They walked away from Chimera House, putting it all behind them, for the time being at least. Happy looked sideways at JC.

"So," he said casually, "did you really steal that Hand of Glory thing from the Carnacki Institute's Armoury?"

"You'd be surprised at what I've gotten away with, over the years," JC said solemnly.

They all stopped abruptly as Kim clapped both her hands to her head and cried out in pain. The sound rose and rose, a miserable howl of horror and agony, filling the night, continuing on long after living lungs would have been unable to sustain it. She swayed on her feet, eyes clenched shut. JC stood before her, saying her name over and over, trying to make himself heard over the deafening noise she was making, reaching out but unable to touch or comfort her. Melody and Happy looked at each other, both of them lost for anything useful to do. Latimer came hurrying back to join them. And Kim stopped screaming as suddenly as she'd begun. The returning quiet would have been a relief, if it hadn't been for the horror and abject misery still filling her pale face.

"What is it?" said Latimer. "What's happening? Why was she making that God-awful noise?"

"I don't know," said JC. "Nothing happened . . . Kim? Kim, sweetie, what is it? What's upsetting you . . . Kim, look at me!"

Kim finally forced her eyes open but didn't look at JC. She only had eyes for Chimera House, staring at the tall building as though it was the entrance to Hell itself. JC looked, too, but it all seemed perfectly ordinary to him. Everything was as it should be. He could see silhouettes of the Institute people outlined against brightly lit windows, going about their business.

"It's not over," said Kim. "It's not finished. Not yet."

"What do you mean?" said Latimer. "Is it the New People? You said they were gone."

"They are gone," JC said impatiently. "We all saw them move on . . . Kim, did you . . . hear something?"

Kim looked at him for the first time, her pale features still slack with shock. "You didn't hear that? You didn't hear anything?"

"I didn't hear a damned thing," said Melody. "Except you, screaming fit to burst my eardrums." She looked at Happy, and he shrugged quickly.

"Don't look at me. I'm not picking up anything. If this night was any quieter, it would be tucked up in bed with a nice cup of hot milk."

"It sounded . . . like the roar of some great Beast," Kim said slowly. "Nothing human in it, not in intent, or emotion. Just this great roar, of anger and hatred and defiance . . . and evil. An ancient evil, beyond anything human."

Happy's head snapped round, and he stared at Chimera House with wide, shocked eyes. His face screwed up with pain, and he bent over suddenly, as though he'd been hit, and hit hard. He made soft grunting, moaning sounds. Melody moved quickly in beside him but had enough sense not to touch him.

"What is it, Happy? Are you hearing something now?"

"He's killing them," said Happy, forcing the words out between harsh gasps of strained breathing. "He's killing them all! He's going back and forth in the building, killing everyone he finds. Get them out! Get everyone out of there!"

Latimer moved in close, to glare right into his face. "Talk to me, Happy. I need to know what's happening. Concentrate! Follow your training! Find your focus and tell me what the hell is going on inside that building!"

Happy swallowed hard and bit down on his moans, fighting to regain his self-control. He made himself straighten up, by sheer effort of will, though his hands still clenched and unclenched at his sides.

"They're all dead," he said flatly. "Everyone on the upper floors. He killed them all. I heard their terror, their dying screams. He's working his way down through the building, floor by floor, killing everyone he finds. And loving every moment of it."

Latimer glared at JC. "You missed something. Some monster, some hidden killer . . . You told me it was safe to send my people in there! But you left something hidden in some secret place, waiting for its chance because you didn't do your job properly!"

"That's bullshit, and you know it!" said JC, giving the

Boss glare for glare. "Your own psychics told you the place was clean!"

"We didn't miss anything," Happy said flatly. "This is something new."

JC deliberately turned his back on Latimer, to face Happy. "Human? Alive? Dead? What?"

"Yes. No. I don't know!" Happy wiped the sweat from his face with the back of one shaking hand. "There's something new in there, and it's big and powerful . . . Trying to See it is like staring into a spotlight. Its presence is hitting me so hard, I can hardly think straight, barely keep it outside my head . . . It's a man . . . but it's so much more than a man! And there's something very familiar about it . . ."

They were all looking at Chimera House by then. Latimer took out her cell phone and tried to raise someone, anyone, on the upper floors of the building, but no-one answered. She put the phone away and gave a series of quiet orders to the commander in charge of her security people. They moved quickly forward to form a semicircle facing the building, guns at the ready. Everyone else left, clearing the area, followed by all the other vehicles, and the ambulance. Kim hovered beside JC, fading in and out as her concentration wavered under the onslaught of so many unpleasant emotions. Happy was still breathing hard but was as back in control as he ever was. Melody looked briefly at her instruments but stuck with Happy, for the moment. Every time she saw him wince, she knew he was hearing someone die.

There was a burst of gunfire from the lobby. Chattering

bullets, shouted orders, jagged screams suddenly cut off. The security people tensed but held their positions. Everyone strained their eyes, but none of them could see what was happening in the lobby. All the glass had suddenly become opaque. And then, suddenly, all the windows were spattered with crimson, thick blood sliding down their insides. The gunfire died away and stopped. Latimer looked at Happy, who shook his head sickly. Latimer beckoned to the commander, and he hurried over.

"Send half your people to join the established perimeter," she said crisply. "Tell them no-one gets in or out until I say otherwise, in person. And no—I don't care who they are, or who they say they are. I want this whole area sealed off until we know for sure what we're dealing with. Contact Institute Headquarters, and have them send every special force and field agent they can find. They're to reinforce the perimeter, but not come in until I say so. When you've done that, take the rest of your people and secure the situation inside that lobby. You are authorised to shoot the shit out of anything you see. Go."

The commander nodded quickly, and moved off to follow Latimer's orders quietly and efficiently. JC and his people stood close together, shivering in the cold, gusting wind. They all watched silently at the commander led his people towards the now-entirely-quiet lobby. Latimer glared at Happy.

"Happy Jack Palmer! Look at me!"

Happy looked at her. His face was still slack with shock. "You don't have to shout. I'm not deaf."

"I need to know what you're hearing," said Latimer.

"What's going on in the lobby, right now? Who or what is killing my people?"

"They're all dead now," Happy said dully. "Everyone in the building. Bullets couldn't stop him. They never stood a chance, any of them."

"What about the other field team? Can you reach their telepath?"

"You're not listening to me! They're all dead, all of them! Including your precious Jeremy Diego, Monica Odini, and Ivar ap Owen! Your legendary A team, the best you had, your most experienced field team, were nothing to him! He killed them as easily as you would swat a fly. All their power, all their weapons, all their legendary experience, didn't make a damned bit of difference. I heard Monica crying out to me with her mind, trying to reach me . . . but he wouldn't let her. He . . . walked right over them. They didn't even slow him down."

Latimer actually looked shocked, for the first time. "But . . . Diego was one of my best! I would have trusted him to deal with anything! What the hell is going on in there . . ."

"All the training in the world won't help," said Happy, almost dreamily. "Something bad has come here, to teach us a lesson. To teach us our proper place in the scheme of things."

"You're still listening in, aren't you, Happy?" JC said quietly. "Is it the New People? Are they back?"

"No," said Happy. "It's not them. Look. There he is."

He gestured at the lobby door with a shaking hand,

and they all turned to look. The commander held up one hand as the door opened, and his men froze in place, guns trained on the door. The door swung open, and a man stepped out into the night. One man, walking unsteadily because most of his bones were broken, because he was dead. Robert Patterson. His once-splendid clothes were tattered and torn, and soaked with blood. It dripped thickly from him, leaving a messy trail back into the lobby. It was far too much blood for it to have been only his—too much, and too fresh. He carried the marks of his murders on him. Some of it fell in thick drips from his clenched fists.

His body had been broken and shattered by the long fall and sudden impact that had killed him. Every time he moved, the sound of splintered bones scraping against each other came clearly across the quiet. Broken limbs and broken back, broken neck and smashed head. His right eye had been pushed forward, straining half out of its socket, so that he seemed to stare at them all with a fierce, manic gaze. He was grinning widely.

"Robert Patterson," said Happy. "He died and came back from the dead. And he's brought something back with him."

Latimer called out to the dead man, and he stopped and turned to look at her. His neck made sickening grinding noises.

"Robert!" said Latimer. "Robert, it's me, Catherine! They said you were dead! What's happened to you, Robert?"

He looked at her, still grinning his humourless grin.

He didn't move, and he didn't answer her. JC stepped in beside Latimer.

"I don't think that is Patterson any more, Boss," he said carefully. "Or at least, not the Patterson you knew. Happy, talk to me . . . what's going on inside that dead man's head?"

"He's not alone in there," said Happy. "He's hardly there at all. More like a memory, now, pressed down and supplanted by something else. Someone else has . . . moved in and taken over. Riding him."

"And that's what killed everyone?" said Melody. "One dead man, with a rider in his head?"

"He's not like any dead man we've ever encountered," said Happy. "Not a zombie, not any kind of lich . . . Whatever's riding Patterson has suffused his body with so much power, it's a wonder the world is able to bear his presence. This is far more than a simple possession. This is a Power, walking unfettered in the world."

"I don't care what it is," said Latimer. "It's killed my people. No-one gets away with that." She nodded quickly to the commander. "Blessed and cursed bullets, half and half. Take that thing down."

The commander nodded easily and turned to his men. He didn't seem too bothered at the idea of shooting Patterson. JC wondered briefly if perhaps the commander had known Patterson, before. The commander moved easily among his people. His voice was calm, professional, assured. "Target dead ahead. Put him down."

The security people all opened fire at once, and the quiet night was filled with the roar of massed gunfire. Bullets pounded into Patterson, over and over again, and he stood there and took it. Every single bullet hit him, not one miss, and none of them did him any harm. The dead body soaked up the punishment, and the horrid smile on the dead face didn't waver in the least. He didn't even rock on his feet under the multiple impacts. The bullets made holes in his flesh, but that was all they did. He felt no pain, took no injury. The occasional head shots blasted the back of his skull away, blowing out long streams of grey and pink brains, but his awful gaze never wavered. He was dead, and there was nothing more the guns could do to him.

The gunfire died slowly away, as one by one guns ran out of ammunition. The security people lowered their weapons. The echoes died away, and Patterson was still standing. The security men looked at each other and muttered uneasily; but not one of them retreated. The commander opened his mouth to give new orders, but he never got to say them because Patterson was already off and moving. He raced forward with inhuman, unnatural speed, arms and legs moving without grace or efficiency. Shattered bones in his arms and legs made harsh protesting sounds as the possessing will drove them on. Patterson hit the commander first. One punch ripped the man's head right off, and Patterson was already moving on before the body hit the ground. He was in and among the security people in a moment, striking them down with closed fists, breaking their necks and clubbing them down, ripping out throats with clawlike fingers. Most of them didn't even have time to scream before they died. He tore arms out of their sockets with inhuman strength, his dead fingers sinking deep into mortal flesh, laughing silently as blood sprayed over him. He crushed skulls and punched out hearts, and stalked over fallen bodies to get to those who remained. None of them ran. They fought him with gunbutts and knives and bare hands; and none of it did any good.

It was all over very quickly. In the end, Patterson stood alone, surrounded by the dead, with fresh blood dripping from his hands. He laughed soundlessly. And then he turned to look at Catherine Latimer.

He nodded cheerfully to her, and she stared back at him with stiff, frozen features. Patterson took a step towards her, and JC, Melody, and Happy immediately moved forward, putting themselves between their Boss and the dead man. Latimer started to say something, then stopped herself. They were following their training. Patterson studied them all thoughtfully.

"Who are you?" said JC.

Patterson stood very still, not breathing hard, not breathing at all. He nodded slowly to JC, still smiling his wide, wide smile, as though this was the finest thing ever, the most fun he'd ever had.

"You'd know my name if I said it," the dead man said in a breathy, scratchy voice. "So I won't say it."

The voice grated on everyone's nerves. It was only breath, moving over vocal cords. Nothing human in it at all.

"All right," said JC. "Let's try an easier one. What do you want?"

"I will kill you all," said the dead man. "And you can't stop me. You should never have come here. You should never have interfered."

"I hate to be picky about this, oh high-and-mighty dead person," said JC, "but you brought us here. Or at least Patterson did, presumably on your orders."

"You were supposed to fail," said the dead man. "I chose you, above all the other A teams, because you had the least experience. I had to get you in place before someone better turned up. You were supposed to walk in there, like good little sacrificial lambs, and fall to the New People. Or their creatures. The New People were taking too long. They needed a nudge, some exterior pressure, to get them moving. We arranged for their creation, you see, so they would damage reality . . . break it open from within. Smash the walls of the world."

"You wanted the New People to destroy the world?" said Latimer. "Why?"

"The world doesn't matter," said Patterson. "It's merely a cage, from which we will escape. The New People were only ever a means to an end."

Latimer's phone rang. Everything stopped for a moment, reacting to the harsh ringing tone. Latimer took out the phone and put it to her ear, never taking her gaze off the dead man before her. He looked vaguely annoyed at being interrupted but let her answer it. Presumably some reactions are ingrained, even on the dead.

"Yes, I know," said Latimer. "Yes, I'm looking right at him. No! Stay where you are! That's an order! Maintain the perimeter at all costs. Nothing else matters. Hold the line until I tell you otherwise . . . or until it's clear I'm no longer in charge. Then you take your orders from the Second In Command. God help you. Now don't bother me again. I'm busy."

She put the phone away. Happy looked at her, almost in shock.

"That's it? Shouldn't we contact Institute Headquarters, get some serious reinforcements down here, with really serious weapons?"

"By the time they could get here, this will all be over," Latimer said flatly. "One way or the other."

"You should get the hell out of here, Boss," said JC. "You're too valuable to the Institute to put yourself at risk."

"Yes, I am," said Latimer. "Good of you to remember that, for once. Unfortunately, my emergency teleport button isn't working. It should have removed me to safety the moment it became clear brute force wouldn't stop that thing but it would appear something . . . is blocking it. Which isn't supposed to be possible. I can only assume Patterson betrayed us on a great many levels, sharing his insider knowledge with whoever or whatever is riding him now. I could run, I suppose but I doubt I'd get very far."

"Typical," Happy said bitterly. "The Boss gets an emergency teleport button, but we don't. I didn't even know there was such a thing as an emergency teleport button."

"I did," said Melody. "I've been trying to hack its files for months, so I could build one of my own."

"Oh, that was you, was it?" said Latimer. "We will discuss that later, young lady."

"Excuse me," said JC. "Do you think we could all concentrate on the matter at hand, pretty please? Namely, the dead man with the blood of many on his hands, standing right in front of us? And no, I wouldn't try out-running him, Boss. You saw how fast whatever it is moved. I suppose once you're dead, human limitations don't apply any more."

"No," said Kim. "They don't. But there are other limits."

JC looked at her. "Anything you can See, anything you can tell us, about the dead man?"

"He's got one hell of an aura. Lots of purple. Just by being present, he's burning up that body. Though probably not soon enough to do us any good. So much power . . . Whatever it is that's riding Patterson, I don't think it's human. Or at least, not human any more."

JC nodded quickly, as though that was nothing more than he'd expected, and turned his attention back to Latimer.

"Have you got any special weapons about you? Objects of Power, that kind of thing?"

"Not actually on me," said Latimer. "Didn't think I'd be needing them. I wasn't even expecting to be up and about at this ungodly hour of the morning."

"It's a pity you haven't got that Hand of Glory monkey's paw thing any more," Kim said artlessly. "I'm almost sure it would have helped."

Latimer glared at JC. "I knew it! It was you! The moment I heard another of those things had gone missing from the Armoury, I knew it was down to you!"

"Another?" said Happy. "How many of those things have you got in storage? They're dangerous and damned, and I think I'll stop talking so you'll stop glaring at me in that really quite scary way ooh look a sparrow."

"Something else we should perhaps discuss at a later time," said JC, ignoring Happy with the ease of long practice. "The point is, I don't have it any longer."

"What? What have you done with it?"

"I sort of . . . lost it," said JC.

"I will have your balls for this," said Latimer.

"Melody, Happy," said JC. "Do you have any weapons, legal or otherwise, about your person and please say yes."

"I've still got my machine pistol," said Melody. "But it's out of ammo, remember? And there's probably some useful things I could be doing with my instruments if I'd only had time to activate them." She scowled. "I hate being caught unprepared."

"She does," said Happy. "She really does." He stuck both hands in his pockets and glowered at the dead man. "And don't look at me, either, JC. I've got nothing that could even touch Patterson. He's got shields you wouldn't believe. We are all seriously outclassed here."

"You mean, like we were with the New People?" said JC.

"Well, no, not on that level," Happy said immediately. "He's a Power. They were more like gods."

"We won out over the New People," said JC. "So, we should be able to beat Patterson if we put our minds to it."

"Confidence is a wonderful thing," said Happy. "Where did I put my pills . . ."

And then he broke off, as he realised Patterson wasn't looking at them. The dead man was giving his full attention to Kim. She rose and fell slowly in place, her eyes locked with his, unable to look away.

"Little ghost girl," said Patterson. "You shouldn't still be here. Flaunting your undecided status. You're staying for him, aren't you? He can't ever love you, not really, because you're not a real girl."

"He knows me," Kim whispered. "The thing inside Patterson. He can see inside me. I can hear him, he wants to do things to me. Awful things. Things he can't do to the living . . ."

JC moved forward, deliberately putting himself between Kim and the dead man. He took off his sunglasses with a sharp flourish, and fixed Patterson with his glowing eyes. And for the first time, Patterson stopped smiling.

"Abomination," he said tonelessly. "Unnatural thing. You don't even know what you are, do you?"

"Leave the girl alone," said JC.

"Or what?" said Patterson. "What will you do? What can you do? The terrible thing that reached down and touched you, and changed you, and gave you those eyes . . . wasn't what you think it was. It can't help you against me. You're on your own here." He was smiling again now. "You think you're so important—the great white-suited ghost hunter—but what have you ever really achieved? The world still turns as it always has, and the night is still full of monsters. Like me."

"Then why is it so important to you, to kill us?" said JC.

"You know too much," said Patterson. "Far more than you were ever meant to."

"Okay," said Happy, actually brightening up a little. "Now that's interesting. Which of the many things I know, or think I know, are important enough to kill me over?"

"Not now, Happy," said JC.

"Yes, now! This is proof! If I'm worth killing, then at least some of the things I've always believed have to be true!"

"He sort of has a point," JC said to Latimer, putting his sunglasses back on. "If we do know really important things . . . we should get a raise."

"What do you want?" said Latimer. "Danger money?"

"Oh, please," said Happy.

Patterson looked back and forth as they talked. He seemed to be having trouble accepting that he wasn't holding their full attention.

"Keep him busy," Melody said suddenly.

"What?" said JC.

"Patterson! Keep the dead man occupied! I've got an idea."

She turned and ran, sprinting down the street. Everyone else stood there and watched her go. Happy looked longingly after her.

"Running away looks like a really good idea to me. Wish I'd thought of it first."

"Stand fast!" JC said immediately. "She's not running out on us. She'll be back."

"You think she has a plan?" said Happy.

"Hopefully."

"A cunning plan?"

"Let's not set our hopes too high."

Happy sighed heavily. "What if we all ran in different directions at once?"

"We can't abandon the Boss," said JC. "The dead man would kill her in a moment if we weren't here to protect her."

"Well, yes," said Happy. "But you say that like it's a bad thing."

"I am still here!" said Latimer. "I can still hear you! There will be discussions about this later."

Happy looked down his nose at her. "I never liked you. I'm only still here because of the principle of the thing, so shut your cake-hole and let us concentrate."

Latimer looked at JC. "When did he grow a pair?"

"My little boy is all grown-up," said JC. "I couldn't be more proud. Now do as the terrified but still somehow holding his ground telepath says, and keep the dead man occupied while Happy and I try to think of something. You might try asking him why he hasn't killed us yet, a question that has been much on my mind."

"Don't give the dead thing ideas," growled Happy. "He's probably got a very good reason, and I don't want him doubting it."

Latimer sniffed loudly. "I do not negotiate with monsters. And I am not helpless! I didn't get to where I am in the Carnacki Institute without learning a few useful and really unpleasant tricks along the way . . . Like this one." She glared at Patterson. "You! Dead thing! Pay attention! Whatever you are, within my old friend's body. You think you're so hard, cope with this!"

She slammed her wrinkled hands together while speaking aloud a Word of Power, and the ground shuddered under everyone's feet. A harsh grinding noise filled the night air, and the ground tore itself apart. A huge split opened up, zigzagging its crooked way across the street between Patterson and the others, then the split widened abruptly into a crack, enlarging into a great crevice that opened up beneath the dead man's feet. He fell into the wide gap without a sound, and it swallowed him up. Latimer brought her hands together again, and the two sides of the crevice slammed together. The loud, grinding noises stopped immediately, and the ground settled. The night air was still. All that remained of the crevice was a long, jagged crack in the street. JC looked at Latimer with new respect.

"I didn't know you could do that."

"Not many do," said Latimer. "That's the point."

"And the dead man is toast!" said Happy, doing an ecstatic little jig on the spot. "He is flatter than toast! He is dead and very definitely departed." He stopped dancing and nodded brusquely to Latimer. "I may be a little more respectful at future meetings. It's possible."

Then the ground shuddered under their feet again. They all looked down. The ground shook again, more insistently, then groaned loudly as the jagged split jerked itself apart, opening up foot by foot, until it was a crevice again. And from that crevice, up out of the dark, Patterson rose. He soared into the air, like a dark bird of ill omen, hanging in the air above them, held there in defiance of all natural laws by sheer force of will. The two sides of the crevice slammed together again, and Patterson sank slowly down to stand exactly where he had before. Unhurt, untouched, unruffled. He smiled condescendingly at Latimer.

"Is that really the best you've got?"

"There is no way you did that on your own!" snapped Latimer. "You had help. Powerful help. Outside help. *Who are your masters?*"

Patterson nodded slowly. He looked heavier now, more solid. More *real*, as though he was several things in one place. The ground cracked and broke beneath his feet, as though he weighed more heavily on the world than a real thing should.

"Ah, Catherine," he said. "I have always enjoyed our little chats. You're quite right. I'm not alone. You have no idea who and what you're facing."

"Happy," JC said quietly, "I need you to look inside that thing's head. No excuses. Get me some idea of what's going on in there."

Happy sighed, in his best put-upon way, and reached out to the dead man with his most powerful and subtle probe, only to recoil immediately, shaking violently.

"He let me See!" he said, breathlessly. "Just for a moment, just for a glimpse . . . Whatever's riding Patterson was human once, but it's a whole different thing now. Something horribly powerful. I couldn't even look at it straight on! Man is not meant to look into the face of the Medusa . . ."

"It's not Patterson," said Latimer. "It doesn't talk like him, or move like him. My dear friend is gone."

"Oh, he's still in here somewhere," said the dead man. "So I can enjoy his suffering. He was never your friend . . ."

"Excuse me!" Latimer said sharply, "But I think I knew him better, and longer, than you ever did! He may have . . . drifted away, wandered off the proper path, but I have no doubt he would have found his way back, eventually."

JC could have said something there, about Patterson, but he didn't.

Latimer fitted one of her dark Turkish cigarettes into her long ivory holder, lit it with her monogrammed gold Zippo lighter, and blew a mouthful of smoke at Patterson. She looked him over disparagingly.

"You said . . . you enjoyed our little chats. So I do know who you really are. Do you really think you can hide from me?"

"Ah, Catherine," said the dead man. "I'm afraid you've left it for too late. You never did appreciate me."

Latimer blew a perfect smoke ring. "Why haven't you killed us yet?"

"Because I'm having so much fun," said Patterson.

"If we're having a civilised little discussion before the slaughter," said JC, "can I ask again—what is it we know that we're not supposed to know?"

"I don't know anything," Happy said immediately. "I never know anything. I am famous for not knowing anything, so there is absolutely no point in killing me."

"This is true," said JC. "He doesn't know anything. Or at least, not anything you can prove."

"Your whole team was a mistake," Patterson said flatly. "You were getting too good, too quickly. We couldn't allow that. And if you don't know what you know, all the

better. You can die ignorant. Yes. Enough talk. I have
more important things to be about. Die, little things."

Suddenly, Patterson's stretch limo came squealing
round the corner at high speed, Melody behind the wheel.
She fought to keep the speeding car under control, and
aimed it right at Patterson. He barely had time to react
before the limo screamed across the intervening space,
tyres howling, and ploughed right into him. She hit him
dead-on, the impact breaking his legs again and throwing him forward across the long bonnet. His arms flailed
wildly, his hands scrabbling for a hold on the smooth
metal. Melody kept her foot hard down, hauled the car
around, and drove it right at Chimera House. Patterson
was yelling something, but no-one could make it out
over the roar of the car's motor.

The stretch limo slammed into the building and crashed
to a halt half-way into the lobby. Broken glass pelted
down from the shattered windows, like jagged rain. The
car's engine cut off abruptly. The driver's door flew open,
and Melody half fell out. Happy and JC ran forward, with
Kim swooping along beside them. Melody stood up,
slowly and painfully. Happy got to her first, took her arm,
and slipped it over his shoulders, so he could take some
of her weight. It was a mark of how shaken Melody was
that she let him do it. She limped away from the scene of
the crash, leaning heavily on Happy, while JC and Kim
hovered beside them.

Latimer approached them, smiling broadly around
her cigarette holder, and surprised them all by applaud-
ing loudly.

"Nice use of improvisation!" she said. "Gold stars all round when we get back."

"Bloody airbag smacked me in the face," mumbled Melody. "I know I'm going to have two black eyes."

Then they all stopped and looked back, as the limo shifted suddenly to one side. Happy handed Melody over to Latimer, and he and JC moved to stand between the women and whatever was moving underneath the car. The limo tilted onto one side and fell over, as Patterson rose out of the wreckage, pushing the car off him with almost contemptuous ease. His clothes were even more of a mess than before, and jagged slivers of glass protruded from his dead flesh, but his gaze was steady, and his awful smile was broader than ever. He stood in the wreckage of the lobby like a conquering hero, posing and preening and showing himself off so they could all get a good look at him.

"I'm thinking this would be a really good time to start running," Happy said quietly. "I won't point a finger if you won't. I'm in the mood to cover a lot of ground in a really short time."

"Do you want to leave Melody and the Boss behind?" said JC.

"Well no, not as such, but . . ."

"No buts. This is the job." JC looked Patterson over carefully. "Besides, whatever's holding that body together has got to be really powerful. I don't think you could outrun that with your best running shoes on. And anyway, I don't run. It's bad for the image."

"When all else fails, try diplomacy," said Latimer. She handed the still-groggy Melody back to Happy and gave

the dead man her full attention. "Robert, if there's any of you left in there, please listen to me. You know me. I knew your grandfather, and your father. Both of them excellent field agents. They wanted something better for you, and I did all I could for you . . . I watched you grow up, watched you rise through the ranks . . . You believed in the Institute! I know you did."

"I'm here, Grandmother," said the dead man, and the voice sounded suddenly different. There was a whisper of life, of Patterson, in the voice. "I'm lost. I'm damned. I rolled the dice in the name of ambition, and they came up devil's eyes. Don't make my mistakes. Don't try and fight the rider. You can't win."

"Stop that, Robert!" Latimer said fiercely. "I won't have it! I taught you better than that. Fight him, boy! Fight for your body, and your soul!"

"That's enough of that," said the dead man, and once again the voice was dead air moving in a dead throat. "Robert isn't here any more. I am. He betrayed you and the Institute of his own free will. His body serves me now, as he served me in life. He sold his soul to us long ago, so why should he begrudge me his body? You shouldn't grieve so, Catherine. It really was a very small soul."

"Who are you?" said JC. "Come on—you know you want to tell us."

"Ah, wouldn't you like to know?" The teasing tone sounded very out of place in a dead man's mouth. "See if you can guess. I'm not Carnacki Institute, and I'm not Crowley Project. But you people aren't the only players in the game. You really should have paid more attention to what was going on around you. Now playtime's over.

Time to get down to business and remove some more than usually troublesome pieces from the board."

Melody pushed herself away from Latimer. She straightened up and glared at JC. "Come on! You're the clever one! Think of something!"

JC looked back and forth, frowning hard, then his gaze stopped on Happy. "You know . . . I do have an idea . . ."

"Oh bugger," said Happy. "That's never good. I'm really not going to like this, am I?"

"I said, time for you all to die!" said the dead man.

"Oh hush," JC said coldly. "We're talking.

"Go ahead," said Patterson. "Plot and plan. I do so love to watch my prey squirm."

"Listen, Happy," said JC urgently. "You couldn't get inside his head before, through all the mental shields, but that was only you. What if you had help? What if you linked your mind with mine, with my extra power? And Melody, with her scientific self-control? Could you do that?"

"Well, probably," said Happy. "These aren't the best conditions, but stark terror motivates the mind wonderfully. And if I can tap the power within you, use that to strengthen the link . . . But what then?"

"Then we push the rider out," said JC.

Happy was already shaking his head. "Even if we could do that, it would step right back in the moment we stopped pushing."

"Not if we put someone else inside," said Latimer. They all turned to look at her, but she was looking dispassionately at Kim. The ghost girl stared back at her with wide, frightened eyes. And now JC was shaking his head.

"No. We're not putting Kim at risk."

"She's already dead," Latimer said ruthlessly. "Nothing more can harm her in this world. She can inhabit Patterson's body and hold it, deny the rider access. After a while, he'll have to depart, or risk dissipation. Then she can come back out of the body and let it fall."

"No," said JC. "This is a bad idea. A really bad idea. Somebody else come up with another idea."

"It will work, and you know it," said Latimer. "And it's the only real chance we've got. You haven't any more weapons, and I'm completely out of tricks. The ghost girl is our only chance, our only hope."

"She has a name," JC said tightly. "Her name is Kim."

"Of course," said Latimer. She bowed very slightly to the ghost. "I'm sorry, my dear. I can't make you do anything. But if you want to save your young man here, it's the only way."

"It's all right, JC," said Kim. "I'll do it. I quite like the idea of being the only one of the team left to save the day. It's not as if anything could go wrong. I'm dead. That's as bad as it gets. Just . . . don't leave me inside that thing any longer than you have to."

"I'm not sure I like this," said Happy.

"Do you have a better idea?" JC said savagely. "I'd really love to hear a better idea! No? Then let's do it. Happy—link us."

It only took a moment. Happy concentrated, reached out, and brought the three of them together into a single unit. Three minds meshed together, like the working parts of a single great mechanism. Fitting as though they'd always belonged together. They still knew who they were, but now they possessed all of each other's strengths and none of their weaknesses. They turned to look at Patterson, at the dead man, and he flinched suddenly because now all three of them had glowing golden eyes. The glare burned brightly in the dark of the night, so very bright, and the dead man had to turn his dead gaze away from it. He couldn't even move, held where he was, but even so, the three minds working together still weren't strong enough to punch through his shields. Latimer stepped forward.

"Robert! This is your chance! Your last chance to be the man I always knew you were! Break the shields from your side! Let them in!"

And whether what was left of Robert heard her, or whether the linked trio finally won through, or whether the rider's power wore out . . . the shields fell, and JC and Melody and Happy rushed in. They reached out to Kim and urged her on. The ghost girl smiled bravely and moved towards the dead man. Some unfelt breeze swept her on, flapping her dress and ruffling her long hair. She drifted up to the dead man and on into him, disappearing inside as though walking on in a direction none of the others could follow. In a moment, she was gone, and the dead man swayed and almost fell. A great mental cry of rage and pain and horror briefly filled the night, then was gone. The dead man slowly straightened up, broken bones scraping loudly against each other, and for a moment someone new looked out of the dead man's eyes.

And then it was only a corpse, standing still, and Happy broke the link.

JC and Melody cried out briefly as they dropped back into their own heads. They were already forgetting what it had been like to be so much more, because deep down they knew that was necessary for their continued sanity. Happy could have remembered if he'd wanted; but he already had enough problems. Latimer looked at them all expectantly, but they had nothing to say to her.

"Is it done?" she said finally.

"Of course it's done," said Happy. "Look at the bloody thing. Not an ounce of malice left in it. Probably fall over if you breathed on it. And I feel much the same, thank you for asking."

JC moved forward to stare right into the dead face. "Kim? Are you in there?"

"She can't answer you," said Happy. "She is occupying the body, not possessing it. Give her a few minutes, to be sure the rider isn't coming back, and I'll haul her out of there."

JC nodded slowly, only half-convinced. "Hang in there, sweetie. I have to talk to the Boss about something."

"Right," said Happy. "Boss, while we were linked, and touching the rider's mind, we Saw something."

"Something important," said Melody. "Something bad."

They all stood close together, as though afraid of being overheard, even though there was no-one else in the quiet, deserted street.

"Is this something to do with the rider's identity?" said Latimer. "Did you See who it was?"

"No," said Happy. "He's gone. No trace of him in the body, or anywhere in the area. I'd know." He looked briefly about him. "Quite a few other ghosts, though. Lot of good people died here. Most are already dissipating, fading away, passing on . . . You'd better bring another field team in to do the mopping up. This place is going to be a spiritual black spot for years. Too much has happened here."

"Are you sure the other A team is dead?" said Latimer. "I mean—Diego and his people . . . I depended on them for years! They always got the job done!"

"They got arrogant and cocky," said JC. "And they got caught by surprise. Can happen to the best of us."

"None of them are here," said Happy. "No ghosts, nothing. They're gone."

"Pity," said JC. "I would have liked a chance to say *I told you so.*"

"Cold, JC," said Melody.

"Stick to the point," Latimer said sternly. "What is so important that you need to tell me all about it right now?"

"We found something inside the dead man's head," said JC. "A memory, but not from Patterson. Maybe not even from the rider. Maybe something the rider saw, or was exposed to . . . A memory or recording of past events, featuring the appearance on this Earth of something from Outside."

"A memory, or a vision," said Happy. "I stored it, because I knew you'd want to see it. So come here, oh Boss and mighty one, and See what we Saw."

Latimer moved forward, one slow step at a time. Not because she didn't trust Happy but because part of her really didn't want to see what he had to show her. Happy thrust the memory into her head, and she cried out in spite of herself.

The ocean, blue and grey and green, a choppy surface stretching away forever, miles and miles and far and far from land, under a clear blue sky. And then a door opened in that sky, and something fell through. A great crack in the sky, dark and crimson and full of roiling energies like the opening of some great eye of terrible aspect. A crack in Time & Space & Other Things, a split in Reality itself, and a brief glimpse into what lay beyond. Things came and went on the other side of the door, huge and awful shapes, big as cities, then a bright shaft of light shone through from the other place, into this world. A light that was so much more than any light should be. It scorched through the air, slammed down into the sea, and ploughed on down through the waters like some great driven force. Even in the stored memory, so many years after the original intrusion, the light was unbearably bright to look at, overpowering to merely human eyes. A kind of light that didn't belong in this world, this smaller reality.

And in the short moment the door was open, Something came through. It fell down through the light, huge and awful, its shape meaningless to human eyes and consciousness. It existed in more than three spatial dimensions, its extremities stretching off in directions the human mind couldn't follow. It fell into the sea like a falling mountain, and the waters rose violently as it plunged deep beneath the surface. The waters boiled,

and dead fish rose in their thousands, to float on the sur-
face and stare up at the broken sky with unseeing eyes.
The door closed, and the light snapped off. Everything
returned to normal.

Except, nothing would ever be the same again, be-
cause something new and terrible and utterly Other had
come into this world, and it would not rest until it could
find a way back again.

Latimer swayed on her feet as the mental images came
to an end. Happy put out a hand to steady her, then
snatched it back as she shot him a hard look. She shuddered once, then stood up straight, immediately back in
control again. The others looked at her carefully to see
what she made of what they'd all Seen in the dead man's
head. There was something new in the world, and it was
not good.

"I suppose the first question," JC said finally, "has to
be—did it fall, or was it pushed? Was it some kind of
accident, or did Something Else push that thing through
the door, against its will?"

"No, that can wait," Happy said immediately. "What
matters is, something really quite appalling has entered
our world from the Outer Reaches, and we have no idea
what it is, or what it can do. It's trapped here . . . and you
all felt the same things I did. It's awful and it's vast and
it's powerful, and it wants to go home. Back to where it
came from, where it did awful things and loved it. This
thing is what's been working behind the scenes of our
reality all this time, weakening the walls of the world, so
it can break out of it. It sees this world, our reality, as a

prison! It doesn't care if it destroys this whole world and everything that lives on it, as long as it gets to go home again!"

"Stop hyperventilating," Melody said coldly. "You know what that does to your sinuses. JC's got a point. Even if we could open the door to send it back, would what lives there take it back? Would they fight to keep it out?"

"We're getting ahead of ourselves," said Latimer. "We have to identify this Entity first, then decide what to do about it. There are options . . ."

"Really?" said Happy. "I would love to know what the options are for dealing with a Power and Domination from the Outer Reaches!"

"Am I going to have to get you a brown paper bag to breathe into?" said Melody.

"We've dealt with such threats before," Latimer said firmly. "We identify it, contain it, then either destroy it or send it somewhere else. The Carnacki Institute has a long history of knowing what to do with Abhuman Monstrosities. Did any of you pick up a name from that memory, or a description . . ."

"I got something," Happy said reluctantly. "But you're really not going to like it."

"There's been precious little about this day I've enjoyed," said Latimer. "What have you got?"

"Might be a name, or a description," said Happy. "Or maybe even a warning . . . The Flesh Undying."

There was a long pause as they all thought about that, none of them happily. Latimer shook her head slowly.

"Doesn't ring any bells. I'll have to do some research.

Did any of you get a sense of time? How long ago did this incursion into our space happen?"

"Hard to say," said JC. "I got the sense we were looking at an historical record, of something that happened years ago. How long have there been stories about something untoward going on behind the scenes? Of people working to destroy the walls of the world?"

"Decades," Happy said immediately, taking an entirely inappropriate pleasure in presenting the bad news. "I've been saying all along, there are all kinds of stories, of varying reliability. I believe them all, of course, on general principles, but that's just me . . . We have to ask—how long has this thing had to build an army of followers, or fellow travellers, the dupes and the possessed? If they could get their hooks into someone like Patterson, the public face of the Institute . . . How long has he been secretly working against us? How many others like him are there? How deep has the infiltration of the Institute gone?"

"Okay, you're scaring me now," said Melody.

"Welcome to my world," said Happy. "Cold and spooky, isn't it?"

"As always, you think too small," said Latimer. She wasn't even looking at Happy, her gaze far away. "The question is how many of the secret organisations of this world might The Flesh Undying have infiltrated? Not only the Institute, but the Crowley Project, the London Knights, perhaps even the Droods . . . We've always suspected their power source originated in another dimension . . . If that's the case, how do we warn people?

Should we warn anyone and perhaps give away how much we know?"

"The rider was human," said JC. "Or at least, was human once. He said we'd know his name . . . But he could have been saying that to mess with our heads."

"He called me by my first name," said Latimer. "Not many have ever done that . . . And there was something about the way he said it . . ."

"I was right!" said Happy triumphantly. "All along, I was right! You all said I was paranoid, well you didn't say it, but I knew you were thinking it, when I told you Something was going on behind the scenes, but you didn't believe me! You said I'd been working too hard, reading too many forbidden texts, taking too many of my little chemical helpers, but I was right all along! Forces from Outside are working to destroy the world, using traitors inside our organisations! Ow!"

"It was either a slap round the head, or a major tranquiliser," said Melody. "And you'd probably have enjoyed the latter."

"Quite right," said JC. "You are enjoying this entirely too much, Happy. And anyway, it's only one Force from Outside. Like the Boss said, the Carnacki Institute has a very successful history in dealing with such things."

"Victors write the histories," Happy said darkly, rubbing at the back of his head. "And they tend to leave out all the times when it all went horribly wrong."

"If you don't knock off the X-Files shit right now, I foresee a whole bunch of slaps in your immediate future," said Melody.

"Sorry," said Happy. "I'm not used to being right."

"But . . . why would anyone, any human being, ally themselves with such a thing?" said JC. "Why aid something that wants to destroy the whole world?"

"Don't be naive," said Latimer. "Why do Satanists sign away their souls when they must know that Hell is real? For power, or money, or to be major players in the game. And most of them probably don't know the whole story anyway. They could be lied to, manipulated, even possessed. Some people will always go where the power is, planning to jump off at exactly the right moment and avoid paying the bill when it comes due. Fools. We need to know a lot more about The Flesh Undying."

"We don't even know what it is!" said Melody. "What we Saw could have been a vision, or an interpretation, of what actually happened! We couldn't even look at the thing directly!"

"Could be one of the Great Beasts," said JC. "Or one of the Abominations from the Outer Rings . . . We need to consult the Institute Libraries, Boss, and not only the official ones. We need to see everything."

"Ooh!" said Happy, brightening suddenly. "I've always wanted access to the Secret Libraries!"

"I'll think about it," said Latimer. "Letting you run loose in those stacks would probably be more dangerous than anything The Flesh Undying would come up with."

"I resent that," said Happy.

"I notice you're not denying it," said JC.

"All right!" said Latimer, "Very much against my better judgement, I will authorise you to enter the Secret

Files. But no-one is to know what you're looking for.
Anything you sign out will be under my name, which
should keep anyone else from looking at it, and I will
expect to see full reports from each of you on whatever
you discover." She looked at all three of them in turn, and
her eyes were very cold. "I'm trusting you in this because
I have no choice. You are not the team, or even the individual agents, I would have chosen for a matter as important as this, but . . . it's clear I don't know my own people
as well as I thought I did. You're all new to the Institute,
and to field work, so hopefully that means you haven't
been got at yet. You did good work against Fenris Tenebrae. I haven't forgotten. I do wish you had more experience. Then I wouldn't feel quite so guilty about kicking
you in the deep end to play with the sharks."

"We may not have the experience," said JC. "But
we're sneaky."

"Oh we are," said Happy. "Really. You have no idea."

"Right," said Melody, smiling in a really quite unpleasant way.

But Latimer was looking at JC thoughtfully. "Why
didn't you check in with the Institute before you started
this case? You know that's official procedure."

"Because of Patterson," said JC. "We all knew him,
trusted him. Never liked the man, but we were all aware
of his long service. And he was one of yours. We were
used to hearing your words, from his lips. Never occurred
to any of us that he might be speaking off his own bat."

"Yes," said Latimer. "He always was one of my
favourites."

"He called you 'Grandmother,'" Happy pointed out.

"You should still have followed the official proto-cols," said Latimer, ignoring Happy.

"It was an emergency," said JC. "Not the first time we've been dropped into a case without a proper brief-ing, because there wasn't the time."

"I'm going to have to lay down some new guidelines," said Latimer. "Backed up by heavy fines, demotions, and the threat of actual physical violence. It's the only way to get anything done."

"I have to ask," said JC. "Don't we have compacts, agreements, with . . . well, other Forces and Powers? Other organisations? People, and others, who operate in the same field as us, that we could turn to for help and support in an extreme situation like this?"

"We can't talk to anyone about this!" Latimer said immediately. "If any of them were to discover that the Institute has become . . . compromised, they'd stop co-operating with us, stop sharing the kind of information we need to be able to do our job. And since we can't know how deep or how far this infiltration has spread . . . we can't risk sharing what we know with the wrong people. I won't even be able to report all of what's hap-pened here at the next Summit Meeting."

"Hold everything!" said JC. "The next Summit Meet-ing? This is the first I've heard about any Summit Meeting! Who, exactly, does the Carnacki Institute hold Summits with?"

"Yeah!" said Happy, annoyed at JC for getting in first.

"We hold a Summit twice every year, in neutral terri-tory," Latimer said calmly. "And you didn't know because you didn't need to know. The Institute meets with representatives from the Crowley Project and certain others. We've been holding these very cautious arm's-length little get-togethers for many years. Because for all their bad intentions and very real threats to the world, the Project still needs a world to live on. Which means that sometimes we find ourselves on the same side, opposed to some Force or Entity that wants to destroy the world. Something too big for either of us to combat on our own. As you found out, when you teamed up with those two Project agents down in the Underground.

"A lot of groups and organisations, and certain vested interests, send delegates to the Summit Meetings. The Droods, the London Knights, the Regent of Shadows. Hadleigh Oblivion turned up one year, not long after he was made Detective Inspectre. Shadows Fall usually sends Old Father Time, but once we got Bruin Bear and the Sea Goat. We had to lock up all the silver cutlery. And the expensive wines. And send out for more food for the buffet. Damn, that Goat can put away pizza." She stopped, to smile a surprisingly gentle smile. "Bruin Bear, on the other hand, was a real sweetie. I always loved his books, when I was a child."

"Doesn't everyone?" said JC. "I'm still not happy with these meetings being kept secret. What purpose do they serve?"

"Keep your enemies close and your friends closer," said Latimer. "Because you always know where you are with your enemies . . . but your friends and allies can always surprise you."

"So what do you talk about?" said Happy, actually

bobbing up and down on the spot in excitement at discovering something even he hadn't suspected.

"We have many things in common," said Latimer, not giving an inch. "Enemies in common. Just like in the Underground. And I should point out that I am quite capable of reading between the lines of an official report and noting the points where you were deliberately vague or even evasive about what actually happened. The Summit . . . is necessary. To pool our resources, to share useful information. Of course, there's always a certain amount of deliberate disinformation going on, from all sides, where we spread a little false information around, to see who'll bite and who already knows better. The Summit has always served many purposes."

"There is a theory," said JC, carefully not even glancing in Happy's direction, "that somebody, or perhaps some group of somebodies, really high up in . . . some organisation, did something they weren't supposed to, and it all went horribly wrong. As a result of which, the barriers between the dimensions were weakened. And that was why the door was able to open, and The Flesh Undying was able to come through . . ."

"Or even," said Happy, determined not to be left out, "that these somebodies opened the door deliberately, hoping Something would come through that they could control!"

"Rubbish," said Latimer. "Never happened. I would know."

"Yes, well," Happy said darkly. "You would say that, wouldn't you?"

"Don't push your luck, Palmer," said Latimer.

"You didn't know about Patterson," said Melody, and Latimer had no answer to that.

"Enough," said JC. "We're talking in circles, and getting nowhere. It's late . . . or really early. It's cold, and I'm tired. Time to go home, boys and girls." He turned to smile at the dead body. "Sorry we've kept you waiting so long, Kim. It's all right—you can come out now. Kim?"

There was no response from the dead man. Nothing to indicate there was anyone at home behind the unseeing eyes. JC strode up to Patterson, and thrust his face right into the dead man's.

"Kim! Come out of there! You've held the fort long enough. There's no way the rider's going to come back now!"

There was still no response. JC grabbed the front of Patterson's tattered jacket, took two great handfuls, and shook the dead man hard. The dead head lolled limply on its shoulders, rolling back and forth as though mocking him. The dead knees buckled, and the dead man crashed to the ground, the weight pulling JC down with it, for all his attempts to hold the corpse upright. JC bent over Patterson, still shaking him violently, screaming into the dead and unresponsive face.

"Kim! Stop messing around! You come out of there right now! Do you hear me! Kim!"

Happy and Melody stood close beside him but had enough sense not to interfere. There was as much anger as fear in his voice, and there was no telling who he might lash out at.

"JC," said Happy, "she's not in there. There's no-one in there. The body is empty."

"You're wrong!"

"I'm not wrong, JC. If she were there, I'd be able to See her. No-one's there."

"You've got to be wrong . . ."

JC finally let go of the dead man and threw him away. Patterson lay sprawling on his back, staring up at the night sky with indifferent, empty eyes. JC sat down suddenly, as all the strength went out of his legs. He looked tired and confused and utterly bereft.

"Where is she?" he said. "What happened to her? You all saw her go into the dead man . . . Did the rider grab onto her, overpower her, take her with him when he left? Then why didn't I hear her? She would have called out to me, I know she would . . . Or did the rider call something else, something far more powerful, to bear them both away? While we were all preoccupied, all too busy talking, to pay proper attention to her? Did they take her, and I didn't even notice?"

His voice had risen almost to a scream, his face drawn and strained. Happy and Melody stood as close as they could, and shot a harsh warning glance at Latimer when it looked like she might say something.

"I didn't detect anything," Happy said carefully. "And if I didn't, you certainly wouldn't have. There's no sign to show she was taken. She just . . . isn't in there."

JC glared at the dead body. "Give her back! Give her back to me, you bastards!"

The dead body lay there. JC's hands clenched into fists before him, and when he spoke, his voice was cold, and hard, and little more than a whisper.

"I have to know. I need to know what's happened to

her. Where she is. I have to track her down, and save her, and bring her home. I can't lose her, not so soon after finding her."

"If there's no sign she was taken, she might have . . . wandered off," said Latimer.

JC stood up, brushing at his clothes in an absent, unthinking way. "No. She wouldn't leave me. She wouldn't."

"So," said Latimer. "You and the ghost girl are . . . emotionally involved. Even though you know such relationships are expressly forbidden. Because they never work out well."

"Really not a good time to go into that, Boss," said Happy.

"Right," said Melody, in an only moderately threatening way.

Latimer looked at JC, standing alone, looking as though something had punched his heart out, and surprised them all by nodding.

"I have to get back to the Institute," she said evenly. "I have to make a report . . . of some kind. You can all come in . . . when you're ready."

She walked away, back straight and head held high, not looking back. Happy and Melody watched her go.

"Kim is out there, somewhere," said JC. "And I will find her."

"Of course we will," said Happy. "We're ghost finders."

"Damn right," said Melody.

From *New York Times* bestselling author
SIMON R. GREEN

For Heaven's Eyes Only
– A SECRET HISTORIES NOVEL –

I'm Eddie Drood, aka Shaman Bond, a member of the Drood family. We Droods have been holding back the forces of darkness for generations. It's a hell of a job—and we're good at it.

But right at this moment, the Droods have hit a bad patch, what with the death of our Matriarch and the discovery that she was killed by one of our own. It's left us in more than a bit of disarray, I can tell you. And it goes without saying that those forces of darkness are wasting no time in taking advantage of the situation. There's a Satanic Conspiracy brewing, one that could throw humanity directly into the clutches of the biggest of the big bads—forever.

Things are looking grim—and here I am, not able to be of any help. On account of I'm dead.

penguin.com

M863T0411